BY THE SAME AUTHOR

Innocence Lost
The Polish Connection
A Woman Undefeated
Dreams Can Come True

Ping Pong Poms

Vivienne Dockerty

DISCLAIMER.
Although places and events exist in my story, this is a work of fiction.
All the characters, names, incidents and dialogue is from my imagination
or have been used fictitiously.

Matador
5 Weir Road
Kibworth Beauchamp
Leicester LE8 0LQ, UK
Tel: (+44) 116 279 2299
Fax: (+44) 116 279 2277
Email: books@troubador.co.uk
Web: www.troubador.co.uk/matador

ISBN 978 1848766 358

British Library Cataloguing in Publication Data.
A catalogue record for this book is available from the British Library.

Printed and bound in Great Britain by TJI Digital, Padstow, Cornwall

Typeset in 11pt Aldine401 BT Roman by Troubador Publishing Ltd, Leicester, UK

Matador is an imprint of Troubador Publishing Ltd

AUTHOR'S NOTE

The word "POM" according to research done in the Holdfast Bay, South Australia area, applied to emigrants who travelled by ship to Australia. The people who could afford to accommodate themselves in a cabin were called "People of Means." This slightly disparaging term has been adopted by the Aussies and used mostly to describe anyone of British descent and more recently during Britain/Australia sporting events. Two other explanations for the word "POM", which may be theory rather than fact, according to the English Oxford Dictionary, are Prisoner Of Mother England (P.O.M.E.) which doesn't apply to those who came to settle in South Australia, and Pomegranite (Pommy) because many fair skins became the colour of the fruit after experiencing an Australian summer.

PROLOGUE

Gone are the days of the £10 Poms. The new generation of migrant Poms now have to be accepted by Australia, as "beneficial to the country".

As they leave their relatives, friends and all they have known, for the land of sunshine, cuddly koalas and hopping kangaroos, expectations are usually high. It's got to be familiar, with English being the spoken word, left-handed driving and a large community of Brits already there. It's a fresh start, away from the stress of modern day living and the kids will grow fit and healthy in their new adopted land.

It isn't long before reality dawns. This will be no picnic. There's still the anxiety of retaining that job or searching for one when you get there; good schools need to be found for the kids, while chasing around for that perfect long-term rental, while the funds brought across are dwindling away.

Don't get me wrong. Life in Oz for some is perfection. The sunshine, the beaches, the barbies, the relaxed way of life. Some people are happy and would never go back, but others find the difference in their new lifestyle far too much.

Who will survive and who will become a Ping Pong Pom, as the Aussies love to call the people who decide to go back home?

CHAPTER ONE

Paul stood at the foot of the stairs looking at his watch impatiently. Sounds of a heavy bag being dragged across the carpet in the room above met his ears.

"Amanda, will you get a move on," he shouted. "Taxi'll be here in a minute and we've got to pick the kids up yet from their gran's!"

Paul's normally pleasant looking face began to wear a scowl. It was just becoming light outside and he and his wife had hardly slept that night, due to the enormity of what lay ahead of them. He gave a sigh of relief as Amanda appeared at the top of the stairs.

Dressed in a pair of black boot cut jeans, a pale blue polo neck sweater, a matching fleece and black high heeled shoes, Amanda Dickinson was ready. The makeup was perfect on her attractive face. Her dark brown hair, which was cut in a short bob, was in shiny condition, as were her newly manicured nails.

"Help me down with this, will you," she said, reaching down to lift a large black holdall in front of her. "And have you checked everything, Paul? Passports, visas, tickets, currency and did you lock the back door?"

"I've checked everything, got everything and why the hell you're still messing about up here, I don't know," he said irritably, hurrying up the stairs to do as he was asked.

"Last minute stuff, Paul. I don't want that friend of your mother's who's renting from us, finding things I've forgotten to put away in the loft. I just wanted to check there was nothing of mine still around. I hope your mother's remembered to put the kids' things in their holdalls, I don't want to be having to buy bits at the airport."

Paul heaved the bag down the stairs in front of him, with Amanda close behind carrying her black patent leather vanity case.

"I wish we'd managed to sell this place, instead of having to rent it out," said Paul, as Amanda took a last look in the hall mirror and smoothed a finger over her left eyebrow.

"Yeah, it'll be a bugger to shift her if we want to come back," she replied.

"But we're *going* to like it." Paul sounded adamant. "It's always been a dream of mine to give the kids a better life than this one. When the economy here gets better, we'll sell this and I'll buy you a beautiful place overlooking the sea."

Amanda pulled a wry face behind his back as he opened the front door to see if it was their taxi he had heard entering the cul-de-sac. The driver flashed him and drew up at the bottom of the path.

"Put the kitchen light out, Amanda, while I take the bags down. And check the gas fire in the living room, I had it on earlier. And you haven't left the tap running in the bathroom, have you? That's your usual trick."

"Yes, all right, no, the gas fire isn't on and I haven't left the tap running. I'll be with you in a sec'. Anyway, your mother said she'll look in and check everything later."

"Manchester Airport, is it, Mate?" asked the Asian taxi driver as the couple settled in the back of his vehicle, their luggage safely packed in the boot.

"Via Halliwell," Paul replied. "We've got to pick our kids up from their gran's. Go down Halliwell Road and it's second right."

Amanda took a last look at the semi-detached house, where she and Paul had lived since they were married, eleven years ago. Brand new and built by a local developer, the couple had felt very fortunate when they had managed to scrape together a deposit and meet the mortgage payments too. Paul had been a surveyor in the building department at the local town hall and Amanda had a good job as a hotel receptionist. She had given up work when Emily, who was now eight, had made her appearance and settled down to being a stay-at-home mummy when Cody, her son, came along. She hadn't been bored. Once Cody had gone to school she had joined Total Fitness, then a netball team and she did the round of coffee mornings with the other young mums on the estate. So, when Paul said he wanted to give Australia a try, as there must be more to life than a nine to five job in perpetuity, she tried to ignore his aspirations to a life "down under", hoping he'd snap out of it.

She had dismissed as escapism his prolonged absences in the study each evening, where he researched visas, employer sponsorships and migration agents, and brushed aside his plea for her involvement. There was no way she was going to leave the area where she had been brought up, desert her friends and uproot the kids from the school that they attended. She had thought she had made herself very clear on the subject, until one night they'd had an almighty great row over it, with Paul accusing her of spoiling his life.

It had come as a shock. Paul had always loved her right down to her little fingers, with disagreements always put aside at bedtime and he had *never ever* refused to speak to her, as he had over those next few days. In fact he had begun to come in late, although later he admitted he'd been at his mother's, but she had started to wonder if Paul had another woman tucked away. He might have had. He was still good looking, according to the friends she had a girly night out with now and again. And as fear clutched her heart that he might make a break for it, even if he did profess his love for her and the children, Amanda forced herself to take an interest in his plans.

According to Paul, Adelaide, known as the "City of Churches", the place where he had managed to secure employer sponsorship, had one long beach on one side and hills and country on the other. And from other migrants, who posted things on the website "Poms in Adelaide", that Paul was now an active member of, life there seemed to be rather bright. She felt swept along, on a tide of Paul's creation, but she really had no option in the end.

Still, their house was only rented, she comforted herself as the taxi gathered speed along the ring road towards Halliwell and they could always come back if things didn't work out.

Muriel Dickinson gathered her granddaughter into her arms and gave her another hug. She seemed to have been hugging Emily and Cody, her grandson, every few minutes since their father had dropped them off to stay over the afternoon before. She was "topping herself up", according to her very intelligent grandson, who assured her that his daddy would buy her a Skype, whatever that was, and they could see each other every day. And when they had settled in, over in the country where kangaroos hopped around everywhere, she could come and visit them. Best to come in the winter, when it was cold and rainy in England.

Cody was very excited about this new country that his daddy had said he was going to love, because there were lots of beaches and open spaces and koala bears up every tree, even in your garden! Emily was looking forward to joining a surf club because she loved to swim and had already won a medal at her school.

"My, you're looking bonny, our Emily," Muriel said as she tied a pink ribbon around the fair haired little girl's ponytail, then fastened the top button on the child's white faux fur jacket. She wore it over a pink long sleeved blouse and black cord trousers, with black small heeled boots on her feet. She was quite warmly dressed for a September day, but already the temperatures were falling and autumn leaves scrunched on the floor.

"And me, Granny." Cody didn't want to be left out if there were any compliments to be had. He was dressed in a warm zip up navy fleece with a Ben 10 logo, dark blue denims and navy trainers and his light brown hair had been brushed back in an old fashioned "granny" hair do.

"You as well, my love, you're both looking bonny. Oh, I'm really going to miss you two."

She took out a hanky from her cardigan sleeve and dabbed at the tears that were never far away. She'd looked after these children since they were babies, always on hand for baby sitting for her son and his wife, or if Amanda wanted a break.

"Don't cry, Granny," Cody said in an effort to cheer his grandma up, getting down from the table, where he had been busy with a sticker book. "Mummy says we'll be back by next Christmas. It's only really a long holiday we're going on."

"She did, did she?" Muriel sniffed, thinking of how her son would feel if he found out that his wife had different plans from him. And Gladys Thompson, from church, if she thought she'd have to look for another place to rent so quickly. Paul had given up a good job to realise his dream, but Amanda had always been a bit flighty in her opinion. It had been a surprise when Paul had brought Amanda home to introduce her to her and his father. Overdid it a bit on the makeup and her hair colour was certainly out of a bottle. But there was Paul aged twenty-five, with only one previous relationship under his belt, still living at home and working his way up in the building department.

He had met Amanda at the Icon (the Palais in Muriel's day), when he'd been persuaded by one of his colleagues to have a night out. He usually liked to watch a bit of telly then spend most of the evening on the computer, and at the weekends he liked to go walking up on the moors. Amanda had been at the nightclub with her girlfriends, in an effort to cheer herself up after her partner of three years had walked out. Partner indeed, she meant the man she'd been co-habiting with, but still, mustn't grumble, here they were, still together after eleven years. Muriel's husband had passed on, but she had two wonderful grandchildren.

Muriel looked at her watch. It was ten minutes to seven. Paul and Amanda would be there soon, the children should be ready and waiting when the taxi arrived.

"Right, you two. Last minute trip to the toilet, then we'll get your cases into the hall. Cody, go first, there's a love. Are you sure you want to carry Mr. Furryfeet with you?"

"Of course I do." Six year old Cody sounded scathing. "Mr. Furryfeet goes everywhere."

"And don't let me forget Jimjam," said Emily, picking up a white plastic pony with a bright red mane and a row of beads

5

around its neck. "Hurry up, Cody, I'm dying to go."

"There you are, Paul," Muriel said, unnecessarily, as the taxi drew up outside her terraced house and, upon hearing the engine she opened the door.

"They're just paying a call and they'll be with you in a minute. They've both had porridge and I've put their pyjamas back into their…"

Her eyes suddenly filled up with tears as she thought that this could be the last time she saw her sweet little grandchildren. She hadn't really taken to flying, though she and her husband had done quite a lot of travelling abroad, once he'd retired. Australia was such a long way away to attempt the journey on her own.

Her son gathered her into his arms and gave her a bear like hug. His voice sounded gruff as he assured her that he'd be on the phone every week and he would send her the air fare as soon as he could. Amanda stood there stiffly, waiting for her children to appear. She'd be glad when they were away in the taxi. Emotional farewells were not her thing.

"Bye, Granny. Bye, Granny. Love you, Granny." The children waved from the window until the taxi drove out of the street.

Muriel wept into her pinny then went inside to make herself a cup of tea.

CHAPTER TWO

"Which terminal, Mate?" asked the driver as he drove down Halliwell Road towards St.Peter's Way.

"Terminal 2," answered Paul, who was sitting in the front passenger seat now that the children had been collected. He turned his face to look out of the window. This might be his last glimpse of Bolton, if they settled in to their new life.

There was B&Q, a place he had spent many hours in since his marriage to Amanda. She was always wanting some DIY or improvements done to the house or garden. There was the Audi garage, where he'd bought his first brand new car, letting Amanda have his second hand Honda Civic after he'd taught her to drive. Both cars were gone now. A colleague from work had bought his Audi, he'd taken possession of it the night before, and they'd sold Amanda's in the *Bolton News*. Not to be missed, Bolton Parish Church which they had just passed by. A significant local landmark, having stood there for a couple of hundred years.

"Going far?" the driver continued, seemingly having missed the emotional goodbyes on Muriel's doorstep.

"Australia. We're emigrating. Looking for a better life than here."

"Yeah, definitely going down the pan, isn't it? I'm going off myself in a couple of weeks. Back to Mumbai."

"Oh," said Paul, sounding disinterested.

The driver began to fiddle with his trip-meter. Some passengers couldn't be bothered to talk.

"We had a lovely time at Granny's, Mummy," Cody piped up, after abandoning his CD and headphones for a moment to make his report. "She made us popcorn and we had her special hamburgers that she makes herself. Oh and crisps."

"Yes and you ate most of them," Emily cut in. "He's a little piggy, isn't he, Mummy?" She reared back as Cody tried to slap at her over Amanda's knee.

"That's enough, the pair of you. And what time did your granny put you to bed?"

"Well, we were allowed to watch our programmes and then she wanted to watch Coronation Street, so we took ourselves off to bed," Emily replied. "We knew you would be cross if we didn't get up early. After Coronation Street, Granny came up and read us a story. She said it was probably the last time she would have the opportunity."

Amanda said nothing. If Paul had his way, Muriel was probably right.

Seeing the town hall in the distance, as the dawn had broken and it was daylight now, Amanda thought back to her "going away" party. Her mate, Frannie, had organised it. Just a booze up really. A pub crawl with four other girlfriends, starting off at the Pack Horse and visiting each bar until they got to Churchgate. Then, starting back at the first bar on Bradshawgate, they wove their way towards Tiggy's restaurant, intending to have a meal then call it a night. But who should they happen to meet? Amanda's old boyfriend, who professed his undying love when he heard she was off to Australia! It had been tempting to abandon Paul and his unpopular future and throw her lot back in with Ned, but caution intruded into her intoxicated state and she gave him the knock back.

She was glad she had, she reflected, looking over at Paul, who had been her rock for all these years and a loving dad to Emily and Cody. Better the devil you knew, definitely.

"Which terminal did yer say, Mate?" asked the taxi driver, breaking into the silence that the family had fallen into, as he turned the taxi off the motorway and headed for the airport.

"Terminal 2," Paul replied. He turned around to face Amanda, who had been sitting with her eyes closed for the last few miles.

"You make sure the kids have got their luggage and I'll see to ours. See if you can get a trolley and I'll put everything on."

Amanda nodded, while both children started to bounce up and down with excitement.

"Pack it in, you two," Paul said quietly and felt surprised when they did as they were told.

"That'll be 30," said the driver as the taxi came to a halt outside Departures and his passengers, clutching their belongings that they had carried with them in the taxi, looked in amazement at all the people and cars that were milling around.

"Keep the change," said Paul as he handed over two twenty pound notes, then the man jumped out to help him get the baggage from the boot.

"Singapore Airways!" Look, Daddy, over there," said Emily, pulling behind her a pink holdall adorned with My Little Pony that had a set of wheels of its own.

"Clever you," Paul replied, looking in dismay at the huge queue of people that snaked around the holding area.

"Is it three hours or two, the check in?" asked Amanda. "Only we could go for a drink first, then the queue might have gone down."

"It's three hours. Come on, let's go for it, it may be quicker than we think."

And it was. With personnel checking their tickets first, to make sure the family was in the correct queue, the hardworking check-in girl was soon weighing their luggage.

"Thank heavens for that." Amanda breathed a sigh of relief when she found her holdall was only a couple of pounds over. It must have been her last minute toiletries, as it had been a perfect weight on their bathroom scales.

"Let's head for the café," said Paul, feeling happier now he had the boarding cards, their holdalls had gone off on the conveyer belt and they were left with only hand luggage.

"Who wants a sticky cake?"

"Daddy, is that our plane over there?" asked Cody later as he spotted a large white Boeing 777 sporting a navy tail fin with a gold ensign on it, as the family walked along to the departure gate.

"I should think so," Paul replied, seeing that the Singapore Airlines Airbus 330-300 had the baggage handlers working busily beside it and that someone was testing the windscreen wipers inside the cockpit.

"Good, then it won't be long before we get on it. I'm getting very bored, you know."

"I think we all are." Paul smiled at the earnest face of his little son. Although the child had a multitude of things to play with in the small haversack he was carrying, his interest in them was beginning to fade.

"Can I have a window seat, Daddy?" asked Emily, who had been reading a magazine before her father said it was time to go to the boarding gate. She loved to read them, especially anything to do with young girls' fashion.

"I think we have seats in the middle, Emily. I believe this plane has three seats, four seats, then three. So we'll be able to sit together."

"I want to sit by Daddy," Cody said, as his father usually had interesting facts to tell him if they went anywhere.

"Then I'll sit with Mummy," said Emily loyally, not wanting her mother to feel left out.

Amanda smiled. They could choose a film together that they'd both enjoy.

"We'll be landing at Changai Airport in twenty minutes," the chief steward announced, much to the relief of most passengers, who had achy legs and sore posteriors and to those who were smokers, who were beginning to twitch with stress. "Please put your seats in an upright position and check that your seat belts are fastened."

Everyone did as he asked and the Dickinson family, amongst others, watched the map on the monitors in front of them to see if the little plane, which had been with them since Manchester

Airport on the flight map, had landed. Cody, in particular, had been fascinated with its progress, switching channels at various intervals to check on the air speed and the countries they were flying above.

He and his father had watched *Ice Age*, whilst Emily and her mother had watched *Hairspray* on their monitors. They'd all chosen from the menu that the pretty, orientally styled stewardesses brought around for them, eaten well, gone to sleep, eaten again and lately had all been reading. The twelve hour flight seemed to have gone quickly, but it would be good to walk on terra firma again.

The family's luggage had been put on "follow on", so once they had cleared the Singaporean customs they went in search of somewhere that Amanda could have a smoke. Not that Amanda was a regular smoker. She was more of what was called a social smoker, but the lure of the twenty pack of Silk Cut residing in her vanity case was overwhelming her. The family found themselves on the "Sunflower terrace", where other smokers from the plane had headed. The humidity of the place was causing everyone to at least take off their jackets and the Dickinson family all did the same.

"Do you have a light?" asked Amanda of a woman in her late thirties sitting with three teenage children nearby, two of whom were smoking. "I had to put my matches in the bin when we went through security."

The boy, who looked to be the eldest, produced a lighter from his jeans pocket. He lit Amanda's cigarette and with a grin said, "Don't ask!"

"Amanda, would you mind if I take the children to look at that pond we saw when we came in?" asked Paul once his wife had started puffing on her cigarette and was beginning to relax.

"You know where I mean, don't you? I don't want Cody to start coughing." Meaning, "Why haven't you packed up smoking when you're such a fitness freak? And I don't like the kids seeing you," Amanda thought, as he was always saying that to her. That's why she probably didn't give cigarettes up, just to spite him!

"Are *you* going to Adelaide?" asked the woman, who had lit up another cigarette with her son's lighter. "Only I saw you and your family in the queue at Manchester and noticed your luggage labels."

"Yes, a place called Brighton, I believe. My husband made all the arrangements, but I have the accommodation brochure here." Amanda started to rummage about in her vanity case for the leaflet that Paul had given her.

"Oh, I don't know Brighton," the woman replied. "We're going to a place called Port Lincoln. We've another plane to catch after. My husband's got a job in a garage there and we're hoping they'll take our Tommy on or he'll have to go on a TAFE. We'll have to find a school for the other two, but the man who's employed my husband said there's one locally."

"Your husband not with you?" Amanda asked, looking around as if she could spot a likely candidate.

"No, he came over a couple of months ago. To be honest, our Tommy's not happy about us emigrating. He's got a girlfriend who he's had to leave behind and the other two aren't that fussed, what with having to leave their mates. We were all hoping, me included, that he'd do a few weeks there, get fed up and come back home again. Anyhow, we said we'd try it, then he can't accuse us of not being up for it. Who knows, we might get to like the place."

"Exactly my sentiments," said Amanda, putting her cigarette butt into a nearby ashtray. "I'm not fussed about being there either, but I have to make the effort and I'm willing to give it a go."

She picked up her vanity case and stood up, stretching her spine, which seemed to have stiffened. "See you later on."

The children were hanging over the little wooden bridge, fascinated with the Koi Carp that were swimming lazily about in the pond below. All around it were beautiful tropical plants of every colour and hue. It was like sitting in a botanical garden.

Paul was doing just that, sitting on a bench checking his watch then scrutinising an email print-out he'd received from the Transit Hotel.

"Oh, there you are," he said when he saw Amanda approach

them. "I thought you might have decided to look around the shops, but I think it's time we booked into the hotel. It's six o'clock in the morning here, but it will be midnight at home and I think we should try to keep the children in some sort of routine."

"I totally agree, Paul. I'd love a shower and a lie down for a few hours. Hey, you two, over here."

"Have you seen the fishes, Mummy?" Cody said, sounding very excited as he ran to her. "They're called Koi Carp and Daddy says they are worth a lot of money."

"Hundreds of pounds," said Emily, not to be outdone, taking a seat at the side of her father.

"Don't make yourself comfortable, Em," Paul said. "We're going off to find the Transit Hotel. We'll have a rest, then we'll get something to eat."

The room they were given was quite comfortably furnished, with two double size beds pushed up to each other and a small en-suite with a shower over the bath. It was plain but functional, given that each client could book a six-hour block then a cleaner would service the room for the next client. They helped themselves to the hostess tray provided, with tea and coffee, plenty of biscuits and bottles of water for the kids. The children didn't need persuading to have a lie down. As Amanda headed for the bathroom, Emily and Cody were nearly asleep!

Sleep wouldn't come to Amanda. Refreshed from her shower and now dressed in her ongoing flight outfit, a pair of blue tracksuit bottoms with matching fleece over a white camisole and white Nike trainers, she just wanted to get on with the journey and get it over and done with. According to Paul's calculations, she knew she would have been tucked up in bed back in England, but she had slept twice on the journey and hadn't had her usual nightly glasses of wine. Paul's travel clock was ticking valiantly on the bedside table, making her conscious that in five hours' time they would all be back in the airport terminal and hanging around again. Paul had just lain down beside her, after taking his shower. He was also wearing a tracksuit to travel in, navy blue like Cody's. He smelt of deodorant and aftershave and his brown hair, which he wore in a short back and sides, was still a little damp.

"Happy?" he said, putting his arm under her waist and drawing her to him.

"Not really. I feel sort of on edge, jumpy. I just wish we were back in Bolton and we were tucked up in bed."

"You always feel that way when we go on a long journey. Once we're up in the air again it's only another six or seven hours. You can watch another video, read another book and before you know it we'll have landed. Have you put your watch forward? It's best to stick to the time zones if we can."

Paul turned away and closed his eyes. That was nearest he was going to get to asking his wife about her feelings. If he took on board the emotions he knew that she'd be feeling, everything would go pear shaped and they may as well go back home now. He wasn't going to let her stand in the way of this new life that he had been planning over the last two years. It could be the best decision he had ever made.

Amanda sighed and turned her back on her husband. What option did she have if she wanted to remain married to Paul? She didn't want to end up like her mother, going from bloke to bloke after she and Amanda's father had split up and last heard of living in Torremolinos, making a living as a singer in the local bars. No, she wanted stability for her children. They deserved it, seeing as it was she and Paul who had wanted to bring them into the world. She and her elder sister, Donna, had been dragged from pillar to post, never knowing who their mother would bring home from the pub where she worked. Her father had since died, but she hadn't known him very well anyway and her sister lived in Glasgow, with a guy she had been shacked up with for many years. They didn't keep in touch as Donna thought her little sister was a bit of a snob, seeing as Amanda lived in a nice semi and she lived in a council flat. She'd get a shock if Amanda sent a postcard from Adelaide!

Five hours later they were sitting in an Indian vegetarian café with trays piled up with yummy looking dishes that had been chosen from the counter display. Strangely enough, the children were partial to mild tasting curries and poppadoms, as their parents had often bought a selection of takeaway foods from their local Asda store.

Amanda related her meeting with the Port Lincoln travellers, marvelling that the woman had been persuaded to make the flight on her own.

"Hardly on her own, with those big strapping lads I saw accompanying her," Paul remarked, "but yes, I suppose she must be admired. I couldn't see you coping with our two alone."

"Anyway, her husband's got a job in a garage," Amanda continued, feeling a little stung by her husband's candid criticism. "She was saying that if her son didn't get a job, he'd have to join a TAFE. What's a TAFE? Could I join one?"

"I believe it's a college course. Say, if he wanted to qualify as a mechanic, he could do the theory there. I don't think it would have a fitness centre."

Amanda suddenly felt the urge to smoke a cigarette. Paul was beginning to aggravate her!

She took out her packet of cigarettes, once again seated on the Sunflower terrace looking around for someone to ask for a light. A man, a cheeky looking chappie in his late thirties, sat nearby reading an English newspaper. He felt her scrutiny and got up to offer her a light.

"Still ten hours to go, if you're waitin' for the Adelaide flight," he said and she realised that he must have seen her on the plane.

"I know, it's a drag," she said, pulling hard on her cigarette in an effort to calm her nerves down.

"The wife and kids are still at the restaurant," he said, perhaps in an effort to assure her that he wasn't going to give her a chat-up line. "I'm not a good flyer meself and didn't feel like any grub. If we were allowed to smoke on the plane, I'd be on me second packet by now."

Amanda nodded, as if in agreement.

"Been to Australia before?"

"No, this is our first time. My husband has been offered a job over there."

"Same for me, but we came over last year to validate our visa. We stayed for a couple of weeks in a very nice rental, south of Adelaide. We've booked the same place again, until we can find somewhere else."

"Is it difficult? Paul, that's my husband, was saying it can be quite expensive for the short term rentals, but there are lots of people chasing the long term ones."

"Well, it depends on where you want to live. The nearer the city, the higher the rents. It doesn't bother us about living close to the city, as I've got a job as a brickie with a developer who's buildin' a big estate down in the south. We're hopin' to buy a plot of land ourselves and have a house built."

"Oh, we'll have to depend on the rental market. We did have our house up for sale but we couldn't get what we wanted for it, so we've rented it out. Our rental house is in Brighton."

"Oh, you'll like Brighton. We used to take the kids there, last time we were here. They've got a jetty you can have a walk on and there's a crackin' beach. It might be a bit cool though at this time of year, with it just comin' out of the Aussie winter. I hope you've brought some warmer things."

Amanda blushed as she realised her cami had worked itself down and she was showing quite a bit of cleavage. She stood up and docked her cigarette.

"Right, I'll be off then to find my husband and kids. Thanks for the light."

She pulled up the zip on her fleece and walked back to the restaurant.

CHAPTER THREE

At last the plane had landed and, having cleared passport control, everyone stood by the luggage carousel waiting for the conveyer to start. A brown spaniel, accompanied by its handler, sniffed at each passenger's hand baggage whilst they waited. Luckily, no one from their plane got taken away.

It was crowded in the baggage hall. Another plane had landed before the one from Singapore and the queue before them still drifted whilst custom officials checked documents before allowing the arrivals to continue on.

"What time did you tell the man from the car rental company to meet us, Paul?" asked Amanda as she set her watch to Adelaide time. "Only it looks as if we've got quite a wait. Is it right that we're now eight and half hours ahead?"

Paul nodded. "Eight and half hours until the clocks go back in October. I took into account that the plane could be late, or Customs would be slow, so I told the man half past eight."

"And what about the woman from N and T Rentals?"

"Oh, she said she'd get to the house for nine, but as she only lives around the corner she didn't mind if we were late."

There was no more time for discussion as the conveyer belt started and Amanda stood back with the children, whilst Paul waited to heave their holdalls off and the spaniel set off in pursuit of other interesting smells.

"Any products in your bags that are not allowed into Australia?" asked the female official, who scrutinised the customs forms that Paul had handed her when they got to her at last.

"No nuts, shells, or food that we might be concerned about?"

"No, only a couple of bottles of spirits that we purchased duty free in Singapore," said Paul, proffering the white paper bag, where two bottles of gin resided, for her inspection.

"Then off you go," she said, pointing the way to Arrivals that didn't involve going via an inspection desk. "Have a good stay in Adelaide."

Phew! The family almost ran to the exit!

"Mum, Dad!" A young auburn haired woman almost leapt the barrier when she saw her parents pushing their trolley into the arrivals hall. A large crowd had gathered beyond the railing, waiting to greet their friends and loved ones. Amanda felt a lump in her throat when a tiny boy who had been sitting on his haunches near his mother ran to the older couple ahead of them.

"Granddad, Grandma," he shouted, hugging first the leg of his grandmother before being swept up into the arms of his grandfather.

The crowd sighed then applause broke out as the young woman joined her parents too.

"That was the couple you were chatting to, Paul," said Amanda as they stood watching the heartwarming sight for a moment, before continuing. "They gave Em and Cody some chocolate bars."

"Yeah, they've sold up and they're waiting for a parent visa. I was asking how easy it would be to get my mother here too."

"Oh," was all Amanda could find to say.

It was true that Paul had already looked into the possibility of Muriel joining them at a later date. He'd checked out the aged parent visa as there was no way that his mother could afford the contributory parent visa, which demanded a payment of over thirty thousand dollars! It appeared that Australia's policy towards the more mature was a negative one. Those migrants hadn't contributed anything towards the country in the past, so why should they be able to retire at the expense of the Australian government in the future? A contribution had to be made for Medicare, which was the government's answer to healthcare and a bond placed with Centrelink, a type of social service, should they fall on hard times.

Paul hadn't discussed this with Muriel. It would be like getting a winkle out of its shell if he ever tried to get his mother out of Halliwell. She had lived there all her life and it would only be if she seriously missed him and the grandchildren that he thought she would consider joining them. Then there was Sue, his unattached elder sister, who lived in London. She would have a lot to say on the matter, even though she only saw her mother once a year. He sighed as he pushed the trolley out onto the concourse. Life was never simple and who was to say whether things would work out for him. His sponsorship was only for two years anyway.

"There's a man over there with a card saying "DICKENS", said Amanda, breaking into Paul's thoughts.

"Do you think he means us, Daddy?" said Cody, looking over to where a tall black man was holding up a piece of white cardboard.

"Probably." Paul pushed their trolley towards the man.

"I'm Paul Dickinson. Are you from Jasper's Jetty Car Hire?"

"I sure am," the man grinned, showing his lovely white even teeth. "Sorry about the name shortening, the piece of card wasn't big enough for all your name. Look, the car's in the car park, so we'll get on over. I'll take you to the office for the paperwork."

He strode off, having taken over possession of the loaded trolley. The family trailed behind, as jet lag started to take its toll.

"Granny said we wouldn't see any immigrants when we got to Australia," Emily said to Paul, as she clung to his hand, suddenly deciding she wanted her father's big presence close to her.

"Everyone in Australia is an immigrant in some shape or form, Emily. People have been coming here for a better life for over two hundred years. There was no one here except the aborigines before then. Perhaps your granny was talking about the ethnic minorities that seem to have taken over certain areas of Bolton."

Emily nodded. She wasn't sure about what her father was saying but there had seemed to be a lot of brown-faced children joining her class at school lately.

The sun was shining weakly from a cloudy sky as the family got into a red Holden estate car. Paul sat in the front with the driver, whilst Amanda and the children settled in the back.

"This is the car that you ordered over the Internet, mate," the man explained. "You can watch me drive first, with it being automatic. I hear that you use a gear shift over in England."

Paul nodded. It had seemed a bit of an adventure ordering an automatic car to drive about in when he had sat at home in the comfort of his study, but seeing only two foot pedals and a strange looking gear control made him a little nervous, now he came to think of it.

"It's easy," the man assured him, starting up the engine while the car was in Park. "Look, foot on brake, until you put it into Reverse. See, like this." He slowly manoeuvred the car out of the parking space. "Then through Neutral, into Drive. Easy."

Paul nodded again, feeling a bit more confident. It did look easy.

"So, what part of England are you from, mate? I went to London once. A long time ago now." The driver slowed down to put a card into a PAY machine.

"From the north. You may have heard of Manchester?"

"Yeah. Manchester United. My boy's crazy about them."

Amanda sat in the back, sandwiched once more between Emily and Cody. She shivered and wished she'd kept her polo neck on. Wasn't Australia supposed to be hot and sunny all the time? She didn't like the thought of having to learn how to drive an automatic. Hopefully there would be a supermarket close to hand and a school that the children could walk to. She fished inside her vanity case until she found the leaflet supplied by N and T Rentals. She'd have another look, to familiarise herself with the house again.

"Will Cody and I have to share a bedroom?" asked Emily, taking the leaflet from her mother whilst she studied the front of it. It showed the exterior of a new looking bungalow, with one main window and a garage on the front.

"No, it has three bedrooms. The main one will be for Daddy and me."

"It says here, "Only a short walk to the jetty and the ocean," Emily continued, staring at a picture of a structure that looked similar to a pier that she had seen at Southport. "Oh and there's a surf club on the esplanade and good local schools."

"Let me see," said Cody, snatching the leaflet out of his sister's hand. "I'll be able to go to the surf club too, won't I, Mummy?"

"Yes, if you're good."

Amanda took the leaflet away from her son. If the rental had a comfortable bed when she got there, she'd be grateful. Surf clubs and schools could wait until another day.

She closed her eyes, not bothering to look at the Ikea store on her left that might have cheered her spirits a little if she had seen it, nor the shopping outlet that was called Harbour Town further along. She didn't see the black and white pelicans, sitting on the riverbank that was awash with yellow soursobs, nor the quaint elderly villas that lined the tree lined streets towards Glenelg.

"Mummy, we're here!"

Amanda awoke from her doze, as Emily tugged on her arm in an effort to wake her.

"Wake up, sleepyhead."

Paul got out of the now stationary car and followed the driver to the office, which was really only a shed. Amanda didn't bother to follow. If this was to be their car, she'd stay where she was comfortable. Cody made to open the door in an effort to be with his father, but his mother restrained him with her hand. He'd only be a nuisance to the people in the office, prancing around and jumping about.

"Duchy Avenue," read the street sign, as Paul drove into the road where the rental house was situated. The drive there hadn't been as bad as he had feared. Occasionally he had reached for the imaginary gear stick and looked for the clutch with his left foot, but he felt quite satisfied with his driving, overall.

"It's a good job that they drive on the same side as us," Cody remarked from where he sat in the front on a booster seat that the hire company had provided, as Paul was concentrating on pulling out to join the south travelling traffic.

"I've driven on the other side before," said Paul. "I drove in France when we went to that campsite."

"Oh, look, Ducky Avenue!"

Emily thought the name hilarious, though Amanda had explained that the word wasn't pronounced in that way. The houses there seemed rather old, with homestead ornamentation decorating the eaves of the tin or slate roofs. Number 27, though, was different. A smart new yellow brick villa, with a black tin roof, that filled previously vacant land.

"That must be the N part of N and T rentals," joked Paul, as he drew the car up to where a white haired woman in her late fifties, dressed in red jumper, black trousers and red shoes stood. She lifted a hand in greeting then motioned to Paul that he should park on the driveway.

"Safer here than on the road, my dear," she explained to him as he slid the window down to speak to her. "And best put it in the garage overnight."

Amanda and Emily looked at one another. Wasn't Brighton a safe place?

"No dear, no worries. Sometimes we get a hoon driving about at night."

The pair looked again at each other blankly then began to climb out.

"Nettie Sissons. The N part of N and T rentals," she said, causing everyone to stifle a snigger, as she had just parroted Paul.

"My husband's called Trevor. We had this house built on a piece of land at the bottom of an old lady's garden. She wanted to raise some money to keep her above the poverty level and of course buying it was advantageous to Trevor's Super, so we jumped at the chance."

They all nodded politely, as no one had a clue what she was talking about.

"Do come in. I hope you'll be comfortable. It's very basic, as I didn't want families doing any damage if I put in good stuff. But everything is adequate for a short term stay."

She wasn't wrong, thought Amanda, peeping into the main bedroom of "Trevor's Super", as they walked down the hallway. It had a drab brown waffle type carpet, a black iron bed with a white duvet cover and matching pillowcases and one black and white picture on the wall above the bed. The side rooms were similar, down to the white bedcovers on each single bed, and the lounge room held just a dark blue sofa, a cheap looking table and a small T.V. on a plastic stand.

"The dining table seats six," Nettie said, looking beyond the austere looking kitchen, with its white cupboards, white tiles on the walls and cream bench top, to where a pine table and spindle back chairs stood. "And there's a two way bathroom and a laundry down the passage over the there. Now, dears, any questions?"

"Can we go and play in the garden?" asked Cody, as he had seen a strip of grass through the patio windows.

"Yes, dear, but be careful of the bully ants, they are quite prevalent at this time of the year."

"What are bully ants, if you don't mind me asking?" Amanda couldn't let an explanation go.

"Oh, they're bigger than ordinary ants and sometimes they bite."

The children stepped gingerly onto the narrow grey flagged patio. Somehow playing in the garden had lost its appeal.

"There used to be koala bears around here," said Nettie sadly. "They used to sit in the gums, but all the building work around here seems to have chased them away." She appeared to forget that she and her husband were themselves perpetrators.

"Still, this won't get the baby bathed. I've put ten dollars on the electricity card. It should last you a week, if you're not too heavy handed with the roomie." She pointed to the air conditioning unit on the wall. "And you can top up at the newsagent in the Marion Centre." This reference was to a blue card, that sat upon a thin file over on the coffee table.

"The house is south facing which means it doesn't get a lot of sun. But I'm sure you young things don't feel the cold like we older folk do. I've provided a welcome pack for you. It's in the fridge over there. No need to thank me, it's in with what you've paid me. And I would be grateful if you try to limit any breakages. I don't ask for a bond like a lot of other rental people do. Up to now I haven't had any problems. But as I come in to do a service for my clients each week, I can keep my eye on things. You've got my number, if you need me."

Nettie bustled out, her red shoes tapping smartly on the brown tiled floor as she walked. The children came in from exploring the tiny garden, complaining that they hadn't seen any of the bully ants, or even a dangerous spider that they had read about!

"A cup of tea, I think, Amanda," said Paul, as he noticed his wife was swaying a little as she walked to the fridge to inspect the welcome pack. He filled the kettle from the Pura tap. Not that he knew that it would produce drinkable water, but it seemed the right thing to do.

"Eggs, bread, milk, some sort of marge, biscuits, orange juice and yoghurt. I suppose it's a start."

"There's tea, coffee and sugar here in these tins, Amanda. You can't expect the woman to provide a full week's groceries. We'll go on a reccie later and we'll eat at a restaurant tonight."

"I don't see a point for the Internet, Paul," Amanda commented when they were all sitting at the dining table later, nibbling on Tim Tams and sipping their drinks.

"Yes, I remember now that this rental property didn't provide a modem. To be honest, I had to weigh up the cost of renting this place or going for an all singing, all dancing property, with every commodity. But we have to be a bit careful with our money, until the rent from *our* property starts coming through and I'm getting my salary."

"Meantime, how do I keep in contact with the friends I've left behind?" asked Amanda, as she had brought a notebook full of all her girlfriends' email addresses. "It'll be too expensive to use my mobile and what about my Facebook and Twitter… and Skype, if we get it, for the kids to speak to their grandma?"

"Surely we can do without all that until we find a long term rental?" Paul replied irritably. "There's bound to be an internet café around, or sometimes libraries have the facility. Luckily, there's a landline, so we're not quite out in the sticks, as it were."

"Daddy, can I unpack my bag and put my clothes away in the wardrobe?" asked Emily, trying to avert an argument between her parents, as she could feel the tension rising between them.

"I would like the bedroom over there, if that's okay?" She had peeped in earlier when her parents were in discussion with the landlady and had noticed a small paved side garden from the window, with a few potted plants.

"Yes, we'll all start unpacking," said Paul, getting to his feet and smiling gratefully at his daughter.

Amanda was looking sulky and her mood could have gone either way.

"We could ring Gran and tell her we've arrived," said Cody, making a dash for the telephone that sat upon the kitchen bench top.

"We'll need a phone card," Amanda said dully. "I suppose Daddy will get around to arranging that."

"Oh, come on, Amanda, cheer up. We're here in a lovely country, with beaches everywhere you look and the sun's shining outside, when at home you can guarantee it will be raining. We'll have a better standard of living once I'm into the job and the salary cheques start coming and in a couple of days we'll look around the estate agents. See what kind of house we can buy, when we've sold ours."

"I don't like it here. The house feels chilly, there's no proper heating. All these tiles make me feel as if I'm living in a toilet. There's not even a rug to brighten things up."

"My bedroom's nice," Emily chipped in. "I've got lots of big mirrors on the wardrobe and a picture of a curled up cat on the wall."

"And I found a basket of toys in mine," said Cody, coming back from his investigation. "I'm going to get Mr. Furryfeet and show them all to him. Em, did you put him in your bag with Jimjam?"

His howling later was enough to stop a police car if one had been passing by; the occupants would surely have thought that a child was being tormented. Mr. Furryfeet was nowhere to be seen. Not in his parents' bags, Emily's, nor his own little haversack. The sturdy brown bear that had been with Cody since Amanda brought the child home from hospital had disappeared.

"Where did you last see him?", Paul asked gently after Cody had calmed down a little and was able to listen to reason.

"On the tray when I was having my dinner," the child said in a muffled voice.

"On the plane?" Paul asked for confirmation, as Cody could have meant when he was having his Indian meal at Changai airport.

Cody nodded.

"Well, that won't be a problem then," Paul said in a relieved voice. "We'll ring Singapore Airways. They're bound to have a lost property office and a nice air steward will have handed him in."

Cody looked up hopefully from where he had thrown himself on the sofa. His father was usually a great source of knowledge and if he said that Mr. Furryfeet was being looked after at the lost property office, he was bound to be right.

"Can we phone them, Daddy? he asked, wiping his tears away with a grubby hand.

"Yes, if we don't need a phone card," said Amanda spitefully from the kitchen, where she was washing up her coffee cup after having a cigarette and a coffee on the patio.

"I'll look in that file that we saw on the coffee table," Paul said, ignoring what he saw as a sarcastic remark. "It might give useful telephone numbers."

Cody and Emily trailed miserably behind him, while Amanda went to visit the bathroom.

"There's a Yellow Pages book here, Daddy," said Emily, finding a thick looking book on a ledge under the coffee table. "Oh, it's a White Pages. Do you think that will be same?"

"Well done, Em. Yes, we're sure to find the number now."

Paul dialled a number for the airport that he had found very quickly. His call was put through to the Singapore Airways desk.

"They're on to it, Cody!" he said excitedly once he'd had a long discussion with someone and had put down the phone. "The lady is going to telephone the captain of our plane now!"

What he didn't say was, the woman on the desk had said she would contact someone back at Changai and, as the plane was still in the air, it was just possible that they could get one of their Singapore counterparts to look for the missing bear.

"Do you think they'll put Mr. Furryfeet on the very next plane and send him back again?"

"Bound to, Cody. She's taken this telephone number and will ring us as soon as he lands. Isn't he lucky riding backwards and forwards and keeping those lovely stewardesses company?"

"I suppose."

"What say we have a walk down to the sea and have a look for a surf club? Em, you'd like that, wouldn't you? And if we find some shops we could all have an ice cream too. I'll go and get Mummy."

"You can leave me here," Amanda said grumpily when Paul found her outside the white tiled bathroom looking in the linen cupboard for a towel.

"Look, more damn rooms with a white décor. The bathroom, toilet and laundry. The woman must have bought a job lot of white tiles from somewhere."

"Perhaps she used to be a nurse and likes to be reminded of the hospital," Paul tried an attempt at jocularity.

"You could be right. Anyroad, take the kids and I'll put my feet up after I've had a shower. You can have a look around for somewhere to eat. I take it you managed to use the phone without a card."

"I had a quick look in that file she provided. All local calls are free. She's had a bar put on for international."

"Bully for her."

Paul set off confidently down the road with the children. The air was warm and soon their fleece jackets had been discarded. It was best to leave Amanda alone when she got into one of her moods. He made allowances as she was one of the loves of his life, besides his mother and Emily and Cody, and he put it down to her neglected childhood, which still caused her problems in her adult years.

He'd been lucky being brought up by Muriel and Bill. They had always put their children first and had worked together to resolve any differences. They had gone without to ensure their kids had the best education, with Susan first, then Paul, attending Bolton Grammar School. They were happy to live in their three bedroomed terrace, take their annual holiday at a Blackpool boarding house and be careful with the wages that Bill earned. "Look after the pennies and the pounds will look after themselves" was the dogma that they lived by and Paul had tried to live the same. The problem was that Amanda liked the better things in life and it was always him who tried to settle any arguments before they went to bed.

"That looks a good place to eat later," he said, as they came to a crossroads and there was a banner on the side of a corner pub saying that kids could eat free on certain days. "We could go there if we don't see anything else. Look, we'll cross here and then turn left at the next traffic lights. Oh, a church. Your gran will be pleased when she comes over for a holiday."

"Will we go to the Sunday school?" asked Emily. "Only Gran said we must make an effort to find a Sunday school, so we don't end up forgetting about Jesus."

"I think we had best wait and see if we're going to live in this area before you start anything, Em. When I get to see the boss on Friday, I can ask."

Mr. Farrington, the C.E.O. of the building surveyors company that was to employ Paul from the next Monday, had emailed the week before to say that he was looking forward to having Paul on his team and would he call in for an informal get together on Friday morning. Friday afternoon was "walkabout", when most of the staff would repair to the pub or go home early, so if he made it around eleven thirty they could go for lunch. It all sounded very matey, far different than the formal atmosphere that he had experienced so far in his career. The offices were in the city, in the CBD, the (Central Business District), according to Mr. Farrington, or "Call me Eddie' as he kept insisting when Paul had his hour long telephone interview.

"Daddy, I think Mummy will like to have a look in that boutique." Emily broke into her father's thoughts as they passed by a very modern dress shop.

"Then we'll have to keep her away from it, Em," said Paul, jokingly. "She's enough clothes to open a shop herself!"

Cody had been very quiet as they walked down Jetty Road, although he cheered up a little when they crossed a train track and Paul said they would probably travel on a train often in the future. Cody and Emily had never been on a train. If the family had visited the city of Manchester, they had always gone in the car. Paul put his son's subdued mood down to the loss of Mr. Furryfeet, and tiredness of course. He had come a long way for a little nipper and his father admired him for the fortitude he had shown. He was proud of both of his children. They were well mannered and kind and he hoped they'd be happy in the life he had chosen.

The pavement cafés were full of people enjoying a late lunch or liquid refreshment. It was quite busy for an out of season Monday, but dressed warmly in a jacket or thick sweater, most were happy to feel the sun on their face. Down on the esplanade, with a chilly wind coming off the ocean, it was a different story, with not many people strolling about. Of course there were the die-hard anglers, who fished with a rod from the jetty, and the intrepid walkers who would never let inclement weather put them off. The golden beaches were bare and the ocean waves were boisterous, but to Paul it was everything he imagined. There was even a pub on the corner if he wanted to have a pint!

The kiosk on the corner served hot dogs, burgers, ice cream and fish and chips. Uniformed students from a local high school queued and the smell of the food came wafting, reminding Paul that it had been quite a few hours since their breakfast on the plane.

"We must get back to Mummy," he said, after the children had got their cones and he had paid with a fifty dollar note. "She'll be starving, poor love, so we need to take her to a restaurant. We can come for a reccie on another day."

"But, the surf club's over there," pointed Emily, looking past a children's park towards the beach at Seacliff.

"We'll just take a quick look, then it's back to Trevor's Super," he said.

CHAPTER FOUR

"Yer gettin' on me nerves, yer know," said Abbie Foley to her husband, who had lit himself a cigarette as soon as he and his family came out of Arrivals at Adelaide airport.

"That's all yer've done at every opportunity. Yer'll have to start cuttin' them down once we get settled. That rent we've paid in advance 'as seriously cut into our house money and yer've still got to go on that brickie course before yer get a proper wage."

"Listen to yer mother naggin' me, Jodie," Wayne, a seriously henpecked husband, said to his youngest girl, aged nine, who was holding on to the loaded trolley while her father lit up. Jodie nodded in agreement, looking serious. That's all her mother seemed to do.

"Jason, shift yerself. We'll go and see if that hire firm has brought the people carrier we asked for. You'd think they'd send a bloke with a placard, like they did last time."

Jason, the eldest boy, who was seventeen, shuffled along moodily behind his mother, leaving their eldest girl, Molly, looking after three year old Kyle, who was sitting in a pushchair.

"I'll be glad to get back to work," Wayne said to no one in particular. "I wouldn't mind, but it's me own money I'm spendin'. The fat cow's never done a day's work in her life."

"Don't let me mother hear yer say that, Dad," said fifteen year old Molly. "This is supposed to be a fresh start for everyone and I'm hopin' the pair of youse will stop those stupid rows."

"It's just our way, Molly. It's affectionate banter. Do yer think we'd still be together if we didn't care fer one another?"

"Well, yer nearly wasn't. When Mum found out you were sniffin' around Angie from the Claughton hotel, she was goin' to the solicitors. She told me yer were in danger of havin' yer whatsits cut off."

"It was just a blip, queen. Angie kept givin' me the come on. I tried to ignore her, but she wouldn't have it."

"Ah, but she did have it, didn't she, and that's why Mum decided we were all emigratin'. Still, I'm not bothered. I liked that place we stayed in when we came fer the validation and I'm really lookin' forward to getting' a sun tan on Christies beach in the summer."

"I didn't see any kangaroos when we were here last time," said Jodie. "Mum said we'll have to go to the zoo to see them. I thought kangaroos were everywhere."

"Want a wee wee," Kyle said from the depths of his pushchair.

"Molly, tek 'im. Why the hell yer mother didn't put a nappy on 'im, I'll never know."

"He's being potty trained." Molly went off with the pushchair to find a loo.

"Where is she, then?", shouted Abbie from the passenger seat of the dark maroon people carrier that drew up at the road side.

"Gone to the loo," replied Wayne, pushing the trolley towards the vehicle, with Jodie in tow.

"Our Kyle wanted a wee."

Abbie raised her eyebrows to heaven then got out to help her husband stow the luggage and place Jodie onto a booster seat.

"The bloke said he'd drive us to his office, do the paperwork, then he'll hand it over. Do yer know, I think it's the same one as we had last time?"

"It is," said Jason from within. "I remember it had a little tear in the roof and it's still there."

"Well, don't go pokin' at it," said Abbie. "We've enough to pay out without having to pay fer repairs to it."

"I'll start lookin' around fer one of them camper vans," Wayne said. "I bet they'll be a load of them fer sale in the newspaper."

"Oh, 'ere she is," Abbie sounded relieved, as she saw her daughter pushing Kyle through the arrivals door.

"Right, we can get off now. I'll sit in the front seat, there's more room fer me there."

At last it was happening. Abbie sat back and relaxed, whilst the driver navigated his way into the airport traffic. They were back in Adelaide. Back to the place where they could rear their children in sunshine and give them a better crack at life.

She had just given birth to Kyle when she had found out about her Wayne's affair with the local barmaid. It was Gaynor, from next door, that had put her onto him. All those nights when he had said he was working overtime was just a cover. Gaynor's old man had seen Wayne and his bit of skirt wandering off towards Bidston Hill. Abbie had felt a bit suspicious, as the nights were getting dark early and there were not many arc lamps on building sites, but being busy with the new babe and having to see to the other children pushed any malarkey from her thoughts. He got a fright when she lumbered into the lounge bar a week later and beckoned him over, with a pleasant smile pasted on her face. But out of sight, as she pushed him down the road ahead of her, he was made to rue his liaison and had the bruises to show for his sins.

It was then that Abbie Foley made her mind up. Britain was going to the dogs after all.

Immigrants were coming, taking jobs, getting council houses, wanting to build a mosque. They'd sell their house and move out to Australia. She had seen "A Place in the Sun" on their T.V. and it looked like paradise.

Wayne was a skilled craftsman. He'd been working as a brickie since he'd left school. He'd been lucky, they'd always had the readies to pay the mortgage, but how were they going to manage if he had to go on the dole? Then there was their eldest son, Jason. Too many kids were leaving school without qualifications and he wasn't the brightest of the bunch. Molly was attracting the no hopers, the teenage losers who hung around her school. She'd been flattered, like a young girl is when reaching the age of puberty. It wasn't what Abbie wanted for either of them.

Wayne had been against her plan from the onset. His mates were there, he'd lived in Birkenhead forever and he wasn't about to up sticks and go to the other side of the world.

"Okay," she'd said. "Get used to being a loner, 'cos me and the kids are goin' anyway. With yer or without yer, I'm not bothered. I'm goin' to write to our Stanley in Brisbane and he'll give me all the gen."

Abbie Foley was not a woman to be messed with, so Wayne decided to go along with the plan.

And he'd come round to her way of thinking in the end, thought Abbie, as she shifted her bulk a little in order to get comfortable. Stanley, her cousin, had put her in touch with an Adelaide developer who was looking for skilled workmen. An estate of fifteen hundred houses was being built down in the south. They'd been over, validated the employer sponsored visa, visited the place where Wayne would be working and had a very nice holiday. It was better than sitting in their Tollemache Road semi, watching the hearses drive down to Flaybrick cemetery. A place where she surely would have been going one day.

The Southern Expressway was still closed to southbound traffic as Abbie drove the people carrier along the main road. She tutted in exasperation: they still hadn't made the road two way.

"I can't understand why they didn't make that into a proper motorway," she said to no one in particular. "One minute you can go south on it and the next you have to go the long way round!"

"There's lots of things we'll have to get used to," said Wayne. "I was wonderin' what the man was up to when he said yer couldn't drive in thongs. I mean, that's a bit personal, isn't it?"

"He meant Mum couldn't drive in her flip flops," Molly said smiling. "Don't yer remember that's what they were called when we were here before?"

"Oh, I was only joking, our Molly. It just tickles me. I see we're not too far off now. There's the old Stanvac refinery in the distance and eh up, there seems to be a lot of building over there. Looks like I'll be kept busy with all this developing."

"Yeah, let's hope so and let's hope our Jason gets himself a job too."

The young woman who owned the rental house, which was named the "Protea" stood at the top of the small driveway. She had just arrived ahead of them a few minutes before.

"Hi, how's it going?" she asked as Abbie got out of the vehicle and went over to give her a hug.

"Glad to be back, Laura," said Abbie as she gazed at the villa that had been their home briefly, a year before.

"A good flight then." Laura nodded to Wayne, who had got out of the passenger seat and was lighting up a cigarette. "It's a wonder you didn't see me, I was at the airport earlier."

She watched, as Abbie and Jason went to the back of the people carrier and started unloading their luggage. Then Molly picked up her brother, Kyle, and carried him to the front door.

Laura followed Wayne, who was rummaging around in his hand luggage as he walked.

"No need for me to show you around this time." She put the key in the lock and let them in. The house smelt of eucalyptus and oranges. It was like walking back into time again for Abbie.

The room on the right, what the Aussies call the lounge room, held the same navy sofas and a comfortable Lazy Boy chair, a large plasma, a coffee table and a stand for the DVDs. On the left was the master bedroom, with a walk-in wardrobe and access to the two way bathroom and loo. Abbie took note of the duvet cover on the bed, which was different from last time: it was in a pretty shade of green. Ahead was the kitchen and dining room, where Abbie's favourite, a walk-in pantry room, lay. They all watched as Wayne made straight for the patio doors, and once outside, opened a bottle of Coopers Pale Ale from a pack of six he had bought at a bottle shop near the car hire.

"Never changes," Abbie said, shaking her head in mock despair, then opened the fridge to check on the contents of the welcome pack.

"Are yer staying for a cuppa? I don't know about you, but I'm gaspin."

"No, I'll get off, if you don't mind. My mum and dad were on the same flight as you. I've just dropped them off around the corner. They're staying in one of my other rentals for a couple of months, until they find somewhere to buy. You'll be seeing them around, no doubt. Oh and I've topped up the lecky, it should last you a few weeks."

"Ah, yer a doll. Is it still right we have to go to the Colonnades to sort out the Medicare and the post office for our ambulance cover?"

"Yeah, nothing's changed as far as I know and remember you've three months before you have to do something about your English driving licence."

"Okay, queen, yer a goodun. I've got yer number, so I'll give yer a ring or I might send yer an email. I see there's still a modem. Oh and how's the little un?"

"He's good. Growing fast. He'll be going to pre-school soon. Nice to see you all again."

Everyone nodded in agreement, except Kyle, who had gone to rummage through a toy box in the front room, but waved politely as the nice lady walked down the hall to the front door.

"Right, same bedrooms," Abbie said happily. "Molly and Jodie in the back and Jason and Kyle in the side room."

"Well, that's not fair," Jason answered sulkily. "Why do I have to have him in with me?"

"Where do yer expect him to sleep, in the garage?"

"He didn't sleep with me last time."

"That's because he was in a cot and slept with us."

"Then wharrabout he sleeps in that walk-in wardrobe?"

"No, he sleeps in the side room with you," his mother said firmly. And listening to the tone in her voice brooked no argument from her eldest son.

She set about moving all the bags in the direction of the corridor which lead off to the bedrooms and told her kids to get them shifted, quick smart. Even Kyle, called from his futile search of the television channels for CBeebies knew that to argue would be pointless.

"Want any help?" came a voice from the patio outside, where Wayne sat on a sun lounger, his face pointing up to the now warmer sun.

"No, yer all right, we've got it covered. Don't forget you have to put suntan cream on here."

"Slip, slap, slop," said Jodie, coming into the room wearing a pair of yellow shorts and a matching T-shirt she had quickly changed into. "The lady's left some sweeties in a bowl on our dressin' table. Can I have one?"

"Little love," Abbie said. "Yeah, I'm goin' to get Molly to walk up to the supermarket and get us some Vili pies later, so you can 'ave a couple now. Laura's left some juice, would yer like some?"

"It's all right here, isn't it?" said Wayne, coming to the patio door, his cheeky chappie face wearing a happy grin.

"Pity, I 'ave to report fer duty next Monday and I'm goin' to be missin' all the sunshine when I'm on the course."

"Don't blow yer smoke in the 'ouse, Wayne. She must 'ave worked hard to get it so lovely. I noticed there's a new sign up, saying it's a no smokin' 'ouse."

"Bloody no smokers. They'll be stoppin' folk from breathin' soon."

"That can be arranged," said Abbie. "Now, will yer eat a pie, if Molly goes to fetch us some?"

Wayne sat back down on his lounger, after taking the top off his second bottle. She never changed, did Abbie, all there with her cough drops. She'd been a bold piece, even when they had first started courting nearly twenty years ago. He was a mate of one of her brothers. Was a mate. He'd nearly got his eye blacked by the tosser, when word had it he was playing away.

But when Abbie met him, even though she was only fifteen, it had been her who had made a beeline. He supposed it was his blue deep set eyes, fringed with dark curly lashes, and his cheeky smile that attracted the women. That and his aura of sexual prowess of course. He hadn't let her down, neither. There could have been seven kids making a new life in Australia, if she hadn't have had three miscarriages along the way.

That thing with Angie. Just a passing fancy, because Abbie was being stingy in the bedroom department. Angie was up for it. Well, she would be with a face like the back end of a bus, and she had fallen for all his promises. As if he'd leave Abbie. He wouldn't be able to function without the silly mare.

"Molly, yer Dad will have two pies, silly sod must be starvin'. And get an assortment. And keep yer eye out fer that bloody girl that was causin' grief last time we were 'ere. Honestly, I don't know what's up with you young girls, scrappin' over anything."

"They've all got bloody chips on their shoulders, Mum. Anyway, if yer let me go to that technical college on Beach Road where our Jason might be goin', I'll be mixin' with girls who want to get on with their lives, not hangin' round street corners."

"We'll 'ave ter look into it, queen. I suppose we could keep yer off school until yer sixteenth birthday. It's not far off and yer can keep an eye on Kyle fer me. I thought yer wanted ter get into childcare."

"Childcare, hairdressin', beauty, I'm not bothered. The world's me oyster, as they say."

"Well, whatever. Here's fifty, get us some washing powder while yer at it. That Spree was okay last time and if I get a load in now it'll be dry by tea-time."

"Right," said Wayne, shutting the patio door behind him and walking past Abbie on his way to the lounge room. "Where's Jason? Me and him will have a walk to the video shop, get some vids in fer tonight. I had a look through the T.V. guide in the *Messenger*. There's nothing on we'd like."

"Here's fifty," said Abbie, reaching into her purse again. "And don't let that money drip through yer fingers. We have ter keep some back fer the house money, yer know"

How did I ever become such a nag, thought Abbie, not for the first time in her married life. She never used to be, she used to be so easygoing. A bit of a tomboy really, with all her brothers to knock about with. She had three elder brothers and they all treated her as if she was their angel. That was until they got married and their wives became their focus of devotion, and she fell for the charms of the "Claughton Casanova", not to be outdone. She had kept her hand on her halfpenny for a couple of years, knowing that if she got pregnant her brothers would kill the man responsible. But just short of her seventeenth birthday she'd given in, when Wayne had said he was getting fed up with going out with a prick-teaser. She'd always wished they'd had a big fancy wedding instead of ten minutes in the registry office, with the ceremony at a posh church in Oxton and a reception at the Swan hotel. But her father was on the dole, her mother only earned a pittance as a cleaner and *she* only earned buttons in a chip shop down Borough Road.

They had started married life in a flat on Shrewsbury Road with their name down for a council house, which had never materialised because the couple didn't have enough points at that time to climb up the waiting list. It was then that Wayne had become a star and had genuinely worked a lot of overtime, putting his wages into Abbie's hands as soon as he came home. It was the time of the "lump system", when many brickies avoided paying tax on their earnings, so the Foleys soon had a nice deposit for a semi-detached. But all good things come to an end and Wayne was soon having to travel across the Mersey in search of building work. Gone was the time of not having to watch the pennies and Abbie was obliged to take on the role of the shrew, with two young children and a miscarriage under her belt.

"Mum, can I play out in the garden?" Jodie broke into Abbie's thoughts as she set about making cups of tea. "I think I saw a koala bear sittin' up in one of those funny trees."

"I think they call them gum trees, Jodie." There was no way she would trade her life with anyone.

The phone rang later causing everyone to jump, as they were concentrating on tucking into their delicious pies at the dining table. It was Laura Gee, according to Molly, who had been first to reach the kitchen bench top, making Abbie wonder if that no hoper, Neil, who had been sniffing around Molly back home, had been given the rental house telephone number.

"She wants ter talk ter you, Mum."

"Sorry, I forgot to mention before, Abbie," Laura said. "It must be the excitement of having my parents over. We're having a barbecue at ours, tomorrow. It's to welcome Mum and Dad, yourselves of course and there's a family living in my other rental that you'd probably enjoy meeting. I've also invited some other folk that have moved on, but I've kept in touch with. I thought about fiveish. Save you having to cook dinner." She gave her address, which Abbie knew already as it was on the tenancy agreement. It was a place in Kingston, which Abbie couldn't wait to view.

She went into the master bedroom later. Master bedroom, what would all the folks back home think? Putting all her things on hangers in the walk-in wardrobe, she lamented her lack of decent clothing. What had she got to wear to a barbecue at a posh address? Her thin black seersucker trousers made her backside look like an elephant and she had one decent skirt that fitted well because it wasn't gathered. Her long bottom-covering blouses had been chosen because they hid all her bulges and the only dress she possessed could be used as a tent!

She hadn't had all these problems before she had the children. Perhaps a little plump after Jason, but that could be hereditary and it appeared that Wayne had liked her like that. The tan three quarter pants she wore were fit for the bin really, but they were cheap and very comfortable and went well with her beige hand knitted V-neck sweater and matching camisole. Glancing into the full length mirror that was attached to the back of the door, she vowed to make more effort. Eat less, have her blonde straggly hair cut and buy some new clothes.

"Right, me and Molly are off to do some shopping," she announced after putting her husband's clothes away and changing into her tent-like dress.

"Jodie, you can come or stop with the boys to watch some videos. I'll bring back some fish and chips."

CHAPTER FIVE

The five bedroom superior built double-storey detached house was on a small development of nine houses overlooking the Gulf of St.Vincent, with views towards Brighton and Glenelg. At the head of a horseshoe shaped cul-de-sac lived Laura and her husband, Graham Gee. Along with lawyers, doctors, celebs and members of the local media. Not bad for a couple who had only emigrated to Adelaide some eight years before.

It was whispered that Laura had the backing of her newly arrived to Adelaide parents, who had bankrolled the husband to get his fledgling demolition business up and running. Along with the sale of some of Graham's assets back in Britain, it seemed that the couple had joined the well-to-do. It had begged the question though, amongst Laura's friends and confidants, why were her parents living in one of her rental houses, instead of living in luxury with their daughter and little grandson? All might be revealed at the barbecue, supposedly being held in the parents' honour and as a way of introducing them to some of Laura's friends.

Abbie and her family were the first to arrive. It wasn't B.Y.O. (Bring Your Own), which most people did when invited to a barbecue, but Wayne had brought a six pack of Coopers, just in case they were only serving wine.

Abbie was wearing the dress that she and Molly had chosen at a boutique in the Colonnades on her first day. It suited her perfectly. A white satin decorated bodice, which picked out the dark blue of the long ankle length skirt in a paisley pattern, worn with white block heeled sandals. That morning she'd gone to a local hairdresser and had her hair cut into a shorter, more becoming style. She felt and looked a million dollars, compared to her usual slouchy self, and even Wayne had felt inclined to give some flatter and a promise of an early night.

Her kids were dressed in what she called "their Sunday best" and Wayne had on a Blue Harbour shirt and a pair of black chinos. Their eyes were round with disbelief as they walked through the open front door.

A large hallway laid with a solid timber floor, with an antique grandfather clock standing at the bottom of a mahogany staircase, met their gaze. To their left was an amply furnished room, holding white leather sofas and a large mahogany glass inlaid coffee table, which was positioned on a huge white ornate rug. A display cabinet in the same wood held small ornamental statues that, from the look of them would make a fortune if sold on eBay! To the right of the hall was a comfortably furnished study, with a huge expensive looking desk.

Laura was there to welcome them, dressed rather formally for a barbecue in a pair of black velour trousers and a long sleeved white pin tuck blouse. Her auburn hair was coiled high in a becoming style. There was a smell of food wafting as she walked ahead of her guests to the large family room and white laminate, blue granite work topped kitchen area. Huge windows with patio doors dominated the room, the view so breathtaking that it made you want to stay and look all day. Though the light was beginning to fade, the naphtha flares dotted around outside were beginning to kick in, illuminating the decking and the large garden with its courtyard swimming pool below.

They all walked down the few patio steps to where a dark haired man stood in charge of a stainless steel barbecue, with its built in sink, the size of which you wouldn't believe!

"Hi there, how's it going?" he said, not looking up, nor really waiting for an answer as he turned a few steaks on the griddle.

"Help yourself to drinks from the trolley over there."

"That view's amazin'," said Wayne, wandering over to him, after he had helped himself to one of his own light ales, seeing he didn't know the brand of the ones that were in the Esky, a type of cool box, he had seen at the side of the buffet table.

"Wait until you see the sunset, mate, you'll be blown away."

A man of few words, thought Wayne, but he persisted. A man who might be useful, if what Abbie said was true and he was in the building trade too.

"Yer've a great house," he said admiringly. "Me and Abbie are goin' to build down in Aldinga."

"Ah, you must be Wayne, Abbie's husband. Laura said you're a brickie. Much the same business as me, but I'm in demolition. We knock down the houses then build another on the land. We'll have a talk later when I've got the meat sorted. I don't know about you, but I like to have my meat from the barbecue well done."

Chance would be a fine thing, thought Wayne, having never owned a barbecue. He ambled back to Abbie, who was standing with Jodie, talking to some new arrivals.

"This is Jenny and Finn," Abbie said, looking very happy with herself over something.

"This is Wayne, my husband. Jenny and Finn are in one of the other rentals round the corner from us. And you'll never believe where they're from."

"He will now I've opened me mouth to speak," Finn, a gangly looking chap with dark hair and a stubbly chin, said, holding his hand out to shake Wayne's.

"A scouser," said Wayne, delighted to meet another Merseysider. "Glad ter meet yer. Been over long?"

"We was just tellin' yer missis. We're nearly at the end of our tenancy. Only booked it fer a month, thinkin' that Jen' would 'ave found a job by now. She's a nurse and we came over on her skilled worker visa, but no bugger will give us a long term tenancy unless we 'ave the wage slips ter prove we can manage the rent."

"Oh," said Wayne, thinking he wouldn't have been shifted out of Birkenhead if Abbie hadn't found him a job first. "I'm sure somethin'll pop its head up. Have yer got any kids with yer?"

"Yeah, our littlest is over there playin' with yours, Lucy's talking to yer son and Belle, that's Lucy's twin, is talkin' ter your Molly."

"Well, that'll please Jason," said Wayne, looking over to where

Jason was talking animatedly to a pretty teenage girl with a skirt on that looked like a pelmet. "Get in there, my son!"

"I was saying ter Jen, we should get together tomorrer and take the kids down to Christies beach. I heard that it was goin' ter be 28 degrees. Beats the rainy weather back home."

"Yeah, we should. Fancy 'avin' a beer then, Finn?"

"Just look at that sunset," said Laura, who came onto the decking area with two other couples and their children behind her.

"Never ceases to amaze me, all those fiery colours. How's everyone doing? Help yourselves to drinks, don't be shy. This is Phil and Wendy, they used to be in one of our rentals, but they've bought a house in Blackwood, and Jared and Sam they've been here as long as me and Graham. Jared works in the city and Sam works on Rundle Mall."

"In a dress shop, not on the street," said a well dressed, blonde haired woman in her thirties, smiling at Laura's joke. "Are these all escapees from Britain, or have we got some Aussies here?"

"The Aussies haven't arrived yet. There's still Eddie Farrington, Rhonnda Thornton and their partners and, of course, my parents. Fred and Ginger from next door have gone off on a cruise ship, so they couldn't come. I don't suppose you noticed any movement, Jenny, when you were passing the other rental. My father said they'd get a taxi, save me foregoing a drink."

"No, sorry," Jenny said, her sallow, bespectacled face looking apologetic. "We couldn't even 'ave offered them a lift either, with only 'avin' the one car."

"I'll give them a ring," said Laura, looking worried. "You know where everything is."

The two couples who had just arrived nodded, having enjoyed Laura and Graham's hospitality before.

"I'm surprised her parents aren't stayin' 'ere," said Jenny, once the others had moved to the drinks trolley and out of earshot.

"Exactly my thoughts," Abbie replied. "Yer'd think with all this space they could have had them. And I'd want to be close to the little one, if it were my grandchild. Oh no, our Kyle's hoggin' that car and Laura's boy wants it back again."

"So what did yer do back in Liverpool?" asked Wayne, not interfering with the fight between Kyle and his host's son. That was women's work.

"A bit of this, and bit of that," Finn answered. "I worked on all that new building for the Capital of Culture, as a hod carrier mostly, but I did serve my time as a tiler. It wasn't worth workin' after that. Jen worked out at Halton hospital and I was 'ome for when the girls got back from school and then Brandon came along and it put a whole new slant on things. When Jen said she fancied gerrin' out of Liverpool and tryin' our luck out 'ere, I thought, "Why not?" We didn't have a house to sell, 'cos we were housed by the council and I wasn't happy with the way the girls were beginning to attract a load of wankers. I'd 'ave locked the girls in their bedroom until they were twenty-one, if I had me way."

"But Jen's 'avin' problems gettin' work. What will yer do if nuthin' comes of it?"

"We said we'd give it another few weeks. Laura said she hadn't got another bookin' until November in the house we're rentin' from her, but unfortunately we'll have run out of the readies if we 'ave ter pay her 'til then."

"She seems a nice woman, she might let yer pay on a weekly basis. Anyway, let's get a bevvy. We're 'ere to enjoy ourselves."

"I can come and pick you up, Mum," said Laura, once she had telephoned through to the rental house she called the "Banksia". "I told you we were putting a party on so we could introduce you to everyone. No, there won't be just young people and children. Rhonnda said she might bring her mother. She's come down from Wentworth to live with her. I know it's dark, but if you'd rung for a taxi earlier, you could have come and helped me. Oh, okay, you and Dad are suffering from jet lag. Why didn't you tell me that this morning? Then me and Toby wouldn't have been looking forward to seeing you all day. I think it would be best if we sort you out a hire car. I'll be over in the morning. Give my love to Dad."

She put the receiver down on the landline phone, feeling rather miserable. She'd gone to all this trouble just for them. Wanting to show off her house, her possessions, her friends and how well she and Graham had done. She had wanted them to see that although her marriage to Graham wasn't made in heaven, they were making a fair fist of things. True, he had walked out on his wife and kids when he had met her. True, he was fifteen years older than her, and true, he had no contact with his children back in England. But that wasn't his fault. It was his ex-wife, Dawn, who had called the tune. She had nearly bankrupted Graham with her demands for half the sale of his business, the deeds to the family home and maintenance for her and the kids. He had worked all hours and gone without when he and Laura had decided to come over and start a new life.

Then out of the blue, a few days after she had given birth to Toby, having sent a text message to her father's mobile to say that they had a grandchild, her mother rang, asking for their bank details. It appeared that they'd had a change of heart over their son-in-law now that the marriage had been cemented by their only grandson. They were prepared to make a loan, enough to help Graham with his business, to be repaid if and when the company started to show a profit.

Before her parents' amazing offer, she and Graham had lived on a succession of building sites in a small caravan, whilst the shack they had bought, or run down house that had become uninhabitable, was knocked down to make way for a new one. Graham had managed to convert the remains of his English assets into ready money, helped by the favourable exchange rate of that time. Within six months they had sold their first endeavour and moved onto the next and consecutive ones. Each time they made a handsome profit. It helped that Graham could turn his hand to anything and made use of any unemployed tradies that he met in the local pubs. He eventually came across a man named Eddie Farrington, the owner of a firm who supplied surveyors trained to inspect a would-be purchase and report their findings to the purchaser. The man was a godsend and eventually a sleeping partner. It meant that a bad report knocked down the price, with the vendor grateful he had sold it at all.

Laura took on the loan from her parents instead, as Graham said he wouldn't touch it. It was meant for her and her son's well being after all. She purchased three homes, gave them each a name of a flower that was native to Australia and, with a view to renting them to migrants, resolved to pay her parents back as soon as she could.

Thinking of Eddie seemed to conjure up the very person, as the man himself breezed through her front door, just after she had put the receiver down.

"Laura," he said, his handsome face, sporting a greying moustache, wreathed in a ready smile and his dark blue 'come to bed eyes' looking provocatively into hers.

"Young and beautiful as always, your Graham's a lucky dog. Helen couldn't make it this evening. She said it was too short notice and she'd arranged to go into the city with some friends. Gayla, our Fijian maid, is taking care of the children. Not that they need much looking after with the Foxtel, computers and Nindendo DSIs. Sounds like everyone's through the back. Little Toby doing okay?"

Laura nodded. Eddie tried hard to come across as a bit of a philanderer, but he had been married to Helen for many years and they had three lovely teenage children. It was his way of making a woman feel special and Laura took all his flattery with a pinch of salt. She watched as he sauntered down the hallway, smartly dressed in a pair of navy trousers, a blue and white check shirt, with a white knitted cable sweater thrown carelessly around his shoulders. She had glimpsed another car's headlights coming to a halt outside one of her neighbour's houses. It could be Rhonnda, or one of the girls she had asked from the fitness centre she went to.

It was Rhonnda, that is, Rhonnda Thornton, who worked for a real estate company and tipped Graham off if any dilapidated houses came up for sale. She was helping her mother down the bit of a gradient that the drive was on, assisted by her husband, a great big bear of a man.

In fact both the Thorntons were big boned and larger than life.

47

Rhonnda had been brought up on a farm in Wentworth, a fruit growing area in Victoria, and Anthony was reared on a sheep station at the Top End, that is, in the Northern Territories. Both had craved the city's bright lights and had met whilst backpacking in London. They had settled for a quieter life when they married, with Anthony opening a speciality shop selling lambs' wool rugs and sheepskin products in Adelaide.

"Hi Laura, how's it going? I've brought the old girl. Looking for a knees up, ain't yer, doll?"

This was said in an attempted East End of London accent, as Rhonnda's mother, Betty, had come over from England as a teenager in the 50s and had never really lost hers.

"Yeah and if yer've got a karaoke machine, I'll be in me element," Betty joked happily. It was good to be invited to a party, after living on an isolated farm for so many years.

"Have you settled in? Do you think you'll like Adelaide now you've moved here?"

"I've got to, 'aven't I? Now me husband's gone, it would be difficult to manage alone."

"Ah yes, sorry to hear about your loss. Anyway, come in, I can't promise you a karaoke machine, but we have some pleasant music."

Laura couldn't hear the music from the wrap around sound system they'd had installed in the entertaining area. She had pulled down the café blinds earlier so that the other neighbours wouldn't be disturbed by the noise, but *Matchbox 20*, an album by her favourite singer, Rob Thomas, was being drowned out by the voices of her guests, who had now been added to by Alison and Joanie from the gym and their respective partners and children. Still, everyone seemed happy, from the looks of things.

"Grub's up," shouted Graham, as he finished burning the last of the sausages and steaks and added them to the platters that were piled high with delicious looking meat.

"Get them while they're hot," he continued, sounding like a barker from an old time fete or fair.

"Good, snags," said one of the children, helping himself to a piece of white bread and making himself a sausage sandwich and beckoning over a friend he had made.

"I'll get myself a drink," Graham said to no one in particular, walking to where most of the male guests were either standing or sitting on the heavy wooden slatted table and chairs near the drinks trolley. "That's me finished cooking," he said, after pouring red wine into a large glass and taking a mouthful. "Ah, my favourite. You can't beat a good shiraz. This one I can recommend."

"Yes, we must get a party up again and go down to McLaren," said Eddie. "My stocks are getting very low and yours will be gone by the time we've finished with it."

"I was saying just that before, to Laura. Though she'll probably want to take her parents there."

"Is McLaren Vale the place where they 'ave all those wineries?" asked Wayne.

Now that he was on his fifth beer, he felt relaxed enough to speak to anyone, even if the newly arrived bloke looked a bit intimidating. "We didn't get to go when we were over before and I'm not a wine drinker. The wife likes Lambrusco, so we might make the effort when we've settled in."

Most of the men who were listening looked at him in surprise when he had finished speaking, so he lapsed into silence, as he felt himself a pleb.

"Wayne's a brickie," Graham said, by way of explanation to Eddie, as if it explained why his guest wasn't a lover of good wine.

"Ah, a tradie. Do you have a job to go to? I'm sure Graham could find you something, if not."

"Yeah, I'm here on an employer sponsored visa. I'll be workin' down in Aldinga once I've finished the course. Finn here hasn't got a job yet, 'ave yer, Finn? Didn't yer say yer were a tiler?"

The man next to Wayne shifted uncomfortably.

"Aye, but we're over 'ere fer Jenny's job. I'd 'ave ter look into the visa restrictions."

"Well, whatever," Eddie was dismissive. "I've got one of you Poms starting to work for me on Monday."

"What I feel most miserable about, apart from not getting a job," said Jenny to the women who were sitting with her around a small wicker glass inlaid table on brown wickerwork chairs. "Is the way friends and rellies in England forget yer so quickly. I mean, me sister threw a big going away party fer us at the British Legion and there were at least forty people there. All me friends from the hospital promised faithfully that they'd keep in touch. I give them the twins' email address so they could stay in contact and our Jane even got Talk Talk, so she could ring us fer peanuts. We've 'ad one phone call from her, just ter see if we got 'ere safely and that's been it. The girls are on the computer every day, sendin' messages to their mates on Facebook, but we've 'ad nothin'. It's like they've all give up on us."

Sam, who had been in Adelaide for quite a long time, nodded her head in agreement.

"We came over eight years ago and I had loads of girlfriends, who said they'd keep in touch. I can count the Christmas cards from them on one hand now and my family seem to have forgotten me. My mum's still alive. Granted she's in an old folk's home now and I feel bad about not seeing her, but she could have come over and lived with us. She could have come out on an aged parent visa. I've two sisters and nieces and nephews and they've all got open invitations to visit at any time, but they all have their excuses. That's something that we Poms have to face when we decide to cut and run from whatever urges us out of our comfort zone. We have to remember the reason we came here and not yearn for the nostalgia of home."

"I second that," said Wendy, her face looking flushed with the three glasses of wine she'd consumed, because she was only an occasional drinker. "We actually went back to England. We were from Harrogate, by the way. We missed the lovely green hills, our close family ties, the small community where we lived and the Yorkshire accents. Believe it or not, some Australians couldn't understand what I said. We hadn't got as far as buying property at that time, we were still renting from Laura and I woke up one morning and told Phil that we were going back home. He'd just started his job, he works at the Science Park on Main South, and of course the boss there wasn't very pleased when Phil said he had to go back. Well, he had to, or I would have taken the kids and gone without him. Anyway, to cut a long story short, we'd only been back there a couple of days, we had to bunk up at his mother's because we didn't have a house to go back to, when I looked out at the pouring rain, couldn't see those green hills for the mist on them and woke up from a sort of trance and wondered what I was doing there. We'd left sunshine here, now we were walking around in woolly jumpers and raincoats. We'd actually found a lovely place to live called Blackwood and seen a house we could afford to buy outright before we went back, but I'd been dithering. I said to Phil, 'Get on the phone and ask your boss if he'll take you back again.' And here we are and I've never been troubled by nostalgia again."

"A Ping Pong Pom," said Rhonnda, who had attached herself to the group when she had deposited her mother in a chair next to Wendy. "Mum had no such option when she came over as a teenager with her parents in 1963. They came over on the ten pound scheme, enduring bad weather on the ship to Sydney, then slumming it in the government accommodation that was provided for them. Eventually they made their way to Adelaide, where Mum's family had relatives they could stay with, but they were in no position to go back to England again."

"We never wanted ter go back again, Rhonnda," Betty volunteered. "The East End got rough. Well, it always was a bit rough, but where we lived, it got crowded out when there was problems in Uganda. Anyway, I met your dad here and he wanted me to go and live on his farm and of course you know the rest of the story."

Her daughter nodded and asked her would she like another drink?

"You probably wouldn't like it there now, anyway,"said Abbie. "If yer thought it was crowded with foreigners in the 60s, you'd be

51

amazed to see 'ow many there are of them now. The government decided to let all the Eastern Europeans in and they came in their thousands. It wasn't too bad where we lived, because most people were on the dole anyway, but now there's Poles, Czechs, Latvians and any other bugger who wants to come and work there. But what gets me, the fellers claim family allowance and send the money home!"

"You have to remember that we're all foreigners here too," said Wendy. "Of course this is a bigger country, so depending on where you live, you won't be exposed too much to other races. If you went to Croyden Park you would find yourself in a Polish community, in Hahndorf there's the Germans and there's a large Italian population living in Adelaide too. Australia was obviously built on immigration. The only ones who can honestly say they're truly Australian are the aborigines."

"Who haven't had much of a deal since the Europeans started coming over and colonising," said Rhonnda, handing her mother a glass of white wine and sitting with them all again. "It's time we had another referendum, to vote ourselves a Republic instead of supporting the Queen!"

"Rhonnda!" Betty looked at her scandalised, as did some of the Brits that were listening. "I've always brought you up to respect the Queen and her family!"

"Huh, a Queen who's only shown her face here once or twice."

"I'm sure she's been 'ere more than once or twice, Rhonnda. I know for a fact she came in March 1977 and then in 1986, because your grandma died that year."

"And she was bound to 'ave come over after her Coronation," Abbie chipped in, having always had a fondness for the Queen since her "annus horribilis".

"Whatever. A toast to the queen and her family then!"

CHAPTER SIX

"I think we'd best get off," said Jenny, feeling the atmosphere grow tense after Rhonnda had started spouting and noticing that her five year old was fighting with another boy over a piece of Lego. "He always gets cranky at this time of night. Brandon get over 'ere, immediately!"

The little boy ignored her and started to rain blows on a small unfortunate character. She got up and yanked him away from the other children, who were beginning to watch the fracas with interest. The recipient of Brandon's displeasure ran howling to his mother, who took a dim view of the situation and looked about to get revenge.

"I'll ring you, Laura" said Jenny apologetically, as she fled up the hallway, with a screaming monster, two scowling twins and a half cut husband in tow.

Laura took the opportunity after saying goodbye to them to rinse a few dirty plates that she had collected on her first foray around the entertainment area. She looked over the kitchen bench top, as she did so, to check that all was well. Now that Brandon had gone, Toby, Kyle and another child were playing happily with their newly built Lego castle. Jodie had made friends with a girl similar in age to her and they were sitting together on two child size armchairs that Laura had brought out. The teenagers were nowhere to be seen. They were probably sat on the cubby house decking, or in the garden, out of sight.

Her mind dwelled for a moment on the couple who had just left the party. They seemed to have come over from Britain on a wing and a prayer. Neither had jobs and their contract for the house expired at the end of the month and she might have to charge them, if the child was anything to go by for a tin of wall paint. What must it be like to see no light at the end of the tunnel? At least she'd had Graham to sort things out.

She had never had any regrets about taking Graham away from his wife, back in England. In her opinion his wife had deserved it, but it had caused a rift in her own family.

They had met on several occasions when Laura was a bookkeeper at a local garage and Graham brought his truck, family car and his wife's run about in for service. She had been walking along the high street in her home town of Wheaton one lunchtime and he had pipped the horn of his Ford as he had driven by. She'd waved, recognising the truck as one that the garage serviced, then was taken by surprise when the vehicle came to a halt. He'd been quite brazen in his invitation to have lunch together. He needed to eat, as did she, and what was wrong with getting in the truck with a valued customer and driving out to a pub on the road to Shrewsbury? Well, nothing at the time, but it soon became a habit, as did the assignations on a Thursday night, when he was supposed to be playing pool with his mates.

She had listened sympathetically when Graham told her that his wife had lost interest in their sex life. Of course, he hadn't said anything like that on their first few meetings. No, they talked about Laura's aspirations instead. Her dream was to backpack around Australia, but up to then she hadn't got the courage to leave her parents, who would have talked her out of such a foolish idea. Boyfriends had been few. Only one had matched up to her parents' image of the perfect suitor, but Laura could only see a life of boredom beckoning if she had married him.

They had decided, much later on in their illicit relationship, to find a flat for Laura to move into. It would make it easier, if Graham suddenly found the opportunity to walk out on his wife. As Christmas was just around the corner, it seemed churlish to do such a thing at that time, given that it would upset his kids, though they never saw much of him anyway. Things came to a head with her parents though, when she announced she was moving out.

There were bitter words and recriminations when later they found out her reason, accusing their daughter of being a marriage wrecker and telling her not to darken their door again.

"Ah, there yer are, queen." Abbie's scouser accent broke into Laura's reminiscing and brought her back to the present again.

"I think we'll get off. Thanks so much fer the invite. Our Wayne's 'ad a skin full and I'd best get 'im 'ome ter bed. We're goin' down ter Christies beach tomorrer, if you and Toby are up fer it. Jen and Finn are goin'. We'll be there around eleven or there about."

"Thanks. We'll be over that way to see my parents in the morning, so we might come down and join you. I don't know if you noticed, but my last tenants left some beach stuff in the garage. I know there are water wings and a couple of inflatables. You're welcome to the use of them and the deck chairs."

"Ta, Laura, yer a star. We've only got this week, then Wayne's off doing his brickie course. He's been bricklaying fer years, but he has to get licensed or something."

"Every tradie has to get a licence," Laura replied. "And the Poms have to learn the Aussie way. You might have noticed that the wooden structure of a house can be up in a couple of days. That's with a good team of workers, so brickies from England need to learn what's expected of them too."

"Well, as long as 'e starts getting a wage, I'm not bothered what 'e does. I don't want ter start eatin' into our 'ouse money. We want ter build one from new."

"If I can help you with anything, just shout," said Laura. "I've got contacts that I can put you in touch with. Rental agents if you need a long term rent, or if you want a car at a discount price."

"Good one, I've got your number," said Abbie, before walking back to the decking and rounding up her kids.

"Jason, get 'old of yer father, there's a love, and help 'im up!"

Everyone watched with amusement as the father shrugged his son's hand off, then staggered towards the patio door. Three footsteps forward and two back again, then he lurched up the steps.

"What a tosser," said Graham to the rest of the males standing with him, who were helping him to demolish most of the bottles of wine he had put out. "I hope he's not driving, the police are red hot when it comes to drink driving around here."

"No, I heard his wife saying before to someone that she'd driven over in a people carrier," Phil broke in. "I think most of us get our wives to drive us back again."

"Well, my wife's not here," said Eddie, sounding bitter: something that was beginning to appear in his voice quite often, when he mentioned his wife. "I might have to bed down on one of your sofas."

"Go for it," said Graham, knowing that life in the Farrington household was not as most people assumed it to be. "You could leave a message on the machine, if Gayla doesn't answer."

And Gayla was part and parcel of the problem, in his book, thought Graham. Too much attention given to the live-in maid.

"Sit yourself down, Laura," he shouted, as he saw his wife bobbing around the buffet table, merging uneaten food onto one big platter, so that she could take more plates away for washing. "You can do all that in the morning!"

"I'll help you," said Betty, quickly getting up from her seat. She preferred to be of use, rather than accepting the hospitality for free.

"You'll spoil that nice sparkly jumper," Laura replied, but let the older woman lead the way to the kitchen. It would have been nice, if her own mother had been there offering to help.

"You've a lovely house," Betty said, once she had wrapped herself in one of Graham's chef aprons. "Similar to Rhonnda's, but you're nearer to the sea. I never thought I'd be living in such luxury. Do yer know, I've a bathroom all to meself now? When I went to live on the farm with Rhonnda's father, we 'ad a dunny. No bathroom, and just a bucket fixed up at the bottom of the garden fer a shower, near the chooks' house. Yer can imagine. We lived like that for years and all the time I saved what bit of money I made from selling off a table at the end of our track. I 'ad an honesty box, for it was too far fer people to trail up to the homestead and I sold fresh eggs, veggies and any fruit that were surplus from our trees. Then one day, I told me husband to find a tradie who could fix me up a bathroom and do yer know, I was the cleanest smellin' farmer's wife within the year!"

"Ahhh, bless you," said Laura, giving Rhonnda's mother a pat on the arm. "I'm sure you'll love living in Adelaide, there's so much to do if you look for it."

"Well, there's a senior's club I've got my eye on. They have outings and Bingo and special rates at a lunchtime, so Rhonnda doesn't feel she has to come back to make a meal. I've told her to find me a unit. Yer know, one of those on a retirement site, with a community hall and a warden, but she won't hear of it."

Laura nodded. "And I don't blame her. Now, do you think I could make you a cup of tea?"

The guests were gone by nine and once Toby had been put to bed with his favourite teddy bear, Laura sat with Graham and Eddie, watching the lights of an ocean liner as it drifted towards Port Adelaide.

"Eddie wants us to look into building apartments, Laura," Graham said. "He thinks it's the way to go. More money in it than a couple of small villas, or a semi. Don't you, Eddie?"

"Yeah, I was down at Christies the other day and I saw that development going up on the corner of Beach Road. They'll make a packet. Especially if they can get investors to take up the slack, if they're not bought as holiday homes."

"I could buy one for my rental business," said Laura. "I mean buy one of ours, not one at Christies. You'd have to try and get a piece of land near a beach though."

"Already onto it," said Eddie. "So where're your folks? I though you had invited us all over to meet them."

"They've got jet lag. I suppose I was a bit previous, expecting them to come over when they've just arrived."

"And do you think they'll settle here? I mean at their age it's a bit much to ask, isn't it?"

"Well, they've sold their house back in England," said Graham, helping himself to a handful of peanuts from a bowl nearby. "So I reckon they've come over to keep an eye on me!"

At eleven the next morning, Wayne, dressed in khaki shorts and a blue Hawaiian beach shirt unbuttoned down the front, was seated on a folding chair on Christies Beach. He was lathered in sun cream, sunglasses shaded his eyes and he had chosen a spot near enough to the toilets and café, so if he fancied a coffee and a pee, he wasn't too far away.

Behind him on the esplanade, Abbie and Jodie struggled in the boot of the people carrier, pulling out two more chairs, rubber inflatables, a bag full of food, a small cool box, towels, a picnic rug, and a bucket and spade for Kyle. The child was seated inside the vehicle, wailing, as he wanted to be out as quickly as possible to enjoy the delights below.

"You tek the rug and Kyle's stuff, Jodie," said Abbie, knowing she had made a rod for her own back by not insisting that Wayne help her. But he thought he was helping by carrying down his own beach chair! It was like having five kids, not four. "I'll put Kyle at the bottom of those steps over there and you come back fer 'im. Yer can make a start 'elpin' 'im with a sandcastle and I'll bring down the rest of the stuff."

Her beach wear clad daughter went ahead and Abbie, dressed in a white bustier top and black crinkle ankle length skirt, with pink flip flops on her feet, lifted Kyle from his booster seat. Her legs were itching from the mozzie bites she'd got at Laura's house last night. Wayne's aftershave, which she had dabbed them with, didn't seem to be working. It had been a good do though, especially meeting up with Jenny. She hoped the lass would manage to get herself a job and then the family could stay. Their Jason had seemed very taken with Jenny's Lucy and Molly had got on well with Belle. So much so, that instead of coming down to the beach that morning, the teenagers had walked together to the Colonnades. Of course it had cost Abbie another fifty dollars. The way things were going, *she'd* be looking for a job.

A blue car pulled up behind her and the driver pipped his horn. It was Jenny and Finn in their hire car, waving happily at her. Abbie let out a sigh of relief when she saw them; they could help her down with a couple of things. Jenny, her dark brown hair braided in a plait and wearing a blue strappy top and a short white denim skirt, lifted Brandon down from his seat and handed him over to Finn.

"Good news," she said, after Finn went off with his son to the beach, carrying a cool box and a folding chair too. "Apparently, someone on the books of the agency I'm down with 'as gone off on maternity leave, so I might be coverin' fer them fer the next few months!"

"Where will that be then? At Flinders or Noarlunga?" Abbie was hoping that Jenny didn't say Flinders, because that would mean they would move nearer to the city.

"Flinders, but I can travel in by car if we decide ter stay around 'ere. Though it'll mean Finn will 'ave ter go everywhere by shank's pony. We'll 'ave ter look round fer a banger. What with the rent and the hire car, our money's runnin' very low."

"And when do yer find out if yer've got the job?"

"She said she'd ring back. I think it's because I need to be shown the ropes first, that the 'ospitals 'ave been reluctant to take me on. Which is daft really, when yer think I am trained in intensive care. Oh and I met that couple this mornin'. Laura's mum and dad? Laura and 'er Toby were just gettin' in the car with them. It appears she was takin' them ter 'ave a look around a few car places. They seem nice enough. I'd say they're in their early sixties. What it must be like ter 'ave a load of money, eh?"

Laura drove her Toyota Rav4, with Toby and her parents aboard, down the main road until they came to the car dealership. Seeing as Laura was happy with her Toyota and the good service she had experienced in the past, her parents, new to the country, had to rely on her judgment.

Her father, Barry Webster, a balding, white haired, stern looking man with a dry sense of humour, sat in the front passenger street, recalling all the cars he had owned since becoming a driver. Quite a feat, seeing as he had been driving for over forty years, but it filled the uneasy silence that possibly could have been created, with father and daughter having been apart for so long.

Brenda Webster, a bottle blonde with a short style haircut, was smartly dressed in black tailored walking shorts and a sunshine yellow blouse. She sat in the back with Toby and held onto the little boy's hand as if she never wanted to let it go. With only seeing him via Skype, once per week, it had been difficult to form a bond with the tiny fellow. But she was with him now, feeling his soft pink hand in her hand and seeing his happy smile. He was so like Laura, when she had been Toby's age. Blonde hair, a chubby face, deep blue eyes that held a sparkle. Even his lips were shaped like Laura's; there was nothing of Graham in him at all.

She began to frown as she thought of the man who had brought her daughter to the other side of the world. An unfeeling man, who could leave his wife and family at the drop of a hat. No matter that according to Laura, he had worked hard and given her and Toby all the luxuries that money could buy. What he had done was against all that she and her husband, Barry, believed in. To walk away from the vows of marriage was a mortal sin. Still, she supposed they mustn't dwell on his past misdemeanours now. They were there to forgive. Wasn't that what their religion taught them, to forgive the sins of others and turn the other cheek?

"We can have a look around, Dad, see if there's anything that takes your eye. Then if not, there's a Ford dealer down the road a bit. You've had a few Fords, so perhaps you'd like to have a look there as well."

"I'm more concerned about payment, should I see something, Laura. I should have set up an Australian bank account when we were back in England, but with selling the house and moving into the rental, it didn't even cross my mind."

"Then we'll go to the ANZ in the Colonnades and open a bank account there. I'm sure Mum has your passports tucked away in her handbag and should you need to put a deposit down on a car, your Visa card should do."

Wayne and Finn sat at a table outside the beach front café drinking iced coffee whilst watching the world go by.

"I've heard they're goin' ter build a desalination plant over yonder," Finn said, looking out to where the beach disappeared from view. "I thought I might keep me eye out, ter see if they'll be takin' on labourers. If Jen manages to get this job, I was tellin' yer about."

"It looks as if they're doin' somethin' there already," Wayne observed, noting workmen activity that seemed to involve pipes. "If I were you, I'd turn up at the site one morning and ask if they're takin' anyone on. Or maybe tap that Graham up we met last night, he might 'ave somethin'."

"I'll 'ave ter see. It's all right fer them that's got money behind 'em."

Behind his sunglasses, Wayne closed his eyes in mock despair. This bloke seemed intent on having a permanent holiday if he could get away with it.

A similar conversation was being held by their spouses.

"He didn't do much when we lived in Liverpool," Jenny said, as the two women sat on folding chairs whilst keeping their eyes on their small boys, who were running in and out of the lapping tide with Jodie. "Granted he worked on the Capital of Culture buildings, but that was because the dole said they were withdrawing payments, basically if he didn't get off 'is arse. We put most of what 'e earnt away. That's what I managed ter get off 'im, as he's always liked a pint or three, but I was determined to try a new life 'ere. There's not much goin' fer the girls back 'ome, unless they followed me and got a nurse's training. Neither seemed inclined when I talked to them about it. Lucy says she'd like to work in a dress shop and Belle says she'd like to be a nail technician. There's not much ambition in my family."

"Not much in mine either," Abbie said ruefully. "Without me, they'd be back at 'ome doing the same old, same old everyday. Jason could be anythin' 'e wanted ter be, if 'e put 'is mind ter it, but e's lazy. Do yer know, he could read before 'e went ter school. Of course I encourage all three of them and our Kyle gets read to every night, but once they get into the school system, it's like they can't be bothered. Perhaps it'll be different fer our Kyle, perhaps the schools are better 'ere."

"Let's 'ope so and wouldn't it be the gear if your Kyle and our Brandon become good friends?"

"Well, it looks as if our Jason and Molly 'ave hit it off with your two. Jason 'ad a girlfriend back 'ome and 'e wasn't too pleased about leavin' 'er there."

"Oh, it's puppy love at their age. They think they're in love, 'til someone else they fancy comes along. I got the doctor ter put the twins on the Pill before we came 'ere. There's no way I want the complication of a grandchild. I've enough lookin' after this lot as it is."

"Molly's gonna wait 'til she finds 'erself a boyfriend and I'm not sure yer can get the Pill if yer've only got Medicare."

"So many things, Abbie. So many things ter get yer head around. I seem ter be learning somethin' new every day."

"Yeah, the other day, when me and Molly 'ad a walk round the dress shops, we saw a shop named "Manchester and More". I thought ter meself that it was an outlet sellin' footy merchandise fer Manchester United. And do yer know what it was…?"

"A place that sold duvets and bedding," Jenny finished off for her. "And what about this one. I went into a shop and asked fer a lolly fer Kyle. I meant one yer get out of a freezer, a frozen lolly on a stick. The woman pointed to a counter display that 'ad all sorts of different sweets on. I 'ad to go to an ice cream kiosk in the end. That's where we'll 'ave ter go one day. There's a shop in Glenelg that sells sweets, like those yer can get back in England and perhaps we can go to "Play and Fun" down at Christies Beach or the wooden fort at Port Noarlunga."

"That's one of the things I'm looking forward to over here," said Abbie. "There's so much for the kids to do if we look for it. Our Kyle can join Joey's when he's a bit older, Jodie can go to a surf club, 'cos she loves swimmin', and there's all sorts of after school clubs, if they're so inclined. There didn't seem much for the older kids though, when I looked through all the leaflets that Laura had left us in her folder, but I heard when I was here last time that the supermarkets have lots of teenagers working part-time."

"Yeah, our Belle was telling me. They met a girl in Woolies who does just that. Oh, I do 'ope I get that job with the agency, Abbie. I'd feel a fool if after all the effort getting 'ere, we 'ad ter go back."

CHAPTER SEVEN

Paul had been working at Farrington (Building Surveyors) Pty Ltd for two weeks when Amanda made her announcement. He had come in tired, after travelling from the office in the city by car, to a house in Reynella, where a young couple had commissioned a report to check if a property was a sound investment. Besides attending a three-day module course paid for by his employer, he also had to shadow a chap who had worked in the building business for more years than he cared to remember.

"I want to go back to England," Amanda said quietly, after making sure the children were engrossed in watching the T.V. "I hate it here. This bloody house is freezing, that reverse cycle whatsit is hopeless. I miss my central heating and all I seem to be doing is spending my days wandering around the local shops, or sitting on the beach with the kids!"

"Some people would give their eye teeth for your kind of life," Paul retorted irritably. "Anyway, your job was to check out schools and rental agents and I thought you wanted to join that local gym."

"There doesn't seem to be any point to any of it. I don't like it here. I miss my friends. Speaking to them on the phone isn't the same."

"Well, I *do* like it here, Amanda, and I would advise you to make the best of it. I'm not prepared to up sticks and leave a job that I'm enjoying. Both Emily and Cody seem to be happy here, especially Cody, now he's got Mr. Furryfeet back, and you should try to make an effort too."

"They miss their granny and we never did got one of them Skype things."

"And so do I, miss my mother I mean, and we can't afford

Skype just yet. But surely you knew that settling down in a new country would take time."

"Well, I didn't want to come. I only came with you because of the children."

"Ah, and I thought it was something we both wanted," Paul said sarcastically. "Well, tough, like I said, I advise you to make the best of our new life."

"I could go back home on my own." Amanda looked at him dully, wondering how he would take her announcement.

"If that's what you want, no one is stopping you. But you won't be taking the children. I have their passports and their paperwork in my briefcase, so you would be travelling on your own."

He walked off to get a warming shower, after changing out of the business suit he was required to wear. The house he had seen that day was even colder than this one. It only had a wood burning fire, which hadn't been burning.

"That's better," he said, emerging later, fully restored to good humour and looking forward to eating the lasagne that he could smell wafting from the oven. "Did Nettie come to give you a service? Trevor's Super looks nice and clean!" His attempt at humouring her was met with an icy stare. "Look, Amanda, let's try to be rational about this. It's only you that feels homesick. Both Emily and Cody are looking forward to starting school and joining the surf club. You should try to find something that you would enjoy. What's wrong with that gym you saw?"

"I can't be bothered and until the kids start going to school, there's no point in enrolling."

"Then why don't you and the kids come up to the city tomorrow lunchtime? It's walkabout day, so I'll be finishing early. We'll go the market and have a meal in China Town."

Laura managed to find a parking space in the multi storey quite easily. It was unusual on a Friday, when everyone seemed to want to be at the Central Market, looking for bargains among the rows of stalls piled high with fruit and vegetables and other fresh products.

"What would you like to do first?" she asked her parents once they had gone down in the lift to ground level.

"You choose," said her father uncertainly, sounding a bit out of his depth. "Did you want to get some shopping, Brenda, or did you want to eat first?"

"Well, we could look around and Laura could tell us whether things are cheaper here, or if it would be best to visit that Woolworth store on our way home. Are you sure that Graham will remember to pick Toby up from pre-school?"

"He hasn't forgotten to do so before now, Mum," Laura replied, "but it's not worth trekking to the city, if we have to go rushing back."

"Oh, don't mind me, Laura, I know I'm fussing. It's just that now I've got to know the little fellow, I worry, naturally. That's what grandmas do."

"We'll start here at the cheese counter." Laura ignored her mother's professed interest in her grandson's well-being, as she hadn't given a hoot about her daughter's. It had been nearly five years; five years when her parents had chosen to pretend they *hadn't* got a daughter. In that time, Graham had divorced his wife on the grounds of incompatibility, applied for a business visa in Australia, paid for him and Laura to visit all the places she had always dreamt of seeing, culminating in an exotic wedding on the island of Fiji!

Laura knew her parents' problem. It was a moral thing and they hadn't been prepared to move with the times. It was Toby's birth that had healed the rift. That and their sudden yearning to do something amazing before they got too old. And it was amazing. How many couples of sixty-one could up sticks and travel to the other side of the world?

"I love coming here," Laura said. "Before we had Toby, we used to come to the city every Friday night. We'd come here and stock up for the weekend, then we'd go to a little Chinese restaurant in the shopping mall. Sometimes, we'd have a change and go to a place called the "Hog's Breath" café. They do a lovely steak and in the summer there's nothing nicer than sitting outside at one of the pavement tables. I thought this time though, we'd go to the Chinese food hall. It's always full of Chinese people eating, which tells you the food must be up to their standard and you can choose whatever you like from the hot food stalls."

"Sounds good to me," said her father, "and it will be my treat."

After filling a plastic bag full of bananas, apples, walnuts and a wedge of brie, they wandered through alleyways full of jewellery, toys, Akubra hats, knitwear and tourist memorabilia, until they came to a large rectangular hall that was filled with hot food stalls, selling meals from China, Taiwan, Vietnam, Japan and India. As Laura had said, the place was full of people who could be described as hailing from the Orient, and one of the stalls had a queue of people waiting to choose their buffet lunch. Of course that was the stall that they made for.

"Beats sitting in our house back home wondering what to cook for dinner," said Brenda contentedly, after she had finished her noodles, prawns and bok choi dish.

"You never cease to amaze me, Mum," said Laura. "When I lived at home, we always had English food. You never seemed to experiment very much."

"Things have changed since your father retired from the Post Office, Laura. We realised that life is passing us by. If we had stayed in Wheaton, we'd have gone downhill in a matter of months. Bothering the doctor every time we got a twinge, taking our holidays down on the Isle of Wight each year. We may as well have booked ourselves into the local old people's home and be done with it. Now a whole new life beckons. And in the sunshine, which has been proven to aid longevity."

"Amen to that," said Barry.

"Well, we'll have a little wander now and I can show you Victoria Square. I believe there's a lot of history attached to that area, but I don't know much about it. Once you've found your feet, you'll be able to come on your own and have a look around. There's a market on Rundle Mall every Sunday morning, as well."

"Sounds good to me," said Brenda. "We could come after we've been to church, when we find one we like, and we'll also need to find our way here in a couple of weeks, when we have to go to D.I.A.C. I believe it's in Currie Street."

"Oh, why do you have to go to the Department of Immigration and Customs? I thought you had applied for an offshore visa."

"Someone said that once we're granted our parent visa from Perth, we might be able to change it to an onshore one. Save us having to go to a consulate somewhere abroad and then having to come back to validate. We thought we'd visit Currie Street to see if that's the case," said Barry.

"Well, you've plenty of time left on your tourist visa, so I wouldn't be in a hurry," said Laura.

It was sunny as they came out of the food hall and walked onto Grote Street. Laura took her jacket off, feeling the warmth on her arms. She had worn a sleeveless dress that day, a navy and white floral one, which was caught around the waist with a narrow navy buckle belt.

"That's a familiar figure walking in front of us," she said, spotting Eddie, in his brown pinstriped suit, walking along with a group of people that she hadn't seen before.

"It's Eddie, Graham's partner. You would have met him if you had come to the barbecue. I'll catch him up and introduce him to you. Hi, Eddie!"

He turned straight away when he saw who had waylaid him, his face wreathed with a happy smile.

"Laura!" He walked back to where she and her parents stood.

Kissing her on the cheek then giving her a quick hug, he turned his attention to Barry and Brenda, who were standing with bemused looks on their faces, shocked at the unreserved way the man was treating their daughter. He kissed Brenda on the cheek after Laura had introduced her, telling her that she could have been Laura's elder sister she looked so young, then pumped Barry's hand and said how pleased he was to meet them.

The group he was with, consisting of a man, a woman and two

children, one a boy who was carrying a brown furry teddy bear, stopped in front of a bank and were looking at the display of adverts whilst they were waiting.

"Come and meet my newest employee and his wife, *they're* from England." Eddie said, looking over to where the family stood. "In fact, we've just eaten, but if you'd care to join us for a drink, that would be bonzer."

"If you're sure they won't object," said Laura. "Would you like that, Dad? I was only planning to drop in to see Graham and Toby, before I ran you and Mum home."

"Go for it," said Barry, using a term he had heard when he had been watching Channel 7. Anything to put off seeing his son-in-law again. It had been bad enough last Sunday, when Laura had insisted that she was going to pick them up and take them to see her new house. Of course, they had no option but to go and they *had* wanted to see where their grandson was being brought up.

They were astounded, to say the least. They had thought their four bedroom detached house was rather nice, back in the countryside outside Wheaton, but Laura's took the biscuit. To say it was grand was an understatement, especially the beautiful view, but it was their son-in-law's attitude that had got to them. He was rude to the point of embarrassment. Not rude verbally, but he made a point of being very busy somewhere and made no effort to receive their olive branch.

"This is Paul and Amanda," said Eddie. "And Emily and Cody, their very polite children. Paul has come from Manchester to help me with my very heavy workload. We're building surveyors by the way. Guys, this is Laura, wife of one of my associates and her parents. Sorry, Laura did tell me your names."

"Barry and Brenda," Barry supplied. "Very pleased to meet you. Nice to meet other Brits."

"Apprentice Aussies, now," said Paul affably. "So where are you from in England?"

"I think we should get a move on, if you don't mind," said Eddie. "We appear to be blocking the pavement. We were on our way to a place just off Rundle Mall. They serve excellent coffee."

Later, when the children had been put to bed and Paul and Amanda were relaxing with a glass of wine, after Amanda had been out on the patio smoking a cigarette, she announced to Paul that she had changed her mind about going back to England.

"Any reason why?" Paul asked, trying to appear nonchalant but hoping Amanda couldn't hear the relief in his voice.

"I don't think I've given it much of a chance. I mean, look at that couple we met today, Laura's parents. They've given up everything, just to be with their daughter and grandson. They've come all this way, not knowing what to expect, only seen their grandson on Skype. It's been a leap of faith for them really. I'll make a greater effort next week and take the children to look around a couple of primary schools in the area and perhaps tomorrow we could visit a few estate agents and look for a long term rental."

"Sounds good to me," Paul said, putting his arms around her and giving her a hug. "But actually, Laura, the girl we met today, has a friend called Rhonnda, who may be able to help us. She's in real estate, I believe."

"Yes, Eddie said. I was talking to him when you were chatting to Laura's parents. He said he would be willing to take me around any of the houses we were interested in, especially if we saw any that were out of the area. That's if you were tied up with work and things."

"He's a good bloke, is Eddie. We get on like a house on fire."

On a cloudy Saturday a few weeks later, Abbie and Jenny, with their younger children, were walking along the main street of Glenelg, tourist attraction area, which bustles with visitors from interstate and sightseers from all quarters of the world, all intent on enjoying the well stocked shops, full of everything a tourist might like to purchase as souvenirs.

That day was looked upon as a well earned day out for the two women. They had quickly become fast friends and when Jenny had managed to be taken on as a "stand in" for the nurse who was going on maternity leave, Abbie couldn't have been happier for her.

Laura had put Jenny in touch with Rhonnda, who had found a long term rental for the family in Woodcroft. Of course this had meant rushing around looking for furniture to supplement the goods and chattels that were at that moment locked in a Pickfords container and travelling across on the high seas from Europe, its destination being the docks at Port Adelaide.

Luckily, the purchases were not very big ones as Jenny and Finn's finances were scant to say the least. The twins were the major consumers of their fragile funds, besides having to find a deposit for the new rental, with them wanting the latest this and that, now that they were attending college. Finn, of course, was now back in his role of "house husband", lounging around watching daytime T.V. with Brandon. Venturing into the job market was not an option, as he had to have a meal ready for his wife and family when they came in.

Abbie, too, was becoming concerned that her new house money was becoming seriously eroded. Although Wayne had completed his course and become a fully licensed bricklayer, they were still paying hire fees for the people carrier, Wayne not having sourced a camper van that was suitable. If he did find one for sale, it was usually a wreck or needed substantial work doing on it. Jason and Molly had to walk to the technical college they had both enrolled at, now that Molly had celebrated her sixteenth birthday and until the family found a long term rental, Jodie and Kyle stayed with Abbie at home.

Abbie had parked the people carrier in a small car park at the back of "Cheap as Chips", a discount store. They were on their way to the Beach House, situated near the front of Holdfast Bay. It was a place of fun for youngsters and teenagers alike, with its water slide, crazy golf, dodgem cars and slot machines.

Having visited Glenelg before, on their validation reccie, Abbie was aware that treating her two young ones that day was going to be a costly exercise. The place wasn't cheap, with tickets having to be purchased for each ride or amusement, and she wondered at the folly of her suggestion. A camel or a pony ride on the nature reserve might have served her purpose of treating her two. She cheered her troubled thoughts impatiently. She was in a better position than her good friend, Jenny. At least she got to stay at home and look after her family, while Wayne went out and earned their daily bread. Jenny looked tired and anxious, having worked long traumatic hours in the hospital department she had been assigned to.

Finn was out with Abbie's husband, having a drink at a local bar.

"She won't be 'appy when I tell 'er," Wayne was saying to Finn, as they downed another pale ale at their chosen venue on Main South Road.

"The chap at the display 'ome I visited after work yesterday said that she obviously hadn't taken into account the conveyancer fees and stamp duty when we were over last and, with the mortgage rate now at nine per cent, it's going to cost an arm and a leg. I mean, I'm not goin' to do without the things that make me life bearable, whilst she's sat at home having coffee mornings on some fancy estate."

"Well, you'll 'ave ter tell soon, mate, 'cos she told our Jenny, that you and 'er were off ter look around a new 'ouse tomorrer. Knowin' women, she'll give yer bloody rice if she sets 'er 'eart on summat and then she finds yer can't afford it. Me an' Jenny 'ad a ding dong the other night, when I put me noz in over a coffee table she liked. I mean, let's face it, the plasma's the first thing on the agenda, not a friggin' coffee table."

"Yeah, that an' all. She's not goin' ter be 'appy with some of the stuff we've got comin' over in our container. Not now she's bin with your Jenny ter these furniture warehouses. And I wouldn't mind, but I'm up ter me neck in muck on this site I'm workin' on and she's started givin' me short rations again. Says she's tired with all the walkin' about, now I need the car ter get me there."

"Tell me about it, our Jenny's got an 'eadache every soddin' night."

CHAPTER EIGHT

Laura and her parents stood outside the Bay Discovery Centre in the historic Glenelg Town Hall, deciding whether to go for lunch at the small Dolphin café on the beach front, which Laura said served excellent pancakes with maple syrup and ice cream, or wander along Jetty Road.

It was a Monday lunchtime on a warm sunny day and excited children, who were too young to go to school, ran in and out of the water jets that were a feature of the palm tree lined piazza in front of McDonalds.

"I like a bit of history now and again," said Brenda contentedly. She had enjoyed looking at the mock-up emigrant ship and the factual contents of the museum. "Especially now, when I've just learnt all about the Poms who came over from England in the nineteenth century."

"And now I know why the British are called Poms," said Laura. "Those people who could afford to pay for a cabin on their way over were called People Of Means. I don't think I would have liked to have travelled in steerage."

"Oh, you wouldn't have," said her father. "My forbears would have been able to travel in luxury." Barry's ancestors had been gentry.

"But mine were probably convicts," said Brenda, "and landed here in leg irons."

"No, I know for a fact that they were free settlers who arrived here," said Laura, who, being so fascinated by the thought of it all, had often stood in front of the Holdfast Bay monument on the sea front, which declared that Governer Hindmarsh had established a settlement there in 1836. "Convicts went to Botany Bay. Let's go and look at the monument while we're deciding what to do. If you're not hungry yet, we can go over to the "Buffalo", by the marina. It isn't the original ship that came over with the settlers, the real one sank on another voyage off New Zealand, but it gives you an idea of what kind of ship the people travelled in."

"Isn't that the person you introduced us to when we were in the city?" asked Brenda as they strolled along the pathway on their way to the marina, having decided to put their lunch at the Dolphin café on hold for the time being.

"Where?" asked Laura and her father simultaneously, looking over in the direction of a tall block of apartments that Brenda had pointed to.

"Just by that tree. I'm sure it was him. You know I have a good memory for faces. There, look, he's standing talking to a woman by that red car. She's the one he introduced us to at the market."

"Well, we won't go over," said Laura, some sixth sense telling her that to do so would be an intrusion. "I seem to remember her saying when we were at the coffee shop that Eddie would be helping her find a long term rental around here. Which reminds me, we'll drop in at Rhonnda's on our way back, Dad. We can ask if the vendor will take an offer on the house we saw in Seacliff."

Wayne was surprised, to say the least, when, after plucking up the courage to relate what the salesman on the development site had told him, Abbie hadn't kicked off as he had expected her to. It seemed that having perused the property section in the weekly *Messenger* newspaper, she had seen quite a few houses in their price range around the Woodcroft area. The merits of moving to where Jenny would be living far outweighed her desire to buy a brand new home.

"There's a shoppin' centre that I can walk to, seein' as I don't like drivin' that heap of junk someone offloaded on yer. It's got a Foodland, which is as cheap as the one we've bin shoppin' at, and an ANZ bank, so I can swap over from the HSBC. Accordin' ter Jenny, they've a Montessori kindy fer Kyle and a decent primary fer

Jodie and a bus goes from there to Noarlunga, which is only a stones throw from the tech'. So, I'm not bothered, Wayne. Our funds are gettin' low with all this rent that we're payin' anyway."

"Do yer fancy 'avin' a ride up there then, this mornin'?" said a relieved Wayne, helping himself to another slice of toast from the plate that Abbie had put on the dining room table. With it being a Saturday, it was egg and bacon on toast for all the family.

"Already on to it. We're all goin' to an Open House, 'avin' a look at a place I've got me eye on. It'll need a spot of TLC, but I'm sure it will be within your capabilities."

It was all quiet within when the family arrived on the doorstep of a four bedroom bungalow, which was only a short stroll from the shopping centre and library. The place had a weary look about it, with moss growing in profusion on the red tiled roof, paint chipped window ledges and scuff marks on the front door. The estate agent was pleased to see them. He had settled himself on a stool in the kitchen, checking his laptop for emails.

"Welcome," he said brightly, hurrying up the hallway with his clipboard in readiness.

"Could I have your name and contact details and then I'll show you around?"

"Well, we're just lookin'," said Wayne, worrying already about the time he would have to spend on getting the place up to Abbie's spec'. It was bound to fall to him. She wouldn't pay out for a painter and the garden outside looked as if it hadn't been touched for years.

"Yeah, you can show us around," said Abbie, walking past the smartly suited man to the kitchen, where she proceeded to look through the window. "Look, Jodie, there's room in the back garden fer a trampoline."

"And a cubby 'ouse," said Kyle, who had seen a picture of one in a mailbox flyer and had gone to the patio door to check the garden out.

"And a cubby 'ouse," said Abbie, nodding happily as she stood in the open plan room. "And a separate room where I can have a telly and watch things like "The Farmer Wants A Wife", which you lot aren't interested in." She had spotted a small sun filled morning room just off the hallway.

"It looks a bit run down ter me," said Wayne, seeing that the green painted kitchen with its old glass fronted cupboards, badly needed modernising. Abbie would surely want something similar to the cream laminate kitchen she had left behind.

"Ah, but that's reflected in the price", said the salesman. "The place used to be rented out and the owner has decided to sell it."

"And would 'e be open ter offers?"

Abbie could already visualise her cream kitchen with its green granite work top, a matching round table and six upholstered chairs in the dining room area and two cream leather sofas positioned in front of the plasma. She could probably make do with a couple of wicker chairs and a glass coffee table in the morning room.

"Has it bin on the market long?"

"Long enough for the owner to negotiate." It was said with hope in the salesman's heart, as he wanted to get a settlement on the property as soon as he could.

"Then we'll 'ave a look around at the other rooms and then we'll 'ave a discussion. Come on, kids."

"So the land title and house deeds will have to be put in Laura's name," said Rhonnda, after she had heard back favourably from the owner of the house that Barry and Brenda were interested in.

"Yes, we knew that," said Barry nodding.

"With us being classed as tourists, while we're waiting for our parent visa we knew that we could only buy a new house in our name and go through the F.I.R.B."

"Foreign Investment Review Board?"

"Something like that, Rhonnda, but it seems a lot of messing, especially if we have to go back to England. We really like the house in Seacliff and if we were to buy a new place we would probably have to go further down south and then it's further to travel to visit Laura and Toby."

"Anyway, Laura may as well have it in her name now, as have to wait until we die," Brenda said. "Saves complications in the future and I'm sure she won't chuck us out."

"Graham might," said Rhonnda. It was said tongue in cheek, but she was also a bit of a stirrer. "If anything happened to Laura, *he* might chuck you out."

"Well, we'll see," said Barry, suddenly feeling uncomfortable, even if the woman had been joking with him. "Let's get the paperwork done for the moment and then we'll see."

"Would he do that?" Brenda asked her daughter as they walked to Barry's silver Toyota Camry, which he had taken delivery of two weeks before. "Would Graham try to throw us out?"

"I shouldn't think so." Laura tried to sound reassuring, but knowing Graham and his antipathy, which had grown since her parents' arrival, she wouldn't put it past him.

"Anyway, I'm in the best of health!"

The weather was getting warmer: thirty-four degrees Celsius and hotter than anyone in Abbie's family had experienced. It was their last week in Laura's rental. They had signed the contract for the house in Woodcroft and the settlement date was just around the corner. Abbie felt pleased. Okay, so she didn't get the new house she had set her heart on, but once she had put Wayne to work, with the help of Jason, who had decided he might like an apprenticeship to become a plumber, the house could be tailor made to her liking.

Meanwhile, they had to put up with this heat, which had turned up unexpectedly when they had been shivering under their duvets only the week before. Laura, bless her heart, had turned up with two portable fans and shown Abbie how to use the air conditioner, so most of the time was spent in the house, rather than dehydrating outdoors.

Not that Wayne could escape working in the seriously hot weather, but as he said, sometimes there was a cool wind from off the sea. He was revelling in his job at that moment, having made some mates, or muckers, as he called them, and every afternoon when his work was finished for the day, he could be found in the Aldinga pub. One of the guys had even offered to take him fishing on the Port Noarlunga jetty, one weekend.

Not that he got drunk when his working day was over. He was still able to drive the wreck of a car that he had eventually handed good money over for. And sometimes he won at pokies, the Aussie name for slot machines.

They'd had word that their container was waiting in a warehouse at Port Adelaide. A shared container really, as what they had decided to bring over hadn't filled a whole one. Strangely enough, Abbie couldn't remember what she had given away to members of her extended family and she felt obliged to enlist the help of Jenny to drive her around the discount furniture stores. Meanwhile, the bloke who rang her from Pickfords, or that is, their Australian associates, had arranged delivery on the day that Abbie got her keys.

It had to be said that Jenny's long term rental in Woodcroft wasn't as nice as the house she had rented from Laura. In Abbie's opinion, Jenny should have been more selective and gone for a house that had more room. And it was on a main road, with traffic blaring past until all hours in the morning. It wouldn't have done for Abbie, if it had been her choice. Of course Jenny wasn't in the same position as she was, she reminded herself. Wayne had always been a good provider, while Finn was a lazy sod and, according to Jenny, had always been.

It was the second Sunday of the month and the two women had taken Kyle, Brandon and Jodie to a nearby park, where little trains ran along narrow gauge tracks and people were allowed to ride on them. After treating themselves to a sausage sizzle, they purchased tickets for the children then sat at a picnic table under a shady tree.

"I'm not sure that I can keep going on like this," said Jenny, once they'd settled to watch the passing engines and the cheery passengers. "It appears that Finn is spendin' a lot of his time in the Woodcroft tavern now that Brandon has started school. Lucy and

Belle saw him goin' in yesterday when they finished tech' early and were gettin' off the bus. And, as yer know, he's in there now with your Wayne."

"Yeah, but in my case I've no legs ter stand on, Jenny. Wayne's bin comin' 'ome every night and gettin' stuck into the paintin'. Even Jason's bin a love and 'elped me put the beds up. Molly's bin doin' the washin' and Jodie's bin helpin' with Kyle, while I'm unpackin'. Yer ought ter put yer foot down and tell 'im that 'e 'as ter start lookin' fer a job."

"No, it's more like me wantin' ter go back ter Liverpool, Abbie. Over there I 'ad me mum or me sister as backup and Finn was made ter get a job by the dole. Well, at least 'e 'ad ter turn up fer interviews if 'e wanted ter get paid. 'E can do what 'e likes over 'ere, 'cos 'e got in on the strength of my visa. No bugger's monitoring what 'e does all day and I'm knackered with workin' at the 'ospital."

"Then give 'im a shot over 'is bows then. Warn 'im that unless 'e gets 'is act together yer goin' ter give 'im the flick. Don't go throwing the towel in 'ere, queen. It's bloody freezin' back in England."

"I'm not sure that I've done right by the twins, either. I mean, I don't want yer kickin' off, Abbie, but I'm not 'appy with the amount of time your Jason spends with Lucy in the evenings. She should be getting' 'er 'ead down and bonin' up on this health and environmental course she's enrolled on."

"Then tell 'er, Jenny. Tell 'er she's only ter see 'im at the weekends. Your problem is, yer let the lot of 'em walk over yer. I tell yer, if Finn was my 'usband he'd be dancing to *my* tune."

The lights of the two women's lives were at that moment enjoying a bit of male bonding over a bottle or two. Finn, as usual, was trying to avoid answers to Wayne's questioning about his job prospects.

"I nearly did something about it this week," he said finally, his eyes wandering over to the pokie machines, wondering if he should chance a couple of dollars. "I saw something in the *Messenger* about a traffic manager's job."

"Aye," said Wayne slowly, wondering what had stopped him from applying this time.

"I thought it was somethin' like back home in England and you got to sit at one of them consoles during rush hour and kept changing the traffic lights ter red or green."

"And wasn't it?"

"No, you had ter go on a course, accordin' ter the woman I spoke to on the phone and learn 'ow ter direct the traffic. Yer know, with one of them lollypops that says STOP or SLOW. I didn't fancy being out in all weathers, though I suppose it 'ud be okay nine months of the year."

"I don't know 'ow yer get away with it, Finn. If that was my lass, she'd 'ave bin bagged me by now. 'Er latest craze is a veggie patch in the back garden, though she'll dig it 'erself if I 'old back a bit. She's got me doin' all sorts when I get back from work, but I 'ave ter admit I've done well with the paintin'. Yer'll 'ave ter come over later and 'ave a gander."

"You know, I think our new life is agreeing with you," said Paul as he and Amanda sat at a pavement café on Jetty Road, whilst waiting for Emily and Cody to finish at the surf club.

"I mean, just look at you. Toned and trim again since you started at the fitness centre. You've a new hairstyle and the beginnings of a tan. And you've got that glow about you. Just like when we were first married and hadn't got a care."

"I must admit I'm beginning to enjoy this life down under," Amanda replied. "I feel more settled, especially now we've found our long term rental. I know it's rather expensive with it having an ocean view, but with the rental income from our house back home and your salary, I jumped at the chance when Rhonnda pointed it out to me. And you said Eddie thought the rent was reasonable for Brighton and Hove. Especially with the train station being nearby."

That wasn't all Eddie had said, thought Amanda, smiling brightly at Paul, who had no idea that she had been seeing his boss during most lunch hours for the past few weeks. It was easy. No one questioned where the C.E.O. of the company disappeared to and Amanda was free to do as she pleased while the children were at school. Life was suddenly exciting, right from the time when she and Eddie had felt that sudden fizz between them after Paul had asked her to meet him in the city that fateful day. Not that she had made the first move. This was her husband's employer that she was attracted to. In her opinion, a man who could make or break a person's career.

It had been a few days later, when she was sitting in Trevor's Super, watching a load of women talking drivel on daytime T.V. She had a muzzy head from drinking too much wine the night before, in an attempt to anaesthetise her boredom and withering feelings for the man who had brought her there. The phone rang after she had summoned up the energy to make herself a coffee, whilst wondering if a trip to Foodworks would help to cheer her mind.

It was Eddie.

"Hi, Amanda. How's it going? Did you get in touch with Rhonnda? Did she find you a better place?"

She had felt stunned for a moment. Did the C.E.O. of Aussie companies usually ring up their employees' wives for a chat? Surely he only had to ask her husband about their rental prospects.

"Look, Amanda. If you're ever at a loose end and I can help you, the offer I made the other week regarding showing you around the area still stands. I have plenty of time on my hands and Paul was saying that you only really have the weekends."

"That's true. The kids have joined the surf club, so most of Saturday is taken up and they go to Sunday school, so that only leaves the afternoon. To be honest, I haven't got my act together yet, as we have this place until the end of the month."

"Time flies, Amanda. Tell you what. How about I pick you up tomorrow morning? Around eleven? We'll visit a few places further north, like West Lakes and Henley Beach. I'll take a look at a few websites on the Internet."

Of course Paul was told of Eddie's kind offer and was regaled the following evening with lengthy descriptions of the places that had been visited. But there was no information forthcoming on the successive days, when a couple of hours were spent in the Stamford Grand, inclusive of a dual massage, lunches were taken in out of the way places and there were park ups down at Maslin Beach! And Amanda suddenly had her glow again, courtesy of Farrington (Building Surveyors) Pty Ltd.

"Let me know if you need any help this weekend," Paul's boss said as they walked out of the office together Friday lunchtime. "I presume you've sorted out a removal van."

"No, we don't need one. We only need our holdalls and Amanda's over at the house supervising the delivery of our furniture as we speak."

"I hope you haggled," Eddie said, unnecessarily, as he knew exactly where Amanda had ordered the furniture from, having been to Freedom, Harvey Norman and Le Cornu with her.

"Oh, I left it all to her. She has a better eye than me when it comes to co-ordinating things for the home. We'll have a barbecue when we've settled in and you can come and give it all the once over. And thank you ever so much for all the help you've given Amanda."

"Don't mention it, Mate. Glad to be of service."

What a great bloke, thought Paul, as he walked to the railway station. Amanda had taken over their new Mitsubishi Challenger, (the Holden had gone back to the hire company) so Paul got the train into work. He couldn't remember when he last felt so happy. He had a job he loved, a much better lifestyle for his wife and kids and Amanda seemed more caring and attentive towards him.

CHAPTER NINE

Laura came dashing out of the rental house she called "The Oleander." Her new tenants were due to arrive the next day and she had been putting the finishing touches to the place, to make it look more homely. The welcome pack resided in the fridge, along with a bottle of red wine, and fresh bougainvillaea from the bushes in her garden sat in a long vase on the coffee table.

It was a busy time for Laura. She had received many inquiries recently regarding vacancies at her properties. A sure sign that people in Britain were looking for a better life. Besides cleaning and laundering the bedding at the villas herself, there were her parents, who needed her help until they got their bearings, Toby to see to and her home to run. Still, as she often said to Graham, who was busy on a huge project himself at the moment, she wouldn't have it any other way.

Today was a monumental day for Laura and her parents. They were going to the conveyancer to sign the papers for the Seacliff house. She felt excited. They were all together at last. No more heartaches, finger pointing and volatile accusations, even Graham seemed to accept the inevitable and hadn't been at all disagreeable over her parents moving close by.

They had chosen well. The house was a two storey brick built detached dwelling, circa 1970s, with a balcony upstairs, three streets back from the esplanade and on a block of 800 square metres. That meant there was enough room for a swimming pool in the future should they wish, within an enclosed hibiscus hedged garden, where the previous occupants had planted a small orchard of lemon trees.

Barry was in his element, planning a small vegetable garden that he could watch grow from the patio situated under the Stratco entertainment area. Brenda loved the high ceilings and the long elegant windows in the rooms, which she intended to furnish in a Regency style. One bedroom would be reserved for Toby, decked out with Thomas the Tank Engine regalia, which was his favourite toy at that moment. Another was to be a guest room/study/bail out bedroom, if Barry or Brenda kept the other awake by snoring, and of course the master bedroom, with its en-suite bathroom and walk-in wardrobe, would house a mahogany queen size bed in Regency scroll.

The kitchen, which was downstairs, was a delight with a huge walk-in pantry and a large fitted laundry. The lounge room was huge and very airy and looked out onto a quiet street, from which it was only a short stroll down to the sea. The house was in a perfect spot and they couldn't wait to move into it.

"Do you fancy lunch at the Ikea café?", asked Laura, after they had come out from signing papers and were within a stone's throw of the airport. "They always have a good lunch on and you never know, you may like to buy some things for the new house while you're there."

"I don't think that Ikea furniture would be suitable for our new home," said Brenda. "Ikea is for you young things. Part of the 'throwaway' society. I've never been in one myself."

"Then you're in for a treat, Mother," Laura said mischievously. "We'll have our lunch, then I'll show you around."

To say that the boot of Barry's car was full to the brim was an understatement when, after a tasty sandwich lunch with a side of chips, Laura took her mother shopping around the store. Suddenly Brenda found a need for matching kitchenware, although not cutlery as she had a canteen of Viners cutlery coming over on a container ship. It also seemed important to replace those worn out cushion covers and a couple of sets of anaconda drawers would look really good in the walk-in wardrobe.

Paul and Amanda had been in their new house for three weeks when she decided to have their house warming. Everything had been so exciting: choosing the furniture and the plasma, as the house was let unfurnished, buying things for the kitchen, bedding, towels, glassware and making contact with Telstra, who was to provide them with a telephone and internet package. Many trips had been made to Ikea, although the bulk of the furniture and rugs were bought from Harvey Norman, a place from which Eddie's wife also bought.

Little had been said by Amanda's "bit on the side" about his wife, Helen. Sometimes Eddie called her a moody bitch, sometimes he related a nice thing about her, but most of their encounters were so full of boiling hormones and an over supply of testosterone, that passionless debates never came into it. However, during an afternoon bunk-up in a city hotel, when Amanda mentioned that she and Paul were planning a barbecue and asked would he and his wife like to go to it, she was surprised when Eddie went quiet.

"I mean, I don't know many people, except Paul's work colleagues, a couple of girls I've met at the gym and a mother that I've started to speak to at the children's school. We can pretend that we don't know each other, or at least act as if we've only met a couple of times."

"I don't know that it's a good idea, Mand." Eddie looked worried. "She's been saying a few things lately, as if she knows."

"Knows?" Amanda took in a quick intake of breath then relaxed again. "How could she know?"

"Someone might have seen us."

"According to you, if anyone saw us it could be explained away easily.

"Ah, but not if we've booked in at a hotel as Mr. and Mrs. Farrington, like we have today."

"You said that this could be explained away as a business meeting," said Amanda, jumping away from Eddie's naked body as if he had just touched her with an electric prod. She got out of bed and began to put on her sexy bra and cami-knicks. "If Paul was to find out about you and me…"

"And ditto if Helen was to find out" said Eddie, swinging

himself out of his side of bed and putting his socks on. "That's why I'm not rushing to accept your house warming invitation. In fact, I've been thinking, Mand, perhaps we should cool it for a while. Let the heat die down, as they say. There'll be more people out and about to see us once summer's here."

"Oh, do you think?" Amanda still thrilled to his touch and would miss the way he treated her body as if he had a heat-seeking missile to explode.

"Look, we can take up with each other again after the holidays, when we've done our duty by our spouses and kids."

"Okay then, you're probably right and absence makes the heart grow fonder."

"I wasn't thinking of my heart."

"We're goin' back," said Finn, after taking another swig from the bottle that Wayne had just given him. "She's 'ad enough and she misses her mother and, strangely enough, the 'ospital where she used ter work. I'm not bothered. I'll tek it or leave it. Like I said to 'er, 'Yer've 'ad a go and it's not bin to yer likin', so pack it in.' There's nothin' lost, we'll move in with their Susan 'til we can get another place. The girls are a bit put out, 'cos they were just settlin' in, but they'll get over it. Kids do."

"Ter be 'onest, I'm not surprised," Wayne replied from his deckchair, his eyes looking over to the veggie patch that Abbie had dug out with the help of Jason a few weeks ago, checking to see if any seeds he had sown had started pushing through. "I mean, it's not bin easy. Your lass 'ad ter wait fer somethin' ter come up and I suppose it took a toll on yer savin's. I suppose it would 'ave bin different if she 'ad walked inter summat, or even if *you* 'ad managed to get a job."

"Well, yer win some, yer lose some. Anyroad, we should be 'ome fer Christmas. Doesn't feel right, this change around of seasons. I mean eating Christmas dinner in the middle of a heat wave doesn't do it for me. I like the fog and the snow."

Jenny, on the other hand, sitting with Abbie in the lounge

room, wasn't as upbeat about throwing the towel in as her husband.

"It's really because of 'im that we're goin' back," she said. "Though it grieves me ter say it, he's a drain on me financially and emotionally. We'll never get on 'ere. Never be like you and Wayne, owning our own 'ouse and givin' the kids the good things in life. I'm pretendin' that I'm not 'appy where I'm workin'. It's partially true, as I've bin treated as if I'm the new girl, as if I've not had any trainin' and I should be handin' out bedpans instead. But if I 'ad 'is support and perhaps another wage coming in, I'd decide ter stick with it. But as it is, I may as well be workin' back 'ome."

"Yer'll miss the lovely Aussie summer," said Abbie, trying to joke with Jen, who was really looking quite tired and poorly. "And what'll I do once yer gone? I'll 'ave no one ter keep me company."

"Oh, you'll survive, Abbie. I can't see yer following me back ter Britain and I wouldn't, if I was in your shoes. If I ever manage ter learn how to work a computer, we'll keep in touch by email. I never was much of a letter writer. I didn't know anyone ter write to before."

"Well, all things considered, I'd probably do the same as you, if the boot was on my foot. Is there anythin' I can do ter 'elp? What are yer goin' ter do with all the stuff yer brought over?"

"That's what's worryin' me. We can't afford ter send it back and really there's nothin' much of value. One of the nurses I've met, she's from Oldham by the way, said you can sell stuff on a website called "Poms in Adelaide". So, I don't suppose yer could keep some of it in your garage when we've gone and sell it fer us? And there'll be a few other things ter do, no doubt. Finn says ter dump the banger somewhere, but I still need to get ter the 'ospital and I've 'eard that I can get a refund on me Rego."

"I'll 'elp yer all I can, queen, I could even 'ave a garage sale and I might be able to talk Wayne into 'aving your car. It's in a better state than his old wreck."

Hell, she felt sorry for the poor little mite that she'd quickly made friends with. What was it with some women, who had loyalty to a layabout husband and wouldn't give him the flick? Wayne wouldn't have lasted as long as he had if he sat on his arse like Finn did.

"Tell yer what" said Abbie, feeling a rush of affection for her. "I'll treat yer all ter a farewell dinner at Mick O'Shea's, before yer go. They do a half price menu if yer get there early."

"So, who have you got coming in next door to us?" asked Brenda, as she and Laura sat in the Banksia's lounge room drinking cups of coffee. "Pity we won't get to know them, with us moving out on Friday. Still, we only really nodded to your previous tenants, Jenny and Finn."

"It's a couple on a reccie. No children. It seems the chap wants to set up a business in Adelaide, but instead of renting an apartment in the city, they've decided to have a little beach holiday as well."

"I suppose if you've no children you can do what you like," said Brenda. "It's a different world from when me and your dad got married."

"But you only had me and you didn't have me straight away, so you and Dad could have done anything."

"It was different times, like I said. When a woman got married she gave up work. Stayed at home waiting for the baby to make an appearance. Your grandma would have had a heart attack if we had suddenly decided we were upping sticks and had gone to live in a foreign country. In fact, once, me and your father had a naughty weekend away in London. It was before we were married and I made much of the fact that we had booked separate rooms. Then, when we got back home, I went and put my foot in it by telling your grandparents that the bulb had blown in our room and we had to send for the porter. I don't know who was more embarrassed, me or them." Brenda chuckled girlishly as she related the story.

"And how old were you, Mum?" asked Laura, knowing that her parents hadn't got together when they were teenagers.

"Twenty three and I was mortified."

They finished their coffees and Brenda washed up the cups whilst they waited for Barry to return. He had been at the garage having a complimentary nuts and bolts tightening service done before going to the supermarket petrol station to fill up, as the fuel was cheaper on a Tuesday.

"I heard from Abbie, she was one of my recent tenants, that Jenny and Finn are going back to England at Christmas," Laura said. "According to Abbie, Jen wasn't very happy at the hospital that she worked at. It must be very daunting to make such a big step with three children, as well as an unemployed husband."

"A leap of faith, Laura. We all have to believe that what we are doing is the right thing, or we wouldn't get past base one. It must have felt right when they were applying for their visa, or they wouldn't have gone ahead with it. At least they can say they've tried it, rather than it be something they were always going to do."

"Hark the mother, who said she would never move out of Wheaton. Who said the only way she'd leave her beautiful house would be in a box!"

"Ah, but love is a strong emotion, Laura. And if it wasn't for you and Toby, we wouldn't be standing here now."

"I spoke to Eddie today about our barbecue, Amanda," said Paul, after he had taken his suit jacket off and hung it with his tie on a hanger in the walk-in wardrobe. "I'll tell you in a minute after I've had a shower."

Amanda stopped in her tracks for a moment. She was on her way downstairs, after getting ready to pick the children up from school. Paul had come in on an early train, having finished his assignment for the day.

What was Eddie up to? Had he declined Paul's invitation as she had expected him to?

She lingered by the lounge room windows, not seeing the gentle tide that was lapping onto the golden beach beyond nor the happy toddlers from a nearby kindy, as they frolicked with their helpers on the shore.

For two weeks she and Eddie had been incommunicado. Two weeks in which to examine her feelings for him. She missed his touch, missed the excitement of their clandestine meetings, and wondered if he was feeling the same and was missing her as much. That song, "Like sister and brother we'll wave to each other, we don't want all the world to know, we are really lovers" kept churning through her head and she wondered at the folly of their indiscretions: he was Paul's employer at the end of the day. He might not turn up to their barbecue, but what about if they met at other functions? A Christmas party, say. Most employers put on a do for their workers at Christmas. Would other people notice that frisson of excitement between them, which seemed to happen every time they met?

"So anyway," Paul continued as he came down the stairs looking refreshed in a pair of khaki cargo shorts and a pale green T-shirt, his feet bare and his hair slicked down. "He said, thanks for the invitation and if he can he will. But it all depends on Helen. She might want to go up to the Eyre Peninsular with the kids for the weekend."

"Oh, where's the Eyre Peninsular when it's at home?" Illogically, Amanda wasn't sure whether she was happy or sad, that somewhere called the Eyre Peninsular might be the reason for a no show.

"It's somewhere up north. They've got a place up there, I believe. One of the lads from the office said that Eddie lends it out, if there's some special occasion or he feels we deserve a weekend away."

"It's all right for some," she sniffed. "I'm off to pick up the kids."

Lighting up a cigarette, once she had parked the Challenger in a side street near the children's school, her mood became depressive. It had been the affair with Eddie that had helped her through, blotting out the longing for her old life and fizzing up her sex life with Paul as Eddie's face blurred with her husband's during the expected weekly ritual. She missed the excitement of the random phone calls, the buzz she got from hearing his voice, the electricity between them as they met on their clandestine encounters. All, it seemed, might be consigned into history, if they never managed to see each other alone again. Perhaps it was time to call it a day. Go back home to Bolton, take up where she left off before Paul got his itch to find a better life. If she stayed with him, her days would go back to being boring and predictable, one long round of repetitive cooking, housework and waiting for Eddie to ring, her only respite a cheap holiday somewhere with Paul and the kids. Even more bizarre a holiday on the Eyre Peninsular, imagining herself as Mrs. Farrington at Eddie's seaside home.

There were lots of tears, mainly from Jenny and Finn's daughters, as they said goodbye to Molly and Jason, promising to keep in touch by email. The grownups were more circumspect. Everyday life got in the way of fledgling friendships and a card at Christmas was all you could expect. After they'd got rid of all Jenny and Finn's stuff sitting in their garage, of course!

And it didn't take Abbie very long to find a new best friend.

One morning, after she had flicked through the house with a duster, tidied the kids' bedrooms and given them a quick vacuum, she set off to walk the short distance to the local shopping centre. That morning she was revelling in her freedom. Kyle had started attending the Montessori nursery, Jodie had gone back to her primary school after a two week holiday, Molly was in the middle of a beautician course, Jason had been taken on as an apprentice by Reece Plumbing and she'd got rid of some of the stuff that had been left in the garage. There were lots of people who studied the goods for sale in the Community Noticeboard.

Life had never felt so good, especially as she and Wayne now shared Jenny's old Subaru and although she sometimes missed a bit of a gossip and a coffee with her friend, it was great being mobile at the weekends.

A wander around Sam's warehouse was to be her first port of call. She wasn't someone who liked to lose herself in a book, so she bypassed the library. Sam's warehouse held all sorts of things that people didn't know they wanted until they came across them and twenty minutes later two of her shopping bags were full. It was time for a rest and she knew exactly where to take it. At Drakes Foodland, a few minutes stroll through the shopping mall, where weary shoppers could rest their legs and have a complimentary cup of coffee.

"Hi, how's it going?"

A tall, well built, pleasant looking young woman with fair shoulder length hair, wearing black cargo pants, a pale pink T-shirt and the inevitable matching thongs, plonked herself in a seat at the table where Abbie was sitting, pulling her very full trolley to the side of her. For a moment, Abbie wondered if she had been mistaken for someone else, until she realised that she had seen this woman driving down the cul-de-sac in a green estate car, so perhaps she was a neighbour of hers.

"Thought I'd introduce myself. I live at number twenty-three. I noticed you had moved into Valma's old house. It seemed to be up for sale forever before you moved in."

"Oh," said Abbie, nonplussed, because back in England she wasn't used to people accosting her, unannounced.

"Raelene Buxton, by the way." She held her hand out in a friendly manner.

"Oh, Abbie Foley." She took Raelene's proffered hand and shook it politely. "It's great being able to sit for a while and drink free coffee, isn't it? I don't know of any supermarkets in England that would think of doin' the same". Abbie couldn't think of anything else to say.

"Ah, a Pom. Well, I'm going to get myself a hot chocolate," Raelene replied, smiling broadly. "Can I get you a refill?"

"No, yer all right, I'm goin' to finish this then do a bit of shoppin'. There's some bits and pieces I want ter get fer our dinners."

"You're from England then, hun," said Raelene, when she had brought her hot chocolate in its polystyrene cup back to the table. "I've always wanted to go to England. My grandparents came over after the Second World War. They were farmers and they bought some land up on the Onkaparinga Hills. It's been in the family since then, though one of my brothers runs the place now, the other has a business selling farm machinery, but I never wanted to move out of Woodcroft. Luckily, my husband felt the same. So, how old are *your* kids, hun?"

An hour later, Abbie walked back to her home laden down with shopping bags and an invitation to go to Victor Harbor on the following Saturday, with Raelene and her two boys. It appeared that her neighbour's children were of a similar age to hers.

CHAPTER TEN

"We've been invited to a house warming tomorrow night, Mum," said Laura, as she helped Brenda make the queen-size bed in the master bedroom of the Seacliff house.

"It's someone who works for Eddie. It'll be that chap we met when we went to the city, who started working for him a couple of months ago. He's got a place on the Brighton front. Anyway, it appears he and his wife don't know many people. Just colleagues from the office and a couple of mothers from their children's school. Graham's met Paul and thinks he's a nice bloke and Rhonnda's going with her mother, so she'd be company if you went."

"Don't you think it would be better if you dropped Toby off here and he could have a stop over? I'm dying to see his face when he sees his bedroom and you and Graham could have time to yourself."

"Well, if you're sure, that would be nice, Mum. We haven't had a night out on our own for a long time. No, I'm telling a lie, Fred and Ginger from next door babysat one night, when Eddie invited us over. You think *we've* got a big house, you should see Eddie's. It's like a manor house and they've got a holiday home on the Eyre Peninsular. Of course, Helen's family, that's Eddie's wife, are absolutely loaded. She's always in the 'Show & Tell' section of the *Sunday Mail*, at a fundraising event or something."

"Very nice for her, dear, but who're Fred and Ginger? I've not heard you mention them before. Sounds as if they're dancers like Fred Astaire and Ginger Rogers."

"Oh, it's the nicknames that Graham and I have given them. They *are* professional dancers. They perform all over Australia at theatrical productions and the like. They've just returned from a stint on a cruise ship, teaching the passengers to dance. They've no kids of their own and they seem to have adopted Toby, bringing him little gifts when they come back home. They brought him back a brightly coloured shirt from Fiji this time."

"They sound nice. Yes, you go off and enjoy yourself and we'll take him for a walk along the beach in the morning, if it's fine."

Amanda spent most of Saturday wondering why she had even thought of going to all the trouble of having a house warming party. It wasn't as if they owned the house and until they managed to sell their home in England, they never would. Paul earned far more now at Farrington's than he had at his previous employment, but the rent they were paying was exorbitant because of the ocean view.

"You know, I don't even know how many we're catering for," she complained to Paul as they walked up and down the aisles in Foodland, whilst Cody pushed a trolley with just a cucumber in. "And good job you've decided not to have a barbecue. With not knowing how many, it would be a waste of meat."

"Do you know if there are any children coming, Daddy?" asked Emily. "Because if there are, maybe you could make hot dogs. All children like hot dogs."

"Yes, of course. Well done, Emily. We'll get some bread rolls and then sausages from the meat counter."

"They're called snags, Daddy," said Cody proudly. "Sausages are called snags and yoghurt is called yo-gurt. And children like donuts with frosting on them and coke."

Amanda sniffed. Her children didn't eat any of those things, nor drink cola, but she supposed it wouldn't harm them for one day. As for the grown-ups, she decided to provide buffet food. Just like she would if she was inviting friends around for Christmas tea back home. Chicken legs, ham sandwiches, pork pies, crisps, peanuts and various dressings. A ready-made trifle and a black forest gateau would have to do for dessert.

"Did your boss say whether he was coming or not?" she asked slyly, thinking that if he was, she would get Paul to add a bottle of malt whisky to his liquor list. After all, secretly she had been hoping that he would turn up to the house warming, especially with his wife, so she could see this woman that Eddie was shackled to. She turned her face to inspect a jar of gherkins: it wouldn't do for Paul to see her look of hope.

"He said it was up to his wife. They were supposed to go to their holiday home this weekend, but one of the kids is under the weather. The child's 'crook' to use his exact expression. If they can get their maid to babysit, they'll be right over."

A maid, whatever next? Amanda expelled her breath.

"He did ask if there was anything he could bring. I said you were doing the catering but to bring a bottle if he wished."

"Oh, Paul. Fancy asking your boss to bring a bottle. I'd have died of shame if I'd have been there listening."

"That's what they do over here, Amanda. It's all BYO, bring your own. Everything's shortened. Sunnies, tradies, barbies, tinnies. Sunglasses, tradespeople, barbecues and cans of beer."

"Then I suggest you add a nice bottle of malt to your drinks list, I don't want him thinking that we're poor."

Raelene's kids are little monsters, thought Abbie, as the Toyota estate car chugged up the hill towards the village of Mount Compass on the way to Victor Harbor. Jodie, normally a timid little thing, was holding her own in a verbal altercation with a boy two years older than her who reckoned all girls were sissies. Kyle had already given a good account of himself by hitting out at his tormentor, a boy a year older than him, who looked like a miniature mud wrestler and liked to pinch when parents had their backs turned.

So much for bonding with our Aussie colonial cousins, thought Abbie not looking forward to the rest of the day if she was going to have to be a referee. Raelene didn't seem bothered by the noise coming from the back seats, even when an occasional howl could be heard. She just kept her foot down, her face puckered in concentration, as she negotiated the winding road.

"They have a fair here in January," she said, raising her voice above the radio and the kids' racket, as they started driving through the small country village of Mount Compass, with its pub, general store, café and petrol station. "We call it the dung flinging fair, though its real name is the 'Compass Cup'. The farmers bring their cows and race them against each other and there're lots of silly competitions like wellie throwing, rolling bales of hay and carrying water in a leaky bucket across the field. You have to be there to know what I'm on about, but they also have a pets corner, a bouncy castle and lots of stalls and last year they had camel rides. Our Harrison rode on it. Didn't you, Harrison?"

The elder boy nodded his head, though he couldn't have heard anything she said.

"Of course we know lots of farmers in the area, with my husband being a cattle feed rep. You'll have to come with us, when it's on next time."

Abbie nodded pleasantly. Raelene was doing her best to be friendly: perhaps she should give her kids the benefit this time.

She turned away to look at the passing scenery. Everywhere was lush and green, evidence of a lot of rainfall happening in the winter earlier that year. She'd read all the moaning in the *Messenger's* "Letters", regarding the waste of good water going out to sea via the Onkaparinga River. Why the government didn't build a few more reservoirs was beyond belief. A herd of strange looking creatures caught her eye as she considered it; she thought it strange to see miniature llamas in an Aussie farmer's field.

"Alpacas," Harrison decreed, when his brother, Byron, asked what the funny animals were that he'd just seen.

It was cool as they stepped out onto the pavement, where Raelene had parked in a space just outside the children's adventure playground. There was a dash for the old engine, situated amongst swings, slides and a colourful boat that you could sit in, all the time listening to the sound of the horn from the popular train.

The two women settled on a bench within the enclosure, keeping an eye on the boisterous children and trying to get to know one another at the same time.

"It's usually cooler here at this time of year," said Raelene, pulling up the collar of her red lightweight jacket and tightening her pink woolly scarf. "I'm glad you thought to put coats on Kyle and Jodie. We always rug up in our winter stuff until at least the end of spring."

"And here was me thinking we would only ever wear shorts and T-shirts," Abbie joked, glad of the jacket she had worn. She had heard the saying all "rugged up" before, as Jason was apt to say that before he went to catch his bus in the mornings.

"Oh, it won't be long before you're sweltering under forty degrees, hun."

The day passed pleasantly and the children seemed to settle, most probably because there was so much to do at Victor Harbor that they hadn't time to bicker, nor get up to mischief under both mothers' watchful eyes. After petting the Shire horses in their nearby stable, a ride on the horse drawn tram across to Granite Island was a must, with the children sitting aloft it, and racing across the bridge to the mainland on their return. A ride on the motorised cars was compulsory too, as was an hour spent competing against each other on the miniature golf course. Their packed lunch was eaten at a picnic table under the Norwegian pines, looking out across the bay, and then they wandered through the park, where a whale's fin resided in a splashy pond.

"We can come again," promised Raelene, as groans of disappointment resounded amongst the kids, who had certainly not wanted the day to end.

"We'll take a different route back home and stop at Hungry Jack's."

He'd arrived! Eddie had arrived just as Amanda was about to bring out another plate of sandwiches from the kitchen. Cucumber and Philly cheese seemed a hit with the guests and she had dashed to make a few more, with the verbal help of Rhonnda's mother, Betty, who had settled herself on a kitchen chair.

"Looks like that nice man that Rhonnda knows 'as come with

his spunky looking wife," she remarked, looking down the hallway to the open doorway. "You go and say hello and I'll take the sandwiches through."

"Oh, Paul will see to him," said Amanda, feeling all of a quiver as she glanced towards Eddie, who was looking debonair as usual, in cream knee length shorts, a pink polo shirt and dark blue boat shoes.

Her first impression of the woman who had come in ahead of him, was "Wow!" What the hell had Eddie been doing having an affair with another woman, when he went home to a model from a fashion magazine? She felt jealousy coursing through her body and turned away, so that Rhonnda's mother couldn't see the tears in her eyes. Bile welled up into her throat and she headed for the patio door, until she saw Emily and Cody sitting on the garden swings talking to a couple of little girls. She made a dash for the downstairs loo, where she regarded herself in the vanity unit mirror.

Somehow the revealing little black number that she had purchased from a boutique in the Marion Centre didn't look as exclusive as the exquisitely cut black and white short sleeved calf length A line dress that Eddie's wife was wearing. Worn with high heeled patent leather shoes and matching gold necklace and earrings, she looked as if she was on her way to a dinner party, not to the informal house warming of an employee of her husband. And perhaps she was, thought Amanda, grabbing a piece of toilet paper and carefully wiping her smudged mascara. Perhaps the couple had been invited to another do and they were dutifully making an appearance, as perhaps only an Aussie employer would.

It wouldn't look good, disappearing like she had instead of being by Paul's side putting on a united front, the height of the little wife in her domesticity. And nowhere along the line should this woman smell a rat, or there would be no more afternoons for Amanda spent in pleasurable bliss with the woman's husband.

"Ah, there you are, darling," said Paul as Amanda emerged self-consciously from the downstairs toilet, hoping to escape back to the kitchen unseen.

"Come and meet Helen, Eddie's wife. They can't stop long as they're on their way to another do, a birthday bash or something but it's very nice of them to drop by."

"Of course my father was a judge before we came out to live in Australia," Eddie's wife was saying to Rhonnda and Laura, in her cut glass accent, which sounded rather like the Queen when she was doing her Christmas broadcast to the nation. "I was still at Roedean when my parents first looked around to find a place to settle and they chose Adelaide. In fact they fell in love with the place."

"So not a ten pound Pom then, Helen?" Laura said cheekily.

"Afraid not. Oh, will you both excuse me for a moment? This must be Amanda."

Helen came towards her hosts and made straight for Amanda. The pale blue eyes that looked onto Amanda's face were hostile, though no one would have guessed her animosity from her broad smile. Perfectly groomed, from her pale pink fingernails, immaculate makeup and sun streaked shoulder length hair, she was rigidly polite, as she took Amanda's hand in hers and introduced herself.

"We've only just bobbed in to say hello, as Eddie feels it very important that we socialise with our employees," she gushed patronisingly. "I hope you and your husband will be very happy in Adelaide." She turned away before Amanda could even make an attempt at some polite response. "I'll be in touch, girls. You must come over for supper very soon. We'll be going now, Eddie!"

Helen looked across the lounge room to where Eddie stood chatting with Graham and another couple of men. Eddie had his back to Amanda and seemed unaware of her presence. He turned and nodded in her direction, after Helen had pointed her finger at her rather expensive looking wristwatch.

"Yes, darling, we'll be on our way. Mustn't keep poor Nelly waiting up." It must have been some private joke between them as they both giggled, then Eddie knocked back his glass of whisky and joined his wife. "Thanks for the invite, Paul, and thank you for a very nice tea, Amanda. I'll be starting up the car, darling, don't be long."

He strode through the open front door whilst Helen fussed about making kissing noises around Laura and Rhonnda's ears then waved to Betty down the hallway, who was still sitting on the kitchen chair. She beckoned to Amanda, who had gone to watch whilst her guest walked a little way down the path towards Eddie, who was standing at the side of his black open top Bentley.

"Thank you for your hospitality," she said as Amanda drew near, sounding very much as if she belonged to the upper classes, if Australia had had such a class system.

"Just a word of warning, dear, Adelaide is a small place when it comes to the ex-pat community and gossip is rife within it. You are not the first woman who has fallen for Eddie's charms, you know."

With that, she abruptly turned on her heel, leaving a trail of expensive perfume in her wake!

"Is it all right if Toby stays with you a bit longer, Mum?" asked Laura, who rang early next morning. "I forgot to mention that I have to be at both the Oleander and the Banksia houses this morning. At eleven I have to say goodbye to the couple in the Banksia, they're off to Sydney for a look around. I'll need to collect the bedding and get it laundered before my next guests come in on Thursday and at twelve I have to meet my new tenants in the Oleander. I could leave Toby with Graham, but perhaps you'd like to give him his lunch and I'll come over later."

"Oh, you know we love having him and he's been no trouble, and he's delighted with his room. It's a lovely day so we'll walk along the beach towards Brighton and get him an ice cream at the kiosk. Does he like cheese and tomato? We're just having sandwiches at lunchtime and I've a nice bit of beef that we'll be having for Sunday dinner. You and Graham are welcome to come and join us, there's plenty for everyone."

"No, you're all right, Mum. Graham's not one for formal meals, he's a spag' bol' man. Besides, we're stuffed from last night. You'll never guess what happened. You remember that girl, Amanda? Her husband works for Eddie, Graham's associate. The one you said you thought you saw at Glenelg that time. Well, that's where we went for the housewarming last night. Anyway, we didn't see much of her, she seemed to spend a lot of time talking to Rhonnda's mother in the kitchen and bobbing in and out with food for the table. To be honest, I thought she was a bit standoffish, but maybe she's just shy. Her husband's very nice though. There wasn't many there, just me and Rhonnda, a couple of others that I hadn't met before with their partners and kids and she'd put a load of food on. Nibbles and sandwiches, pies and chicken legs, gateaux and trifle. I was just about to help myself to another bowl of trifle, when Eddie arrived with Helen. You should have seen her, Mum. I mean, I made an effort and put a nice dress on, but Helen looked as if she had just stepped out of a fashion magazine. So, Rhonnda and I stood chatting with Helen and then Amanda walked in. She looked terrible, as if someone had said something to upset her. Helen suddenly announced that they had somewhere else to go on to and they'd only dropped by to say hello. Next thing, Amanda came rushing through the front door after saying goodbye to Helen and ran upstairs! We all left soon after as she didn't make another appearance and Paul looked a bit put out with it all and so we went up to the pub on the corner. Betty, that's Rhonnda's mother, reckons Amanda's pregnant."

Laura straightened the towels in the laundry cupboard of the rental and looked at her watch again. It was twelve thirty and the people who had been booked into the property by the company they worked for were late. According to the woman who had rung her a few weeks before, they were coming over from Victoria to work on a building in a local retail park. The three men were booked in for two weeks and would arrive around midday. They wouldn't need Laura to service the house with a change of bedding, as she usually did if there was no female present, as they were happy to look after themselves.

She heard a vehicle draw up outside and went to look out of the front door, which she had left open. The house hadn't been occupied since her parents had moved out and it had got a little musty. A large white truck had come to a standstill and the driver was just getting out of the cab.

"Hi," he said in greeting, walking down the path to meet her, a large smile showing his very white teeth. "We have come from Victoria to stay in your house." And he produced a few sheets of paperwork.

"I'm expecting someone called John Hacking," said Laura, looking puzzled, as she had thought that the men who were getting out of the truck would be tradesmen, not people who looked as if they had arrived on a people smuggler boat.

"I am Jonny Hakim," he said proudly. "And there are my workers, Rosti and Ferez. We have also brought along Pila who will cook for us."

"Oh," said Laura. "Well, you're very welcome, would you like to ask the others to come in."

As she said to her mother later, she had felt such a fool. Only Jonny Hakim spoke English, but when the young woman had come in, all dressed up in a black burqa, she'd given her a complete tour of the house, showing her how to work the oven, the microwave, the washing machine and where to hang her clothes, and she had left with a horrible suspicion that she hadn't been understood. The men had known how to use the television remote of course and had sat on the sofa while the woman switched the kettle on.

And when she had come to inspect the house and collect the keys, two weeks later, the house was spotless, as if no one had been there.

CHAPTER ELEVEN

It was the second week of December and Abbie felt as if she had lived in her house in Woodcroft all her life. She felt very comfortable and relaxed with everything. Some of her projects that she expected Wayne to get on with hadn't been completed, but at least the place didn't look as down at heel as it had when they first moved in. To give him his due, Wayne had worked hard at his new job and although he usually came in knackered after his day's work, after a quick snooze in his chair after his meal, he was raring to go again.

She had sold a few bits of Jenny's furniture, for peanuts really, but most things were so tatty, she still meant to get around to having that garage sale. Wayne's old car had been towed off to a wrecker's yard in Lonsdale and the sharing of Jenny's Subaru seemed to be working fine.

Abbie cornered him after his snooze one evening. It was always the best time to get his attention.

"You know Raelene, who I've got friendly with up the street?"

"Oh aye, what's she been up to?"

"Nothin'! Well, her lads go to Woodcroft College and I'd like our Jodie to go."

"Yer mean that place just before the shoppin' centre? What's wrong with the one she goes to?"

"Nothin'. I just want one of me kids ter go ter a private school. Jason's doing well with the plumbin', Molly's happy trainin' to be a beautician and that leaves our Jodie. If she does well we can send our Kyle too."

"And who's gonna pay fer all this private education? Don't ask me, Abbie, me wages have to stretch like elastic as it is."

"If yer packed up all them smokes and cut down on yer trips ter

the pub, we could pay at least fer one of them. Okay, I know…"
She held her hands up in mock capitulation. "I know, yer deserve
yer treats at the end of the day. Anyway, where Raelene works,
that's at a shop in Morphett Vale, they're lookin' fer people to help
with the Christmas rush. She says she knows fer a fact one of the
girls there is pregnant and if I act as if I'm indispensable, I might get
her job."

"Might? And how yer goin' ter get there? Yer've no transport
during the week?"

"I'm hopin' I can go in with Raelene. She drops her kids off at
twenty past. I could make arrangements with Kyle's kindy fer 'im
ter go in earlier and Jodie can walk ter school on 'er own."

"And what does Jodie think about it? And 'ave yer bin ter the
posh school ter see if they've any vacancies and if yer can afford it?"

"She's goin', Wayne. If it means I've got ter work, then so be it,
but one of the Foley kids is goin' ter make it big. Oh and by the
way," she continued, as Wayne got up to go to the bathroom in an
effort to get ready for a couple of drinks at the Woodcroft Tavern.
"I'm goin' with Raelene to the Marion Centre on Saturday
afternoon, to watch that film with Nicole Kidman and Hugh
Jackman in it. Seeing as we're going to be permanent residents here
one day, I might as well have a look at some of Australia's history.
Our Molly's got a boyfriend now, so she's reluctant to keep an eye
on Jodie and Kyle and Jason wants to take that girl he met up to the
city."

"What do yer mean, our Molly's got a boyfriend?" Which was
precisely the reaction Abbie expected from him and why she had
kept the information to herself for a couple of weeks. It hadn't
seemed to matter to Wayne when Jason appeared one evening with
a young girl he had met on his arm.

"'Ave yer seen 'im? What does 'e do fer a livin'? She's only
sixteen for heaven's sake."

"The same age as me when we started goin' together."

"Precisely, and maybe our Molly won't be as strong as you were
at givin' in. That's all we'd need, another kid landed on us when

105

youse are wantin' ter get back ter work. Anyway, as it 'appens I was goin' ter take the kids to a Christmas party this Saturday. The developers are havin' a community get-together on the reserve at the estate I'm workin' at. They won't notice if our two are amongst the other kids and I've heard it's goin' ter be a good do. And tell our Molly when she gets in that I want a word with 'er."

The young woman, with her fair hair piled high and secured by a banana clip, pulled onto the drive of the Banksia rental house in a dark blue Corolla hire car the following Thursday. She looked tired as she shook Laura's hand then followed her into the hall.

"Did you have a good journey?" Laura asked, as she carried on to the kitchen, intending to make her new guest a cup of tea.

"Yes, but it seemed to take for ages. I've never done such a long trip before and I hope I'll never have to again."

"Well, sit yourself down on the sofa and I'll make you a drink. When do you have to start your placement? You said you were working locally."

"I don't have to present myself until Monday. Plenty of time to get over the journey and get acclimatised."

"Well, you've chosen a lovely part of Adelaide, with all the beaches and the wineries. Do you want coffee or tea, Melissa? You don't mind me calling you Melissa, do you? Doctor Grainger sounds very formal."

"I'd love a cup of tea, Laura, and I don't mind you calling me Melissa at all. I hope we can be friends. After all, I'm spending six weeks in your property and with all the emails we've been sending each other over the past six months, I feel I know you very well."

"Well, I'm only at the end of the phone if you need to ask me anything and, of course, as you can see there's a modem over on the counter and a desk to do your paperwork on."

"Oh, I'm hoping the paperwork will be left at the surgery, but I guess I'll have some preparation to do. As you know, my placement is for six weeks as a general practitioner and then I'll be working at Flinders Hospital, until I decide what I want to do next."

"Well, I'll leave you to settle in, shall I? I've put money on the electricity and I've left a Welcome Pack in the fridge. There's also a map of the area on the desk and there's sugar in the canister if you take it in your tea."

She left the cup of tea she had been making by the kettle and decided to leave her guest to it. For some reason she suddenly felt nervous and couldn't wait to get away.

"I don't know what came over me," she said to Graham when he came in for his lunch later. "At first I felt a bit intimidated by her because she's a doctor and she was all dressed up in a smart navy trouser suit instead of comfy travel clothes, which most of my guests arrive in and, I don't know, my mother always looked up to doctors as if they're gods. But then I noticed she looked really down, not just tired and jet lagged, her eyes, were sort of, sad, upset looking. You're always telling me not to get involved, it's a business, and I knew that if I didn't leave her to it, I'd still be there holding her hand."

"Your problem is you're too soft with the tenants, Laura. She's probably upset at leaving her family in England and a bit anxious about her new life here. We all had to do it, it's not easy, as you know."

And it still wouldn't be for Graham, Laura thought. Though it had been over eight years since he had left his wife and kids behind to make a new life with her in Adelaide, some emotions you left alone.

"Actually, something was niggling me when I was on my way back here and so I looked up her initial application from six months ago. It was in her name and it has always been her that I dealt with, but when it came to the part about how many adults would be living at the Banksia, she had written two."

After Melissa had brought her two holdalls in from the car and hung most of the contents on hangers in the walk-in wardrobe, she made herself another drink and acquainted herself with the Welcome Pack. It looked as if it was going to be scrambled eggs on toast for her dinner that evening, as she planned to spend the next few hours in bed. The journey down under had been tiring and a lonely one, considering that she would have had a travelling companion up until two weeks ago.

She choked back her ready tears, as she dwelled on the way life could deal you such a blow that you thought there was no way of getting over it. Sympathetic relatives made noises. "It was meant to be", "forget the bastard", "pick yourself up and get on with it". That was from her mother, who had never liked Peter Fanshaw, who had been Melissa's fiancé, until he'd decided he wasn't going to be anymore.

Her controlling mother hadn't been pleased when she had taken up with an ambulance driver, even if he did have aspirations to be a paramedic one day. Surely, if Melissa was training to be a general practitioner, she should set her sights on a surgeon for a husband, at the very least. Her mother had always been a snob, besides controlling, and had always chosen her friends and had pushed her daughters to be the very best they could be. Her elder sister, Sandra, was a lawyer and married to a man who had been selected as the president of the Law Society for the requisite year. Home for the Graingers had been a large house in the rural Cotswolds and a private school had been chosen as soon as the first daughter was born. And father was a retired politician, meaning he hadn't been selected for another term.

What had really upset her was the way that Peter had called the wedding off. They had only decided to get married because the visa had come through for Melissa to live and work in Australia. She had applied for the visa before she had even met Peter and he had known all along that she was going to take up a position in Adelaide, once it had been offered to her. The plan had been that they would get married and then he could come as her spouse. He had already been in contact with the senior officer of an Adelaide ambulance station and an interview had been in the offing, once they had arrived in Australia. He had appeared to be up for it. Right up until two weeks before their wedding, booked at a local country hotel.

She wiped her nose with a piece of kitchen towel and poured herself a drink from the bottle of red wine that Laura had provided. A couple of glasses would certainly help to drift her off to sleep a little later. And of course there was always the duty free she had purchased at the transit airport on her way. That would last her a couple of days, if she needed an analgesic for her pain.

Yes, it was the way he had called the wedding off that had upset her greatly. He had notified her by email! It said that he'd got cold feet and couldn't face her to tell her himself, as then he would lose his nerve and go along with it. Australia wasn't for him. He didn't want to follow her to the ends of the earth. It was her dream, not his. Of course if she was to change her mind, they could continue as they were. It was going to be a sacrifice, having to find somewhere else to live, seeing as Melissa had sold her apartment in Bath and the new people were moving in on the day she was going to emigrate. Of course, he had moved his stuff out and gone to his brother's, to give her a bit of space!

So, Melissa had deleted his email, had a good cry in her humiliation, cancelled the wedding venue, rang her cock-a-hoop mother and asked her to ring around all the companies that were associated with tying the knot, including the wedding dress hire, and had stopped for a bottle of vodka on her way home from the medical practice where she worked. True to his word, Peter had emptied his share of the wardrobe, sorted through the DVDs and even washed his cereal bowl. And her answer machine was full of well meaning messages from everyone.

Christmas in the Foley household was a traditional one. It was not for Abbie, this traipsing down to a local beach, setting up the barbecue and burning a few steaks, while everyone sat around drinking beer and getting plastered. It had been very kind of Laura to invite her and her family to their intended Christmas beachside bash, but you could do that at anytime, unless it was a cold and rainy winter. Okay, so maybe it felt a bit strange cooking a turkey with all the trimmings, boiling the Christmas pudding in the bowl she had brought over in the container and taking out the mince pies that she had made the week before.

Of course, Molly and Jason had tried to buck against it. The weather forecaster on the telly had predicted it would be thirty degrees over the holiday and they had plans to hit the beach with some of their friends. But one look from their mother, that look she gave them when they had upset her and made them feel like naughty schoolchildren, and they gave in and were even now sat in the lounge room with their respective boyfriend and girlfriend, whilst Wayne kept a beady eye on them.

To top the excitement of this traditional Christmas, complete with an artificial silver tree, purple baubles and a red wreath pinned to their front door, was a visit from a special person. Not Father Christmas, who according to Kyle was on his way to England now to visit his cousins, having left an assortment of battery operated cars and robots for him, but Stanley, Abbie's cousin from Brisbane, who had landed the night before at Adelaide Airport, laden with presents for them all.

Stanley's wife had died a year earlier and having spent that first Christmas alone, full of grief and turning down all festive invitations from his three grownup children and their spouses, he had decided to celebrate this one away. Naturally, a visit to meet his second cousin, Abbie, whom he had last seen when she was a toddler and he had been getting ready to embark on his new life as a ten pound Pom, was his first port of call and, let's face it, she owed him one.

"Help yerself ter another tinnie, Stan," said Wayne, who had taken to this big bear of a man as soon as he had met him at the airport.

For some reason, Stanley reminded Wayne of his father. He had been a big guy, with a ready laugh, always standing his mates a drink at The Claughton, and nothing seemed to faze him. The cancer had got him eventually, eating away at the lungs that had smoked up to forty fags a day.

"Don't mind if I do, thanks. Are you' havin' one, Jason? And you, Thornton?"

"Cheers." Both lads got up at the same time, Wayne having been a bit stingy up to that moment.

"Don't let your mother see yer fillin' up on booze before the dinner's put out and our Molly, what yer doin' sittin' on yer backside? Yer should be 'elpin' yer mother."

"She doesn't need no 'elp. She said she'd shout me if she did."

"Then get some of these papers picked up. Here, Jodie, I told you and Kyle before about all that Christmas paper."

Wayne hated seeing Molly sat on the side of the armchair, with her arm draped loosely around this Thornton person. Okay, so he was from a good family. He was at the same tech' as Molly, though doing a course in hospitality and tourism, his aim being to join his father's firm, a McLaren Vale winery. Of course, it was only a fleeting visit. The lad had to celebrate the day with his own family later and had accepted Abbie's invitation for a traditional Christmas roast. Wayne intended to speak to Molly about her provocative behaviour afterwards. That skirt she was wearing was around her bum.

The lass, called Birgit, who had joined Jason for the celebrations, was a comely looking girl. An Aussie who, according to her, had ancestors that hailed back to the German settlers of Hahndorf. She was a big, naturally blonde girl with a loud laugh and seemed very agreeable. Not for her a feminine getup, even for a visit to her boyfriend's mum and dad. Her garb was the compulsory denim shorts, slash neck T-shirt and white roman sandals, which were all the rage. Her Christmas celebration with her family had been the night before, when a suckling pig and roasted duck had been produced with presents exchanged and champagne drunk.

Not that Jason had been invited to the homestead in the hills, where the Schultz family lived. There dwelled another protective father who, according to Birgit, was handy with a shotgun!

"Dinner's nearly ready," shouted a flushed looking Abbie from beyond the kitchen bench top. "Don't all rush at once, but I could do with someone helpin' ter set the table!"

Abbie's traditional Christmas hadn't gone quite as she had

planned. Stanley and Wayne had sat in the lounge room, wearing the paper hats that had been found in the crackers and listening to a recording of Quentin Bryce, the Governer of Australia, who was giving her Christmas wishes to the nation, just as the Queen of England did. But Jason and Birgit had gone off in Birgit's borrowed Ute to Christies Beach to join their friends and Molly had been dropped off by Thornton, in his prestigious Beamer, at a beach party being held at Port Noarlunga. No one was interested in playing party games, as they used to after the Queen's speech back in England. Even Wayne had been a dab hand at Monopoly.

Now the two men had nodded off in their respective armchairs, whilst Jodie and Kyle were playing quietly with their toys.

Neither child had the chance now to go to the school that Abbie had been adamant they would be attending one day. She had visited the administration office and been given a rather smart folder with all the fees and expenses that would be expected to be paid each term. To say she got a shock would be an understatement. If she had been a smoker she'd have had one straight away! With the fees, the voluntary donation and the cost of the school uniforms, Abbie reckoned that even if she worked from morning 'til night for seven days of the week, she wouldn't be able to afford it.

So, there was no point in even trying, she had said to Raelene, when her friend had come for coffee. Nor would she bother taking the job for the Christmas rush that Raelene's boss had been offering. It was a mug's game, all this rushing out to work and still having to keep the house nice and do the cooking, when it was up to Wayne to keep them anyway. How Raelene managed to send her boys to a private school on her and a salesman's wages was beyond her. She had felt very piqued when Raelene said it was a trust fund from her parents that paid for them!

CHAPTER TWELVE

It was a different story in Laura and Graham's household. Christmas dinner would be eaten on the beach, regardless of whether Laura's parents' wished for a traditional celebration or not. Graham had informed his wife, quite curtly she remembered thinking, that it was up to them whether they came to the beach, but he was taking his Weber and that was that. Luckily, Barry and Brenda were quite willing to embrace the Aussie way of celebrating the holiday season and if truth be told, were relieved that they didn't have to go to all the usual trouble. They offered to bring some sort of a pudding and a bowl of coleslaw to go with the meat.

Laura had put a lot of thought into making that first Christmas in Adelaide special for her parents. She had decided to invite as many people as she could to join them on the shore. After all, her parents had been slow at making friends since their arrival and it would be nice if there were other souls who might be lonely too. Graham, she knew, only suffered her parents' presence for her sake, as hurts went deep with her husband and he was slow to forgive.

It came as a blessing in disguise, when on a rare visit to her Facebook page, to wish all her friends a Merry Christmas, one of them had said that her parents-in-law were over on a three month visit and could do with finding a couple of a similar age. "To take them off my hands", were her exact words, as she was finding it difficult to entertain them each day. She was delighted when Laura invited her, her husband, his parents and her three children to join them on Seacliff beach for a festive barbecue.

Along with her Facebook friend, Laura had invited all the existing tenants of her three properties and their respective children, posted something on "Poms in Adelaide" to say that anyone who knew her was welcome to attend, then telephoned a few of the people who were in her address book. Suddenly Graham's small Weber wasn't big enough to cater for around forty plus people and it was decided to move the cooking department to the community park nearby, where a barbecue stood in-situ and toilets were on hand.

Melissa peeped through the bedroom shutters to check if the sun was shining, just like it had been for the past two days. A whole week from work stretched before her, as the partners who owned the surgery where she was carrying out her placement had kindly agreed to hold the fort during the Christmas holidays.

It had to be said that once Melissa had been shown her small office, given the files of her temporary clients and become busy on a daily basis with pap smears, mammogram referrals, birth control and pregnancy tests, she had thrown herself into her new life down under and hadn't looked back. The partners were kind and welcoming, the medical receptionists were good at their job and had tutored her in Medicare and Bulk billing, whilst Melissa, being the philosophical person she was, didn't long for something she couldn't have. True, she grieved for the person she thought was her soul mate, but he couldn't have been much of a soul mate, if he could dump her as he had.

The biggest feeling of liberation was not being nagged on a daily basis by her controlling mother, though having to remember to switch her mobile off when she thought her mother would be up and about in England had been a bit of a nuisance, to say the least. But the icing on the cake by far, was the fact she wouldn't have to endure a whole two days of parental seasonal *bonhomie*. The Aussie way of handling Christmas was something of a relief.

It had started with Dr "call me Alistair, everyone does" Beaumont asking her for a festive lunch at the Caffe Primo. Alistair, who liked to go to work in a polo shirt and blue denims, would have been a "catch", if he hadn't been married to Fiona, who was one of the medical receptionists and who accompanied them to the restaurant. Then there was Dr Brooklyn, another chap who liked to dress down for his patients, but who was "in a relationship", who invited Melissa and the other medical receptionist for a Christmas drink at the Emu pub. There was no embarrassing gestures of little presents offered and received, nor Christmas cards left on someone's desk and that feeling of being slighted if there wasn't one in return. On Christmas Eve, back at the rental, feeling full of *joie-de-vivre* and good will to all men and her mother, Melissa used the international telephone card she had treated herself to and rang her mother.

It seemed as if every family and their dog had come up with the same idea as Graham. The road between Seacliff and Brighton was like the lunch time rush hour, with motorists cruising up and down looking for precious parking.

Graham had been up as soon as the sun was, knowing that the community barbecue in itself would be at a premium, and had paid one of his single, more muscular tradies to stand guard, along with his Weber as a standby. At the last count, there had been thirty-four of their family and friends who had said they would spend the day with them and there was no way, according to Graham, that he was going to let them down.

Brenda and Barry had found a church along the Brighton Road, that they thought might be in tune with their beliefs and had enjoyed a Christmas Holy Communion with other like-minded people. It had seemed rather strange to be celebrating Christmas while the sun was cracking the flags, but that was another thing they would have to get used to. Barry didn't want to sound like a "whinging Pom", but there seemed a lot of differences in this new land they now called home. In England they would call their Anglican priest, Vicar: here the priest was addressed as Father and he was allowed to have a wife. The order of prayer was similar, but the responses were sung to a different tune. And he didn't want to get started about the many Aussie people at the church who didn't seem to understand a word he said. It wasn't as if he even had an accent!

Melissa parked her new Mitsubishi Challenger down a side street. It was quite a way from the park that she had passed along the esplanade, which was milling with people out to have fun. She had never been this far along the coast before, preferring to take her solitary strolls along the shore at Port Noarlunga, and she was amazed to see a pleasant beach that seemed to stretch for miles. Laura had said that she couldn't miss the place where Graham had set up his Christmas barbecue. It was not far from the Seacliff Hotel and the lifeguard station was nearby.

The trick was to spot the man who would be wearing a chef's apron, Melissa thought, as she wended her way through picnicking families wearing red and white Christmas hats, groups of excited children running about and men gathered together drinking bottles of beer.

"There you are," cried Laura, spotting Melissa as she looked around helplessly, Graham having nipped to the toilet just before Melissa appeared. "How's it going? Merry Christmas! Come and sit with us over here."

'Us over here' consisted of Laura's mother, the tenants from the Oleander next door, who were named Cheryl and Todd, and had smiled and waved at Melissa one morning when they were getting in their hire car and a girl called Wendy, who said that her other half was over there and then waved in the direction of the drinking men.

"Melissa's a doctor," said Laura, in reverent tones. "You're going to be working at Flinders soon, isn't that right, Melissa?"

Melissa nodded, feeling-self conscious because Laura had mentioned her profession.

"Yes, for my sins."

"Well, you're just in time. Graham's got everything under control and we should be eating soon".

"It's very kind of you to invite me." Oh, why did she sound so stilted? This was what she was like in new company.

"So where do you come from?" asked Laura's mother. "My name's Brenda, by the way, and that's Laura's father over there, playing with our grandson, Toby. We got him that go-cart for Christmas."

"Oh. I come from the Cotswolds originally."

"Oh, we're from Leeds," Cheryl chimed in. "There's two of ours playing on the swings and this is Ethan. Are you staying in the house next door for long?"

It was a relief when Laura announced that the Christmas fare was ready and to come and help themselves. It seemed that the whole of the community park had been invited, judging by the queue. Brenda and the other women from the picnic table went to help pass around the plastic plates and cutlery and Melissa found herself alone.

"Is Gary in a relationship, Graham?" Laura asked as she saw the tradie who had posted himself as sentry that morning standing in the queue.

"No, his girlfriend gave him the flick a couple of months ago. Pass us over some ketchup."

The tradie blushed as he found himself under scrutiny from his boss's wife. Had he got a zit or something on the end of his nose? She didn't usually look at him so closely.

"Hi, Gary. Merry Christmas. Would you like to do me a huge favour, seeing as it's the season of goodwill?"

"If I can," Gary began cautiously, ignoring for a moment the mountain of succulent looking meat on the platters before him and the crispy looking potato skins. He'd been up since daybreak and his only food had been an egg muffin takeaway, from the franchise at the local garage. Whatever the favour, it would have to be good.

"See that young woman sitting on her own near that tree?"

Gary gazed in that direction. "The one with the floppy hat and red dress on?"

"Yeah," Laura said slowly, seeing there was only one woman sitting alone at the picnic table. "She's new to Adelaide from England and it would be nice if she could get to know someone other than me."

"Come on, shove up!" said another bloke, who was trying to help himself to a couple of chicken legs and Gary was in the way.

"Okay," he said and proceeded to get himself a good helping of all the good stuff that was his for the taking. He'd saunter over, make it look as if he was looking for somewhere to rest his plate.

"Did those people turn up, Laura?", Brenda asked as she brought out another baguette from a large plastic tub under the table and began to hack it into slices.

"Who?" Laura had seen so many people in the last hour, she hadn't a clue who her mother was talking about. As far as she could remember, only her guests from the Protea had turned her invitation down and that was because they were a couple from Victoria, who had only come over for the holiday to visit family and friends.

"Those people who've come from England to stay with their son. I've forgot their names, did you even tell me?"

"I don't know the parents' names, but no, they haven't arrived yet. Fliss and Rob are always last minute merchants anyway."

Melissa stared up in surprise at the thickset, medium height young man with gingery hair and two dimples in his clean shaven, blue eyed face, dressed in dark brown board shorts and a yellow sleeveless T-shirt, who was looking down at her with an embarrassed smile upon his face.

"Would you mind if I sat at the table?" he was asking formally and there was a trace of the Irish brogue in his question.

"No, not at all," Melissa said, a little flustered as she brought her thoughts back to the here and now after she had been gazing into the distance in a world of her own.

"New to the area?" he ventured as he put his loaded plate down on the table and sat down quite closely, Melissa thought.

She nodded and moved along the bench a little, thinking suddenly that perhaps she should go and fill a plate as well.

"It's a good turnout. Judging from how you speak, you'll be used to a snowy Christmas over there."

"In England, you mean? Don't believe all the Christmassy

nonsense of robins sitting on snowy boughs and children dragging yule logs along behind them. We haven't seen any snow for years on Christmas Day, where I used to live."

"Never been to England myself." Gary began to fork his food into his mouth and began to speak in halting sentences.

"The family came over from Ireland when I was ten. Ma went back once when the old granny was dying, but I've never bothered. Seems too much of a trek."

"Oh, Ireland's beautiful, especially the south. Although never having visited the north, it would be unfair to say."

A silence sprang up between them and Gary concentrated on munching through the rest of his meal. She was a classy bird, no doubt about it, he thought, not like his little Noreen, who had a mouth on her like a ship's foghorn when she'd nudged a bottle or three.

"I'll go and get myself a little something," Melissa said, standing up so quickly that she nearly knocked his elbow, as he had shuffled up her way again. Now what could she say? "I'll be back in a minute"? "Will you still be sitting here"? Or should she just move off and leave him to it? She didn't know what to do.

"We'll all be moving down to the beach later, if you fancy sharing the shade sail I brought along. To keep out the sun, that is. I like the sun, but it doesn't like me. I just come out in red blotches."

"Well, that's very kind of you. I hope I won't be an imposition. Surely you have friends that you would like to spend the afternoon with?"

"Not if I can help it. I see enough of them when we've got a job on."

She was surprised at her landlady's reaction when she finally found herself in front of Laura, who was doling out trifle into plastic dishes, much as you would in a caféteria.

"So what do you think? He's a nice bloke, isn't he?"

"Oh, was that a set up? He didn't just wander over and sit at an empty table, as close as he could get?" Melissa felt a little angry and her tone was one of sarcasm. Did she look desperate and dateless? And why was it that every married couple wanted you to be in the same state as them?

Laura held her hands up in mock capitulation and had the grace to redden.

"Sorry, two lonely people, Christmas goodwill and all that. But you must have said something that bowled him over." And she pointed over to where Gary was ambling towards them, ready for seconds, with plate in hand.

"This is Fliss and Rob, Mum, their three kids and you said you were Marge and Ken." She turned towards a couple who looked to be in their sixties. "Am I right?"

More guests of Laura's had appeared just as Melissa had walked away with Gary, who had helped himself to dessert this time.

"This is my mother, Brenda. My Dad, Barry, is over there with my son, Toby. Mum, do you want to take them over to that table and then when they've dropped their beach stuff they can come back and help themselves."

"Thanks, Laura and Merry Christmas. Thanks for inviting us." That was from Fliss, who had been left to carry the inflatables while her three children, ranging from four to ten, ran ahead.

"No worries," Laura said. "It'll be nice for my parents to meet Marge and Ken, as they must get fed up with their own company."

"Tell me about it."

Laura turned away to start piling dirty plastic plates and cutlery into the bin bags she had brought for the occasion. It looked as if most of the guests had taken their fill and after these people had loaded their plates, she planned to start clearing up as much as she could. She had noticed that quite a few were drifting off towards the beach, where brightly coloured gazebos and shade sails had been erected above the shoreline. Many carried holdalls, full of swimwear, towels, bottles of drinks, sun cream and beach toys. Most were wearing shorts and tops, with the obligatory hat and sunglasses.

"Look who's just come through the gate over there," said Graham, who had come over to give her a hand with removing all the debris and cleaning down both barbecues.

"I thought he was having Christmas dinner at a hotel in the city. He must have escaped, 'cos Helen's not with him."

Sure enough, a smartly dressed Eddie in a pale blue shortsleeved shirt and casual navy trousers, strode across the grass, carrying one big present and two smaller ones.

"Oops, looks as if he's bringing presents," said Laura. "He wasn't on the Christmas list you gave me."

"Well, no. I didn't expect him to give us anything. Anyway, we didn't know him that well until earlier this year. Hi, Eddie. Season's greetings. What a surprise. We thought we wouldn't set eyes on you 'til the new year."

"I couldn't let such a special day pass without looking in on you both. Merry Christmas!" He shook Graham's hand, then kissed Laura on both cheeks. "Where's little Toby? Ah, there he is. Toby, over here, Mate. See what Santa left at my house."

The adults sitting with Brenda and Barry sighed sentimentally, as they saw the little boy ripping off the shiny paper as fast as he could, to reveal a huge box of Lego bricks. The structure inside was in the shape of a rather smart house, which Eddie had thought apt, seeing as Toby's father was in the business of knocking them down and building them up again. Excited boys asked could they leave the table.

"Eeh, there was nothin' like that when I were a lad," said Ken, looking at the small crowd of youngsters that had suddenly appeared around Toby. "I were lucky if I got a block of wood and was told it were a sailin' ship."

"Give over," Marge said. "What about all those old Dinky cars you've got, stored in the loft back home. They must be worth a bob or two, so your family wasn't that poor."

"Nay, they weren't, I was only jokin'. We were better off than some of the little blighters that I went to school with."

"Where are you from?" asked Barry, who had now got himself a plate of food and was slowly working his way through it. Secretly though, he would have preferred a sit down traditional roast.

"Preston. I guess from your accent, you're not from up north."

"Near Oswestry, or Shrewsbury, whichever is most familiar to you. I used to hear Preston North End mentioned, if I ever heard the football results on the telly."

"Ever heard the expression, 'Once every Preston Guild'?"

Barry shook his head then wiped his mouth with a paper napkin.

"So how long are you over for, Ken? Do you plan to do as me and Brenda are and apply for a parent visa?"

"Not on yer Nelly. Me and Marge are quite 'appy in our small corner. Isn't that right, Marge?"

"Well, yes, but I do miss the grandkids. I saw them every day when they were back home. It would be nice if we could get one of them visa things."

"Well, we can't. Our Rob's looked into it and yer 'ave to 'ave 'alf your children livin' in England and 'alf your children livin' 'ere, before they'll let you in. We've only got Rob livin' 'ere and the other two are in England."

"Perhaps you could persuade one of the others to emigrate," joked Brenda.

"Then that would be two over 'ere and one back in England," Ken replied, sounding irritated. "Anyroad, I'm not sure I'd want to live 'ere. I'd 'ate to live in a 'ouse with a tin roof; I'd chop the fingers of any little scrote I saw graffitiing and I like to 'ave Christmas when it's freezin' and yer sittin' nice and warm 'round the fire."

"What about you, Brenda? Have you been here long? What made you want to up sticks?" Marge asked, rather wistfully, Brenda thought.

"Well, it's the usual thing. We missed our daughter and grandson and, if you don't mind me saying, we were slipping into old age back in England. We've got a beautiful house just up the road and the weather being warmer is better for our long term health. I feel that we've settled into the Aussie way of life very well. Okay, so there are things that annoy, or you find different to what you are used to, but overall we're happy with the decision to emigrate here."

"And does it take long to get one of these parent visas? Just in case our circumstances change and we were able to apply."

"You'd be comin' on yer own," Marge's husband growled. "Especially if I 'ave to keep puttin' up with all these bloody flies." Ken flapped at a couple that were annoying him.

"Well, we haven't got the visa yet. I believe there's a two year waiting list. There's a possibility that we might have to go back to England, when our one year tourist visa is up. But we do believe in miracles and nearer the time we'll see if we can change our application to an onshore one. Anyway, I hope you won't mind if I leave you for a few moments. There's someone I want to say hello to."

Brenda got up and wandered over to her daughter, who appeared to be having a bit of a flirty conversation with Eddie, judging from her body language.

"Happy Christmas, Eddie. Did Father Christmas bring you something nice in your stocking?"

"Oh, Merry Christmas, Brenda. Yes, he did. I was just telling Laura, he brought me two tickets for a cruise around the Caribbean and seeing as she has turned down my invitation to come with me, I guess I'll have to take the wife."

"Yes, I think you should. Oh and thanks so much for that lovely present you bought Toby, I hope he remembered his manners."

"And so did your daughter. Remember her manners I mean."

Laura laughed and pointed to a pink cashmere shawl she had draped over the back of a camping chair.

"And he got Graham a bottle of whisky. You can come again, Eddie."

"Well, anyway, I'd best get back to the couple from Preston. Talk about a whinging Pom, Laura. I've yet to hear him say anything good about the place."

"Preston or Adelaide, Mum?"

Brenda flapped her hand at her daughter. "Oh you. Oh, by the way, Eddie. I thought I might have seen that nice little family around, that you introduced us to in the city. I believe the husband had just started work for you."

"Paul and Amanda, you mean? Yes, hmm, look, it's a sad story. I had to let him go in the end. What with the financial downturn. You know, it's becoming global. And I wasn't getting enough business to share around. He tried to find someone else to sponsor him, but in the end it was his missis who won. She was never very keen on living here."

CHAPTER THIRTEEN

Gary arranged the two camping chairs he had brought to go under his shade sail so that he and Melissa could sit side by side. The sun was still hot, but a cooler wind was blowing off the ocean, which caused the tide to slap on the shore.

"This is very kind of you," Melissa said, stretching out her long legs before her, showing off her pink painted toenails. " I don't even know your name and here you are sharing your tent with me."

"Sounds like I'm some Arab sheik. I wonder how many camels I could get for you? My name's Gary and I know you're Mel, 'cos I heard Laura calling you Melissa when I was in the queue."

"And that's what I like to be called, Melissa. That's one thing I can't get used to. The way the Aussies shorten everything."

"If you want to be an Aussie, you'll have to get used to it. It's just our way. But I'll call you Melissa if it means so much to you."

The conversation stalled as both participants wondered whether to keep it casual or get a bit more personal, whilst all around were sounds of happy laughter as children played cricket with their fathers and sometimes their mothers, and older children rode their surfboards or raced each other into the waves.

"So, how long have you been in Adelaide? Are you living local?"

"A few weeks. I live in one of Laura's rentals for the time being."

"For the time being? Are you thinking of moving on?"

"I'll have to see. I'm not sure I know what I want to do in the future."

"Not like me then. I know I'll be working for Graham as long as he'll have me."

"In what capacity?"

Jeez, this woman sounded as if she'd swallowed a dictionary!

"By capacity, do you mean, what do I do for a living?"

Melissa nodded.

"I'm a plumber."

"Oh."

A shadow fell across their vision, as both fumbled again for something else to say. Melissa was beginning to feel a little annoyed. What was she doing sitting here on Christmas Day, trying to make conversation with a young man who was probably only interested in getting her knickers off as soon as he could? She just wasn't interested. Having been dumped only weeks ago, by the man she thought she would be with for the rest of her life, getting to know another of the male persuasion wasn't on her "to do" list at this moment in time. She groaned inwardly when she saw Laura peering around the shade sail at them.

"Only me. Just thought I'd see how you two are getting on, seeing as I was the one who thought you'd get on well together. Has Gary been telling you all about his aches and pains?"

Gary looked at a loss for a moment. "Why should I be doing that? Not that I've got any."

"Oh, hasn't Melissa told you?" Laura put her hand up to her face, to stop a snort of laughter! "I should have said. Gary, meet *Doctor* Grainger. Doctor Melissa Grainger."

"Another thing. What about all these hoons? They want sorting. In my day they'd have been put in the army. There's nothing like a bit of discipline. Makes a man of you. These young folk wouldn't have lasted long in my platoon."

"That was years ago, Ken. Times have changed. People get away with more than they used to." Marge was quick to interrupt, as she could see that the others at the table were getting bored with his observations.

"How about we all go down to the shore, Dad," suggested Rob. "I'm sure Laura would let us share their gazebo if we asked nicely and the kids can run a bit of steam off. They can ride on the inflatables, or kick a ball around."

"Yes, why don't we do that," said Barry. "That tent thing that Graham brought down looks as if it could easily hold a small wedding reception. Let's get everyone together and do just that."

Melissa strode along the esplanade. If she had been a cat, her tail would have been erect, swishing angrily. How dare Laura make a fool of her like that? What had her being a doctor got to do with anything? Was it usual in Australia to say in the first instance, "Hi, I'm a doctor, what do *you* do?" Even Gary had looked embarrassed at Laura's brazen affront and had mumbled something about having to see Graham, then rushed off.

"Did I say something wrong?" Laura had gone pink in the face. "Only, I thought, with you two being on your own-somes, you might like a bit of company."

"I was just going actually. I think I'm suffering with a bit of dehydration. Thanks for inviting me."

"Oh, don't go because of me, Melissa. Look, I put my foot in it. I didn't know telling Gary you're a doctor would embarrass you. I'm sorry. Let me get you some water. Come over and join us. Meet my mum and dad."

She had watched sadly as the young woman plodded along the sand, back to the esplanade.

"Well, you *are* apt to say things first and regret them later," Brenda said to Laura, remembering some of the hurts that her daughter had inflicted when they were having problems in their own relationship. "But she's obviously touchy on what she does for a living. Especially if she knew that Gary had a lowlier job, she wouldn't have wanted him to have his nose rubbed in it."

"I thought I was doing both of them a favour." Laura ignored her mother, who she felt was having a go. There was no way she was going to fall out with Brenda again. "Gary hasn't got a girlfriend, his last one dumped him, and Melissa obviously hasn't got a partner now."

"Talking of partners, what's this about Eddie's business being affected by a financial turn down? Will it affect Graham's company and your rental properties?"

"I'm at a loss to know what he's talking about, Mum. Graham hasn't said anything and I'm booked up well into the new year. In fact I'm thinking of employing a cleaner, as at one point I've three turnarounds in one week!"

"Oh, you don't have to do that. I'll come and help you, Laura. I've been itching to offer my assistance, but with just moving into number nineteen, I've had my hands full."

"I'm afraid you're not allowed while you've got a tourist visa, Mum. It crossed my mind, that you would be my best bet to help when I'm short of time, but Immigration doesn't allow it."

"Well, I wouldn't expect you to pay me. I wouldn't be employed by you."

"Makes no difference. I checked it out on the website and I'd be in big trouble, even if I gave you a gift instead of payment."

"What rubbish, your own mother."

"Anyway, I'll ask Graham, Mum, and see what he's got to say about Eddie's downturn in his finances."

In fact it was news to Graham. Both he and Eddie had just sold one of the six units that they had built, after knocking down a dilapidated building on an acre of land. There had also been expressions of interest, via Rhonnda, which meant they could all be sold early in the new year.

"He's either kidding, Laura, or using the downturn as an excuse to get rid of the poor bludger. Eddie's firm will always be watertight, as the company's been put in Helen's name!"

It was enough to spoil his Christmas, thought Wayne, helping himself to a nip of whisky that Stan had brought along with him. Abbie had just announced, having come off the phone to her brothers in England, that Greg, the middle one, was coming over to visit next May.

"They were all there at Terry's house, 'cos Terry's wife is puttin' the dinner on this year."

"Will Uncle Greg be bringin' Becca and Jayden?" asked Jodie, who'd been allowed to shout Merry Christmas down the phone to her cousins, though a shattered Kyle had been put to bed early.

"I think so, I never asked. I presumed they'd all be comin' over, seein' as they're comin' on a reccie."

"I remember Greg better than I remember you really, Abbie," said Stan, who sat stretched out with his feet on the footstool, looking very contented with his life. "I have a feeling he was a little tearaway and Tommy was the quiet one. Greg was always gettin' up to mischief and gettin' the end of your father's belt."

"That was Greg. Me mother would open the back door in the mornin' and he'd be off like a rocket in the school 'olidays. He used to get as far as Arrowe Park when he was seven or eight and that was miles away, as yer know. Do yer remember the time when the polis brought him home, for setting fire to the gorse on Bidston Hill? He swore it wasn't him, but he got the belt anyway, just in case."

"No, I must have left by then. So, Greg's thinkin' of emigratin'?"

"He says so. I thought he was 'appy workin' in the factory at Moreton."

"It's a good job it's not Terry who's thinkin' of comin' over." Wayne's voice sounded slurred, as he'd been drinking for several hours by then.

"Whyever not?" Abbie smiled to herself. If it had been Terry that was coming over, Wayne would be wetting himself!

"If they came to Brisbane first, they could have a bit of a holiday and maybe even look around at any jobs up there. There's plenty of room at my house and I'm not far from Seaworld and the theme parks. In fact, you and Wayne should bring the kids next school holiday, Abbie"

"Abbie could, I've got to work a year before I get a break that's worth 'aving. Anyway, it'll all be pie in the sky with Greg. He's always been the big talker, but never gets round to doing anythin'."

Abbie bit back a sarcastic retort. She couldn't show Wayne up in front of their guest, especially not on Christmas Day.

"Talkin' of holidays, how about if I was to hire a car for a few days, Abbie? I've never been to Adelaide before and it would be grand to have a look around. I don't think your car would be up to carrying all the family, Wayne. If you don't mind me saying so."

"No, yer alright, Stan. It's good enough to get me down to Aldinga and back again, but I wouldn't trust it on a long journey."

"Can we go to Gumeracha?" asked Jodie, her face bright with the thought of seeing the giant wooden rocking horse there. Lots of her friends at school had been there and she had seen the advert on the television.

"I don't see why not, if someone can point me in the direction of this Gummer thingy. Wayne, Abbie? Do you think the big 'uns would want to come as well?"

"Can't see our Jason wantin' to miss seeing his lady love," said Wayne, "but I'll tell our Molly she's comin' with us and of course Jodie and Kyle. That 'ud make six of us, so you'd 'ave ter 'ire a people carrier like we did."

"And I don't think the 'ire place will be open until the 28th, Stan. There seems ter be a lot of public 'olidays in this country. Yer didn't say when yer were thinkin' of goin' back 'ome." Abbie didn't mind her cousin being there, she owed him. But it would be nice to get her sofa back and put the sleeping bag away.

"I thought I'd tootle on back after the new year, if that's okay with you, Abbie? The couch is really comfy and you've made me feel so much a part of the family, it'll feel lonely when I get back home. I miss it, you know. Miss my kids, now I'm an empty nester and, of course, I miss the wife, God bless her."

"Do yer not see the boys?"

"Not much, Abbie. If I'd had a girl, she'd probably be keepin' an eye on me, but the boys have their own lives. Although they did invite me to celebrate Christmas with them."

"Well, perhaps tomorrow we could take a walk around the park. It'll walk some of our Christmas dinner off and sometimes the people from the model car club are there and you can watch them racin' around the track."

"The cars or the people?" Wayne felt he just had to ask.

"Everything all right?"

Melissa nodded rather warily in answer to Cheryl, later that evening, after she had popped her head above the ColorBond fencing, as Melissa sat out at the patio table drinking a glass of red wine.

"Only I saw you rushing off earlier and wondered if you were okay."

"I'm fine, thank you. Just a little dehydrated. I'm trying to compensate for it, as you can see."

"I was going to ask would you like to come around for a Christmas drink with us. The kids are shattered so they've gone to bed."

"No, if you don't mind, I'm expecting a call from my parents any minute."

She got up, picked up her glass and began to open the fly screen door. Her neighbour, who had stood on a chair so she could talk to Melissa over the fence, looked disappointed.

"See you around then. Merry Christmas."

How bizarre was that, Cheryl thought, as she carried the dining room chair back into the lounge room. Saying Merry Christmas to someone who looked as if she was definitely *not* enjoying a merry Christmas and didn't want to.

"Is she coming in then?" asked Todd, her husband, who was lying on the sofa after having demolished what was left of a chocolate log and washing it down with a glass of Chardonnay.

"No. I don't know whether she's 'Miss Starchy Pants' and doesn't want our lowly company, or she's shy and thinks she'll be a party pooper. Ah well, we've done our bit for the season of good will. What did you think of Laura and her family?"

"Well, Graham could be useful, seeing as I've not got a job yet. When they get back from Kangaroo Island, he said to fix up a meet."

CHAPTER FOURTEEN

"Well, thank heavens that's over," said Laura, as Graham drove the car down the Sea Link ferryboat ramp and up the hill to Penneshaw. "I swear that petrol tanker was going to topple over at one point and crush the Rav 4. I wouldn't like to be on that boat in the middle of winter."

"It wasn't so bad," Graham replied. "You can't expect such a great expanse of sea like that to be a mill pond all the way. Anyway, you've always boasted you're a good sailor."

"I am normally. Must have been a freak wave that made me feel seasick. Although, it still looks choppy if you look over there."

"Mummy. When will we get to see the kangaroos?" Toby, who was sitting in his child's seat in the back, was anxious to see these animals he had heard about, but never seen, jumping around.

"I expect we'll see one or two as we're driving over to Kingscote, though I have heard they're nocturnal animals, so we might have to make a special journey to see them one evening. You settle down and look out of the window and let me know if you see one."

"Do you want to stop here in this village and get something to eat?" asked Graham, noticing a few eating places as they drove through Penneshaw.

"I'd rather get the journey over and done with, if you don't mind," said Laura. "I think the heat must be getting to me and that bacon toastie I had earlier keeps repeating on me. I think I might close my eyes for a little while. We were up with the larks and I didn't sleep very well last night. I feel dreadful leaving my parents on their own over New Year."

"Don't harp on about that again, Laura." Graham's face looked grim. "I told you weeks ago that I was booking this three day break and you didn't raise any objections then. It'll do us good to get away on our own for a while. I hardly ever see Toby as it is."

Laura didn't argue. It wasn't worth the aggro to start a fight with him.

The Foleys were on their way to Gumeracha. Abbie had packed a picnic, egg butties and a packet of crisps each, which always went down well with the kids, slathered the two youngest with sun cream, stuffed a small holdall with a change of clothes and sun hats and checked the Esky for drinks. She sat with Stan in the front of the people carrier, Wayne not being renowned as an efficient navigator, even if he had been the holder of the maps.

It was a perfect day to travel to the Adelaide Hills, as it would surely be cooler up there. A wise choice, now that the temperature had already climbed to twenty-eight degrees and it was only ten thirty. Molly had her magazine, Jodie had brought her dress-up doll and Kyle had his Nintendo, as the journey was long from Woodcroft, through hazardous roads and countryside, or so they'd heard.

"So, how many children has your Greg got, Abbie?" Stan asked, after fiddling with the air conditioning knob in an effort to making it less noisy. "Only, I'm thinkin' I might have been a bit hasty when I said he could stop at my place. I've only got a three bedroom house."

"He's just got Rebecca and Jayden. Rebecca's thirteen and Jayden's ten. I'm sure you can sort the bedroom arrangements. I'm more worried about when they come to ours."

"What if we got a caravan?" Jodie piped up from the back when she heard her cousin's names being mentioned.

"We couldn't afford one," said Wayne, thinking that he'd slap that idea down right away. He didn't need any other call on his wages, now that Abbie had decided not to get a job.

"It depends on whether we got a new one or secondhand," said Abbie, warming to the idea immediately and thinking how her poor Jodie would have flourished with a private education.

"We could go on our holidays in it. Save us a fortune on flyin' by plane everywhere and we could even visit Stan."

"Oh, aye, and how do yer think the Subaru 'ud pull the weight of a caravan?"

"We'll get a better car as well. I saw an advert for the Caravan and Camping exhibition at the Adelaide showground in last week's *Sunday Mail*. I expect we could get interest free terms on such a large item and we could pay for it over a couple of years. Anyroad, there's still a bit in the bank account, kept back for a rainy day."

And Wayne didn't argue. It wasn't worth it, she always won.

"Are you sure you'll be up to walking all that way, Brenda? Perhaps you should see a doctor, see if you're starting with arthritis."

Barry was concerned that their proposed trek up to Glenelg from Seacliff that morning would put a strain on his wife's hip joints, which had been giving her a bit of pain recently.

"What do they say? Use them or lose them. It's only the heat that we've been having that seems to dry the joints out. I'll take a bottle of water and I'll be all right. I don't want to see a doctor unless I have to, with having to mess around with this reciprocal healthcare business. Anyway, what else have we got to do while Laura and Toby are away? I think it's a bit much that we've been left to our own devices at New Year, when we came over from England just to be with them."

"I agree, my love. But they have their own lives to lead and it's obvious that Graham wanted them to himself for a few days. And let's be fair, we're very lucky to be here. We've a lovely house, a pleasant climate to live in and before you know it they'll be back again."

"Well, I'm glad you booked a meal for us at the hotel on New Year's Eve. At least we'll feel we're doing something. Instead of going to bed early and ignoring it, like we used to do in Wheaton."

"We'll have to see what Laura thinks of Kangaroo Island. Perhaps *we* can go for a couple of days."

Laura's mobile rang, just as she was using the bathroom, sited off the room they had booked at the Comfort Inn.

"Will you get that for me?" she shouted to Graham, who was changing Toby's T-shirt, as the little chap felt all sweaty.

"It'll only be your mother, seeing if we got here okay. Ring her back later."

"Answer it, Graham. Don't be mean."

He fumbled in her handbag. Something he hated doing, as women's handbags always seemed to be bulging with all sorts of things.

"Graham Gee speaking."

"Oh," came a female voice. "I was hoping to speak to Laura. Is she not available?"

"I'm her husband, Graham. And you are?"

"I'm Melissa Grainger. I'm in one of her rentals."

Ah, the doctor who didn't fancy Gary, Graham thought to himself. Miss Starchy Knickers.

"Can I help you? Laura's away from her phone at the moment."

"Well, I don't want to be a nuisance, but the tap in the vanity unit is spraying out when one turns it on. A small piece of netting appears to have come detached from the inside of it and as I haven't got any glue to re-attach it, I was wondering if next time Laura passes by she could bring some."

"That might not be the problem. I think I should send around one of my workmen. Laura and I are on Kangaroo Island at the moment, so there's no way she can help you."

Graham walked out onto the patio, which overlooked the bay. He had an idea, which he knew that Laura would only talk him out of, if she heard him carry out his mischievous plan.

"I'll phone Dunc' and see if he can get around to you. He only lives up the road, so he can be with you fairly soon."

"Well, that's very kind of you and I'm sorry to have disturbed you."

He put the mobile back into Laura's handbag, grinning to himself as he heard his wife flush the loo.

"Wrong number," he said ruefully, taking his own phone from

135

his trouser pocket and dialling a few digits as he walked back out of the patio door. "Though it reminded me, I promised Duncan I'd ring him this morning. Make us a coffee, there's a love."

"Is that an English accent I can hear?"

The man who was sitting on one of the wooden seats that overlooked the sparkling blue ocean, one that the local council had kindly provided, had heard Brenda speaking to Barry, as she eased herself down beside him.

"Yes, it is," she said, her voice full of relief to be sitting once more, as her trainers had felt a little tight with her feet swelling in the heat. They had walked a long way that morning and were on their way back home again. "I don't know how many miles we've walked this morning, but I think it will be a long time before I do it again."

"A spring chicken like you?" said the man, smiling at her. "Wait until you get to my age and then you'll be grumbling. I walk from Brighton to Somerton Beach every morning and back again."

"Well, we've walked from Seacliff to Glenelg, up as far as Cheap as Chips, stopped for a minute at the café on the sea front for a takeaway coffee and now we're having a rest before we set off again." Brenda wasn't to be outdone.

"So where do you come from in England? Are you on holiday?" His voice held a smidgen of the Scots accent as he spoke.

"Oswestry. Near the Welsh border. No, we've applied for a permanent visa. We're just waiting our tourist visa out." Barry decided to take over the conversation, seeing as he was now sitting on the other side of the man.

The man sucked his breath in when he heard what Barry had said.

"It's a lot more difficult to get in than we when came over. Me and the wife came over twenty years ago, as I had got a job as a carpenter. I was in my fifties, but they snapped me up. I got a visa within months of applying, but of course both our daughters were married to Aussies and the lads could have sponsored us. Nowadays you're in a queue for years, or you have to pay exorbitant amounts to get in here. Someone must have thought at Immi, "Let's charge them for the privilege."

"It's not as if we'll be costing them anything," Barry said. "We've put the money from the house we sold in England in an Aussie bank, we've bought a house here and a new car, so we're putting money into the economy."

"And when we become permanent we'll be paying taxes on our income too." Brenda had to have her say, as Barry had a very good occupational pension and there was a little inherited wealth in the savings account.

"It's a bugger when the kids up sticks and yer have to follow," said the man. "But I suppose I could be sitting in an old folks' home all alone, back in Glasgow."

The couple both nodded, then the thought of sitting in an old folks' home themselves in the future spurred them into action.

"Anyway, mustn't sit here moaning. Perhaps we'll see you again." Brenda was first to her feet.

"No doubt."

"Let's treat ourselves to a bag of chips at that kiosk, when we get back to Seacliff," Brenda said, as they set off again at a slower pace than they had before. "I don't know about you, but I'm starving."

Melissa had just finished eating her lunchtime sandwich when she heard a knocking on the front door. She hastily took her plate to the kitchen sink and swilled the crumbs off, then went along to answer it.

"Gary!" was her surprised reaction when, who should she see, but the young man she had met on Christmas Day.

"What are you doing here? I thought Graham was sending somebody around called Duncan."

"I don't know anything about Dunc' coming round. Graham rang about an hour ago and said he had a lady in distress at one of Laura's rentals. I said, 'I'm your man' and here I am, I didn't know it was you who wanted some plumbing doing."

"My plumbing's fine, as far as I'm aware." Melissa attempted a joke, which fell flat as a pancake on the ears of a flustered Gary.

"I didn't engineer this," he said. "I didn't ask Graham could I come here. I'm only here because my boss asked me."

"Well, standing on the doorstep won't get my tap fixed," said Melissa, suddenly feeling a warmth towards the red faced young man, who obviously thought that someone had set him up again. "Come in and I'll show you the problem."

Melissa left him to it, once she had shown him how the water sprayed out. He thought that long term she would need a new tap, but for the moment he would dismantle it and put the filter back.

"It's not going to affect me, Gary. I'll be moving soon. Once the New Year comes in, I'll be hitting the estate agents. Can I get you a coffee?"

The kettle had barely boiled and Gary was sitting on the sofa, looking in expectation to where Melissa stood in the kitchen. She kept herself busy, fiddling with the coffee jar, sugar bowl and milk jug, all the time self-conscious under his scrutinising gaze.

"So what did you do with yourself over Christmas?" Gary asked, trying to fill in the silence, which was only broken by the ticking of the kitchen clock.

"Nothing much. Spoke to my parents, who had a house full of family and friends around for lunch, so they could only spare me a few minutes. Went for a couple of walks along Christies Beach, sat out on the patio and read my book. Totally chilled and ready for anything."

"So, would you like a trip down to the wineries this afternoon? I'm not on call. I only came over as a favour to Graham." Gary rushed his words out and waited for her excuse.

"Now that I'd love to do, Gary. I've been wanting to visit McLaren Vale, ever since the doctors at the medical centre told me about it. Thank you."

It had been as easy as that, thought Gary, as he stood with Melissa in the Cellar Door at the Coriole Vineyard, a place he had been before with a mate. It was a rather pleasant shiraz he was swilling around his palate: perhaps a couple of bottles of this could be downed between them back at her rental. His uncertain suggestion before had obviously hit the right spot and driving along the country roads, which were lined with acres of vines or olive trees, she had been full of warmth towards him and totally relaxed in his company. Now his confidence had grown in leaps and bounds.

"Phew, that was a long day," said Stan, who was whacked after steering down steep and hazardous roads, via picture postcard scenery and leafy landscapes.

"Sit yerself down and I'll get yer a whisky," said Wayne, who had slept most of the way back home.

"I'll put the kettle on," said Molly, hoping that no one would notice if she slipped away to speak to Thornton on her mobile.

"Can I go round to Talia's house to show her my wooden rockin' horse?" asked Jodie, who had been bought a replica of the real one by cousin Stan.

"And can I go up to Byron's house to show him my car?" Kyle asked. His present from Stan had been a souvenir from the National Car Museum, which they had gone on to visit in nearby Birdwood.

"And then there was three," said Abbie, as she watched her kids rushing out of the lounge room.

"Will anyone be wanting my presence or am I free to start sorting out that stuff for the garage sale I'm plannin'?"

It had to be done. She had put off holding her garage sale for lots of reasons, though mostly it was because she couldn't be bothered at the weekends, when it was her turn for the Subaru. Now that she had decided they were going to have a new car and a caravan, they had to get rid of the clutter and the rest of Jenny and Finn's junk.

Nothing had been heard from the couple, though Belle, one of the twins, had emailed Jason and was now his friend on Facebook. Her mother had gone back to work at the hospital, but her father had said he would like to come back to Australia again, so he hadn't gone after a job. And as Abbie had been kind enough to pay them for the Subaru, over and above what the vehicle was really worth, it had been decided Abbie could keep the little money that was expected to be made from the garage sale.

CHAPTER FIFTEEN

It was the second day of the new year and Cheryl and Todd, tenants of the rental called the "Oleander", were sitting drinking coffee at the table on the patio.

New Year's Eve had been spent with the children, fourteen year old Ethan, eleven year old Lily and eight year old Oliver, walking around the Marion Centre, after treating them to a movie at the Wallis Cinema. New Year's Day had been celebrated by a picnic down on Christies Beach, along with many others who had the same idea.

Today though, Cheryl was going to do something about the rest of her life. Sitting about thinking wasn't an option when you'd got three kids.

"So, when we were at the Marion Centre the other day, there seemed to be a few of those walk in hairdressers', Todd," she said, thinking that her own dark hair could do with trimming back into her usual short bob. "You know, where you don't make an appointment. I was thinking of going back and putting out my C.V."

"Yeah, that could be an option, or nearer still is the Colonnades."

"I suppose, really, we should be making a decision on a long term rental. It's just we didn't see anything we liked when we looked before Christmas."

"What about Hallett Cove? It had good schools and, okay, you're looking for something with two bathrooms, but we only had one in England, so we could make do again."

"It's just now the kids are getting older, I thought it would be great if we could spread out a bit. There was one in Sheidow Park, but we rejected it because it was too far away from the railway station, if I worked in the city. Okay while I'm working and you're at home, but not if you get a job."

"I'll probably get a van or something," said Todd. "Anyway, we've come out on your visa, I'm only the secondary person."

Lazy sod thinks it's a holiday, thought Cheryl, as she got up to check on what the kids were up to. He jumped at the chance of coming out to Adelaide, when I told him what I'd done.

She thought back to that morning, back in Leeds, when she'd turned up at her hairdressing salon and found the door had been jemmied. It had been a heartbreaking moment when she'd walked in and found her mirrors smashed and her takings swiped from the desk in the back room. Of course the police had been called. Was she insured? Had there been a former employee/client who had a grudge against her? Why were her takings in a box on the premises, instead of in the bank? During all this, two valued clients had walked in, seen the scenario and had vanished. She knew, because of the break in, she wouldn't be seeing them again.

To say that the business was in decline would be an understatement really. Situated in a quiet back street in a Leeds suburb, the hairdressers' was used by pensioners and people of limited means. Hence the takings being held on the premises. At the prices she charged, it wasn't worth making a daily trip to the city bank she used. Nor was the business a regular contributor to the tax man. It was enough having to pay the rent to a greedy landlord, without supporting an avaricious government too.

Somewhere in the back of her mind, she remembered that when she was an apprentice at a chic place up in the city, a second year improver had applied to work in a place called Adelaide. It appeared that Australia had been looking for skilled workers. Something about having to support an aging population there. Cheryl decided that she would look into emigration and logged on to the Australian immigration website. With three children under twelve at the time and a husband who could only hand over a decent wage if he worked a lot of overtime, life could only be better down under.

Melissa, next door, was also getting ready to check out a long term rental for the future. Though today, she had someone to accompany her. It was a Saturday and Gary had the day to himself, as his presence on Graham's building site wasn't needed until Monday. Already Melissa had scanned the property section in the *Messenger* for likely places and looked in estate agents' windows when she had a break from work.

It was strange how Melissa and Gary had quickly become an item. From that day spent together at the wineries, it had become apparent that deep down they had a lot in common. Both had recently been dumped by their partners, though Gary hadn't got as far as the wedding nuptials. Both had mothers who had tried their best to control their children's lives and, another coincidence, they were both Leos. Well, Melissa was a true Leo, who had a strong character and liked to roar, whereas Gary was born on the cusp with Virgo and usually his sensible side overrode his stubborn pride. Whatever their reasons for sticking together, they felt suited. Now Melissa had a companion when she took her evening strolls, an attentive ear when she needed to go over a particularly fretful day and Gary had a bolt hole from his domineering mum. It didn't seem to matter to either that Melissa had the more superior brain, whereas Gary was a dab hand at fixing things and hadn't read a book since leaving secondary school.

He was also good in bed, or "under the doona", the Aussie word for duvet, as Gary was fond of saying. Something she had found out on New Year's Eve, after she had let him stay over when he'd drunk too much to drive. A great deal better than her ex-fiancé had been: he tended to get it over with as soon as he could. There had been no bringing her to the boil while he controlled his passion and, as he had been her only lover, she had no one to compare him with. But if all the magazines and medical papers she had read were to believed, Gary certainly knew his way around the female body. Although it was too soon to ask how much practice he'd had.

"What I'd really like to do, is to find somewhere to live in McLaren Vale," Melissa said as she switched on the engine of her Mitsubishi Challenger and looked into her rear view mirror.

"I'm dying to have a good look around the little shops there and have a meal in one of those interesting looking places on the main road. There's a lovely feel of country living, something I was used to in the Cotswolds. But I guess it will be too far away when I start working at Flinders."

"Not necessarily. The Expressway will be open when you want to travel in, if you're on a morning shift, and then it will be to your benefit coming back at night. Anyway, how long will you be working at the hospital? You might decide to work at Noarlunga and there's also a hospital at McLaren Vale."

"I didn't know that, Gary. I'll have to look into working there, maybe when I've finished my two year sponsorship, but according to my map, a good place to start would be Clovelly Park. It's near the hospital because I had a run out the other day and if you stay on the motorway you come onto South Road. Besides, that view as you come down the hill is something to die for. I just said "Wow" when I saw it. City, coastline, the Adelaide Hills, such a panoramic view!"

It wasn't just the choppy sea that had made Laura feel sick, she discovered, after waking up on the day they were due to travel back to Cape Jervis and being sick again. She could have put it down to car sickness, as the past three days had been spent driving around the island, looking for kangaroos. They hadn't seen one, much to Toby's disappointment. Not on the road that led to Kingscote on their first day, nor on the morning they travelled to American River, where the roads were narrow and the fields so full of vegetation that you would expect one or two of the marsupials to be hopping about. But after moaning to the receptionist at the Comfort Inn that the island wasn't living up to it's name, they were directed to Parndana in the middle of the island. A typical Australian country town that had a wildlife park nearby. Here, Toby was in his element, feeding friendly kangaroos and wallabies, patting koalas, listening to the chatty cockatoo and looking with wide eyes at the magnificent display of feathers on the peacocks.

"I don't see how you can be pregnant," Graham said, when Laura came out of the bathroom looking bleary eyed and told him of her suspicion. "You've taken the Pill since a few months after Toby was born and you've never got caught before."

"The doctor said it was unlikely I'd get pregnant again, seeing as it had taken a while to conceive in the first place. Something about a low sperm count, if I remember."

"Which I said was rubbish, seeing as I had three children with my first wife."

"Well, I'll get a pregnancy test kit if we pass a chemist on the way home."

"I can't wait to see Toby and Laura," said Brenda, who was still getting over her hangover that she'd had the day before, after getting very merry in the Seacliff Hotel on New Year's Eve. "I hope Toby enjoyed himself seeing all the animals he was hoping to see."

"I'm sure he did," Barry replied from the kitchen, where he was making a shopping list, as they were about to make a trip to the supermarket. They had come across a Foodland at a shopping centre up the road in Hallett Cove and found the prices most agreeable, compared to the ones in England. It had to be said though that they were still converting the dollar into pounds in their heads.

"Shall we get some Spree washing powder?" he asked, concentrating on a flier from the store that heralded their promotions.

"I know we've got plenty, but it says it's half price this week."

"Put it on the list," said Brenda, as she sipped on her coffee in the morning room.

"And Tetley tea is twenty five per cent extra. Shall we stock up?"

"May as well. I've still not got over the price of PG Tips. They're double the price of Tetley and that's if you can find them."

"What about toilet rolls? Twelve Sorbent for six dollars ninety nine."

"Get two lots. You never know when they'll come in handy. What time do you think Laura and Toby will be back?"

"I'm sure she said the boat from the island was five thirty, so if you add the forty-five minute crossing to Cape Jervis, then perhaps an hour and a half back home."

"We'll get one of those lasagnes from the chilled cabinet for our dinner and they can have it with salad if they call in."

The letting agent was a young woman with a brisk manner. Rental property was at a premium and if this couple with the three children didn't get a wriggle on and make their minds up before her next appointment was due, it would be entirely their fault.

"It seems a bit on the expensive side at two hundred and fifty dollars per week," Cheryl said, after looking around. "And the en-suite is tiny off the master bedroom."

"It has a great view of the sea, Mum," said Ethan. "And I noticed there was a secondary school by the swimming baths. It would be cool if I could continue my training."

"And I like the verandah," Todd said. "I can see myself lounging on a sun chair, having a beer."

So can I, thought Cheryl, whilst trying to be objective about the lack of space in the dining area, the rather dilapidated kitchen and dismal décor.

"Are we allowed to decorate the place with brighter colours?"

"I shouldn't think so. Although I suppose some landlords can be approached." The young woman looked at her watch. "If you don't mind, I have another family coming here in fifteen minutes. I can give you my card if you want."

"Oh, we'll take it," Cheryl said resignedly. It was near to the shopping mall that she might get employment in. There was a train station a few miles away and there were probably a couple of schools as well for the younger children. The décor didn't matter, they'd get used to it and they'd be able to get a mortgage once they both got jobs. "We have to move out of our short term rental at the end of next week, although the container with our furniture hasn't arrived just yet."

"Oh, most people get a Futon and a sofa that converts into a bed. Come by the office on Monday and we'll do the paperwork."

The house in Clovelly Park was in need of a good clean, according to Melissa's standards, of course. But aside from that, it was just what she was looking for. It had three bedrooms, the master en-suite with a spa bathroom, a compact kitchen with plenty of cupboard space, a lounge/dining room and a small sun room with patio doors. There was a medium sized garden area, mostly paved with well filled plant pots. Melissa told the letting agent that she would take it as soon as she and Gary had been shown around.

"Do you have furniture?" asked the well groomed young man, who thought these two people before him seemed oddly matched. She was quite tall and imposing looking, in a well cut trouser suit, like a school teacher he used to have at Westminster College. Her partner was obviously a tradie by the way he spoke. And although he wasn't wearing the usual navy polo shirt, matching shorts and brown calf length boots, the tradie uniform, his clothes were more K Mart than Peter Shearer. And he seemed to hang on every word that Miss Grainger said.

"No, that's next on the list. Hopefully you can point us in the direction of a reputable furniture store."

"Oh, are you not from Adelaide?" The letting agent was intrigued and not a little nosy.

"Gary is, but he is hesitant in his recommendation. Not having shopped for good furniture before."

It was eight thirty before Laura and Toby arrived at the Seacliff house. Brenda had changed into her nightie and dressing gown, thinking that Laura would have put Toby to bed now, so she didn't want to telephone and disturb them. She sat in the lounge room nursing a gin and tonic, whilst Barry checked that his tomato plants weren't covered in white fly, and was quite amazed to see her daughter and grandson standing on the doorstep when her doorbell rang.

"Oh, we'd given you up. Your Dad said you were getting the five thirty boat back home, so we thought you'd have popped in by now."

She gathered Toby into her arms and gave him a hug.

"Hey, Barry. Guess who the wind has just blown in?"

Grandma saying that always made Toby giggle. She often said funny things that him laugh.

"Ah, the wanderers have returned," said Barry, whisking his grandson up, then around in the air.

"Careful with him, Granddad. So, did you see many kangaroos on Kangaroo Island, Toby?"

Their grandson nodded and went into the kitchen to see if Brenda had filled the biscuit tin with chocolate Tim Tams.

"You won't believe this, Mum. We had to go to a wildlife park to see the animals. Although we did see a koala bear up a tree in Parndana when we stopped to ask directions and an echidna crossing the road. I think they must have all been hiding from the tourists. But, when we were coming back through Myponga, there they all were in a field. At least fifty of them. Graham was talking to a tanker driver on the journey back to Cape Jervis and he said they come down from the hills at dusk and to drive slowly as we came out of the town."

"We'll have to have a ride out there one day and have a look," said Barry. "I've only seen a dead one by the roadside since I got here."

"Shh," Brenda said. "The child will hear you. Are you going to stay for dinner, Laura? I've some left over lasagne and salad from our meal. I know Toby likes lasagne."

"Would you mind if we didn't? Toby is very tired and we did get him a hot dog while we were waiting for the boat. Now he's filling up with biscuits, so he'll be fine 'til the morning. I'm not feeling so great, probably the journey, so I'll just have some toast before I go to bed. Mum, you'd love Kingscote. You should get Dad to take you there for a few days. There's a great little bookshop, a pub that serves good food, a pavement café where you can get yummy pizzas, some touristy shops and a hotel called The Ozone. We went pelican watching one evening, just across from there. They come within a few feet of you, they're so tame. And there's a place where you can get local honey. I heard the particular type of bees can only be found on the island."

"Well, once we get our permanent visa we'll be doing all sorts of things. I don't feel very comfortable about leaving this place for too long, don't ask me why. I think we'll go up to the city next week and ask them at Currie Street about changing our visa application mid stream."

"Have Fliss and Rob been in touch while we've been away? I thought you parents were going to have a day out together. Maybe you could all go to the city and have lunch there."

"We're thinking about it," said Barry. "We're not too fond of all that reminiscing and all this sounding like a whinging Pom."

"If you don't mind me saying, Laura, you don't look very well after your long weekend away." Brenda felt a little concerned, as her daughter usually had a bloom on her cheeks. She didn't think there was that much to do on the island that she hadn't been resting.

"Ah, that's something else I have to tell you. I might be a little early in my surmising, but you could be hearing the pitter patter of tiny feet this time next year."

CHAPTER SIXTEEN

A week later, Cheryl and Todd picked up the keys from the letting agent and, with the children, drove to the house to inspect it. They'd been told that all of the carpets would be cleaned at the beginning of their tenancy and a plumber had been in the day before to check on a dripping tap.

It had to be said that the view from the property was well worth the inconvenient size of the en-suite bathroom and, as a pint sized Lily had said, she wouldn't mind using it if her parents didn't. Each child was delighted to have their own bedroom, especially the boys, because of the age gap between them.

Things were looking up for the Gould family. Cheryl, who had just happened to be passing a hairdresser that looked so busy with the clients in a queue at reception, that she had felt the urge to go in and ask to speak to the owner, had been given twenty-five hours' work per week. Her boss, who had been a ten pound Pom, was very pleased at her initiative, as it had saved him the expense of paying an employment agency to find him another member for his crew. She wouldn't have to rent a chair, something that she'd done in England, while waiting for the visa to come through: but she'd be a bona fide employee with all the things that went with the job!

Todd had been offered employment by one of Graham's associates after he had telephoned Laura's husband one evening to see if he knew of any jobs. It involved a trip to the TAFE to learn how to handle a crane wagon and a bobcat, but it would be regular employment as the company were suppliers of in ground swimming pools. There was plenty of work to be had in the new southern suburbs, where people lived the dream with a backyard pool.

A ten year old blue Holden Commodore had become the

family's choice of runabout, mainly because of the price. Cheryl was acutely conscious of the need to conserve the money they had made on their family home in England. It wasn't a lot and they both had to work at least three months before they could apply for a mortgage, if they wanted to buy. As an Aussie might say of their current situation, "They had to do it tough."

There was no such problem for Melissa. Now ensconced in her comfortable home in Clovelly Park, with the occasional visit from Gary when he got an invitation, Melissa's thoughts turned to her future and what she wanted out of life. Her dream had been of a life with her ex-fiancé: marriage, children, an au pair while she worked as a medical practitioner. Eventually, maybe, she would be a stay-at-home mum, meeting friends for coffee and going to the gym. Did she want these things with Gary? The answer was usually "no", or sometimes "don't know".

Gary, God bless him, had been a wonderful support since she'd met him, but did she want this man with the puppy dog eyes in her future? A man who, if she asked him to jump, he would ask "How high?" Didn't she want an equal? Someone with whom she could talk things through, a sounding board at the end of her day. Someone who was familiar with her day to day occupation, as Peter, her fiancé had been, employed as he was as a paramedic. How long would it be before she tired of listening to a plumber's everyday life?

Matters came to a head when, two weeks into the new year, Melissa had switched on her computer, determined to catch up with her Facebook friends. She had one item in her inbox. It was from Peter, the message heading "Happy New Year!" Stunned, she brought up his words.

"Happy New Year, darling. From a very asinine and regretful ex-fiancé, who wishes he wasn't and needs you to forgive."

She was overwhelmed, to say the least, and couldn't stop shaking, even when she put her head between her knees. "Gob smacked" would have been the words her mother's Liverpudlian cleaning lady would have used. What should she do? Her thoughts were all over the place, then she eventually calmed down and reminded herself that she was about to get ready to go to work and doctors didn't fall to pieces when faced with being emotionally overcome!

Why was he doing this now? Why get in touch with her now, when according to her mother he'd been seen out gallivanting with a nurse who worked in the local hospital and they appeared to be getting on very well. Well, she wasn't going to roll over and thank her lucky stars that he had contacted her again. She had a new life now and there wasn't room in it for Peter.

A few days into the new year, with the kids still underfoot and Molly waiting to begin her work placement, Abbie decided that cousin Stan had overstayed his welcome. There seemed to be no inclination on his part to give up his bed on the sofa and gentle hints, such as, "Your mailbox will be overflowin' by now. Are the neighbours emptyin' it?" and, "I was thinkin' of sellin' that sofa when I 'ave me garage sale," didn't seem to sink in. It wasn't as if he was taking the opportunity to get out and about a bit, as the vehicle he had hired had been returned.

On the morning that Abbie had decided enough was enough and she was going to tackle her cousin and his possession of her sofa, they were sitting in Foodland enjoying a complimentary coffee, as Abbie had run out of milk yet again.

"I was thinkin' I should go and get my return ticket, whilst we're passin' the Flight Centre," Stan said suddenly, causing Abbie to take a bigger gulp of coffee than she should have, which brought on a coughing fit.

"Steady on, Abbie. No cause to get excited." He jumped up and thumped her on the back, then waited until she took control of her breathing. "I've really enjoyed meself and your hospitality. It's been a rare treat for me, since my Ada died, but I'm ready for me own bed. I can't thank you enough, Abbie, and you're very welcome at any time to visit me."

"Thanks, Stan." She couldn't manage to say anymore, being

ashamed of her narrow-minded thoughts and lack of sensitivity to her own kin.

"I'll pay for the coffee," he said, in an attempt at being light hearted, as he could see she was feeling upset at the thought of him going home.

Barry and Brenda stood in the queue at the Department of Immigration. They had decided on a trip to the city, they would talk their visa situation over with someone in authority then go to the food hall for another tasty lunch.

The queue was long, consisting mainly of young students from Asia and both felt a little disconcerted, though they were not sure why.

"It looks as if a lot of foreign people are trying to get into the country," Brenda whispered as she saw them being sent over to sit on rows of seats across from the interview booths. "At least they won't have our problems, being young and wanted for their working skills, but it's not as if we're asking for any handouts, being self funded and sponsored by Laura."

The queue got shorter and suddenly the couple were in front of an officious looking young man, who had an air of disdain about him.

"No, you'll have to go back to the UK when your tourist visa expires," he said after Barry had asked if there was a possibility of changing their offshore visa application to an onshore one. "If you want to change your type of visa you'll have to start your application all over again and as you're dealing with the Perth Offshore Parent Visa Department, I'm not sure why you think we can help."

"We were in the city anyway, so we thought perhaps *you* could give us some advice."

"Well, my advice is that you go back to the UK and wait until you hear from the Offshore Visa Department."

"Perhaps we could talk to someone else," Barry said, looking over at the rows of people who were waiting for an interview.

"I'm afraid not."

With that, he beckoned to a young girl who was standing in line. Obviously it was time to go.

Brenda pulled out a paper hanky from her handbag when they got outside and found a bench to sit on.

"How can we go back to England, we've nowhere to live?" she cried, dabbing at her ready tears, which had begun as soon as reality had set in. "Now that Laura's expecting another baby, it's even more important that we stay here. And it's not as if we're sponging off the government. We're self-funding for heaven's sake."

"Look, we've still got a few months before we have to leave the country," said Barry, putting his arm around her comfortingly. "Maybe by that time we'll have been notified of our permanent visas. In fact, why don't I send an email to Perth when we get back to Seacliff? We can ask them where we're up to on the waiting list."

Todd walked along the road after being dropped off by his work mate, who was heading back home for the night. He had completed his TAFE course and had now been put with the regular guy for a couple of days, before being allowed to operate the vehicle on his own.

The sun was still warm on his face as he wandered along, taking a short cut through the wetlands in front of the estate where he and Cheryl were renting. Not that they were wetlands now, with the dried up creek and sun baked earth, as there had been no rain for a couple of months.

Todd smiled to himself as he began to clamber up the hill that ran at the back of their rental property and looked across to the blue of the ocean below. He was a lucky sod, considering that really he should be banged up in jail back in England. How fortunate it was that the very week that he and the family were booked to fly out to Adelaide, that stupid little scrubber back home was going to blow the whistle on him.

It had started months ago, when he had taken pity on a young girl who was always hanging around the haulage depot, where he worked as an HGV driver. She said her name was Vicky when, after he had smiled at her in a friendly fashion, she had followed him to the car park.

"Do you know someone called Alex?" she had asked, after he had opened the car door of his old Nissan.

"Alex Baker? Well I did, but he's gone down to work in Liverpool. He asked for a transfer. Family business I believe."

"Oh." The girl looked as if she was about to burst into tears.

"Anything I can help you with?"

"No, not really. We used to see each other, but I've not been well and as my mother didn't like him much I wasn't able to send him a message."

"You knew he was married?"

"I thought he might be, 'cos he never invited me around to his house. We used to do it in the back of his car."

Then Todd had realised that the girl he was talking to wasn't a full shilling. Either that, or she was so full of teenage hormones that she was begging for it. He wasn't sure which. Before he knew it, the girl was in his car and he was driving the old banger as fast as he could to a secluded lake outside the city, where lovers liked to meet. It became a habit. Once a week he would find her hanging around the depot waiting, just like she had when Alex was there.

She had been there for the taking and, at that time, Todd felt no remorse. Cheryl had never been generous in the bedroom department, more so when the kids were born and it was obvious the girl was up for it, or she wouldn't be waiting for him week after week.

Then one evening a few weeks later, when Todd had given Cheryl the usual excuse that it was Thursday and he had to work late, Vicky hadn't been waiting. No matter, he went to a pub nearby and had a few jars until it was time to make an appearance back home. He had given in his notice first thing that Monday morning as Cheryl's 475 skilled worker, state sponsored visa had finally come through. She had already been down to the travel agents' and made inquiries about their flights; their house had been sold a few months ago and they were in rented accommodation. All she needed to do was book a place to rent in Adelaide and give notice to the children's local schools.

It had come as a bit of a shock when, on the following Monday evening, as he was backing his wagon into the yard, he spotted Vicky standing by the entrance to the car park. He thought perhaps she had got the day wrong, as he had noticed she was a bit of a dozy cow at times.

It had been raining and she still had her umbrella up, something he was about to tell her when he caught her up.

"I know it's not our usual day," she had said, sounding as if she had some sort of an appointment with him each week, "but my mother says she thinks I'm pregnant and I'm not allowed out of the house."

It had been announced in her usual monotone voice, something that had grated on his nerves when he'd had to listen to her on the way to the lake and when he'd dropped her off at the depot again.

"Oh." He had said it quite inanely, he had thought later.

"I managed to escape when she went out to Bingo. She didn't lock the door as she usually does. I told her that you would marry me just as soon as I'm sixteen."

"Jeez, Vicky. I'm already married."

Todd's heart began to hammer as he thought of what Cheryl was likely to do.

"I know that. Mum said, if you weren't, you would have come round to our house. Anyway, she said to tell you that she'll give you until next week to sort yourself out and then she's coming first to see your boss and then the police. She said that married men shouldn't be shagging fourteen year olds."

CHAPTER SEVENTEEN

Laura brought the Rav4 to a halt outside the Oleander. She had been followed closely by the hire car of the family who were about to reside in her rental for the next three weeks.

Beside her in the passenger seat sat a quietly spoken, dark haired woman in her late thirties, who seemed to jump at the chance of some time out when Laura had suggested that the hire car would be more comfortable if there were only three seated in the back. The Hyundai car was renowned for its low petrol consumption and reliability, but not for the space in the rear. The family consisted of two large male teenagers, a rather plump girl and a small boy, who definitely took after his mother's side of the family. Laura wondered if it was money that had played its part in the choice of hire vehicle, as they really could have done with a bigger car.

On the way, the woman, who had introduced herself as Anne-Marie, told her a little of the family's history. This was their second time in Australia. The first had not been a reccie to see if living in Australia was the best place to bring their children up, but many years ago, when she and her husband were in their twenties, they had emigrated from England to Perth.

Ray, that was her husband, had been sponsored by a telephone company, where he had used his expertise in telecommunications for a couple of years. They had settled well and Anne-Marie had given birth to her elder child while she was there, with the intention of following the Aussie doctrine of "One for Mum, one for Dad and one for the country" in matters of childbirth. Then one day they'd got a telephone call from her sister. Her mother had been involved in a bad accident. It was only a matter of days and Anne-

Marie and her small baby were booked on a plane bound for Manchester. Ray followed as soon as his boss could arrange cover, but the family had never returned.

"We just couldn't do it," she said. "Once we'd got back home, back to all that was familiar and saw that Mum needed twenty-four hour care until she got better, we decided to stay. Then our second boy was born, then our Katie and then we got greedy and went for four. But Ray has always had a hankering to come back again and a few years ago he started talking about it seriously. We decided to wait until Liam was a bit older and here we are. We already had the points because we had emigrated before, but we were asked to consider Adelaide. Something about skill shortages in different states. And according to the people that Ray chatted to on 'Poms in Perth', the property there has got really expensive compared to Adelaide."

"So did you have a house to sell back in England?" Laura asked.

"We lived with Mum. When she died she left the house between me and my sister and when we decided to move out here my sister bought us out."

"Well, I think you'll love Adelaide. Not that I've been to many places in Australia myself, but they say that Adelaide has a slower pace than other cities and people are more inclined to be friendly. It took me a while to get used to being called by my first name."

"And what about schools for the children? I hear that the classes are smaller than back home and there's a big choice of private and religious schools."

"Toby, that's my son, has his name down at the Westminster School. It is rather pricey, but there are other private schools which are cheaper and they offer religious education too. Then there are the Christian colleges, but I don't know a lot about them. Unfortunately, the state schools are non-denominational, but they do have chaplains on hand to offer support and guidance, should it be required. Anyway, here we are, your home from home for a few weeks. I'll open up and then I'll be away, as there's another family arriving around the corner in an hour or so."

Abbie was feeling bored and had recently begun to wish that she'd got that job working with Raelene after all. Her daily walk to the Woodcroft shopping centre was not inspiring and sometimes she caught the local bus to the Colonnades shopping mall, just to pass some time away. She had got to thinking that there had to be more to life than housework and gardening. None of it fulfilled her anymore.

She moaned about it to Raelene one morning when her neighbour had dropped in for a coffee, which they drank outside on the patio.

"I mean look at the state of the garden anyway. My stuff in the veggie patch has shrivelled with the hot weather we've been havin' and no one wants cooked dinners anymore. So I'm redundant on both counts. I should have taken that job at your place."

"Look, they probably would have let you go after the Christmas rush," said Raelene seriously. "And there wasn't really a Christmas rush anyway. People seem to be holding onto their money now the government are talking about an economic downturn."

"Hell, what's that?" asked Abbie, wondering if it was going to affect Wayne, as he was the breadwinner, Jason only earning a small amount being an apprentice and usually broke by Monday and Molly having just started at her placement in the Colonnades.

"It's something to do with the Yanks. Some sort of debt they've run up and it's affecting everyone else. I don't know much about it. You just hear it on the news when you switch on the plasma."

"Oh well, that's me shafted. I'll 'ave to get out me knittin' patterns and make a couple of jumpers."

"Now, that's a thought. Knitting. What about knitting for the hospital? When Janae, a mate from work, had her baby, you could buy little hats and jackets outside maternity that volunteers had made. Or you could volunteer yourself. What about working at an Op' shop, or the Salvos? They're always crying out for people. Or you could join a club. I noticed there was a gardening club advertised when I looked at the community noticeboard in the shopping mall. Anyway, I thought last time we spoke you were going to get a caravan and you were going to have a garage sale to get rid of all the stuff."

"I can't get Wayne to agree to it, that's why I 'aven't bothered 'avin' a sale. He says he wants to put his feet up at the weekend, not go racing off towing a caravan all over the place. And he fancies going to Thailand, when he manages to get a holiday. He says all his mates go there and one of them even brought back a wife!"

Brenda, on the other hand, had no problem finding things to do. There were so many pursuits around the place she lived. At first, she and Barry were tempted to get involved with the local church activities, something that they had done back in Wheaton. There was a Men's Club, Mother's Union, Women's Guild and fundraising events, but Brenda remembered all the back biting and bickering that went on in the congregation, behind other people's backs. Someone didn't pull their weight enough, someone, on the other hand, boasted about how much they *did* do, and church politics always seemed to be getting in the way of their worship.

It was Fred and Ginger next door to Laura who encouraged them to join a walking group. They met the infamous pair when they were dropping Toby off, after an hour or so spent at the Beach House in Glenelg.

Ginger, who was really called Aileen, came rushing to the passenger door of their car, as Barry drew up.

"Hi, how's it going?" said this lithe looking woman in her fifties, dressed in a pair of navy cargo pants, a sleeveless white top and a pair of sparkly thongs on her feet. She wore her auburn hair up in a ponytail and the couple could see why she had been nicknamed Ginger, besides the obvious reason of her dancing profession.

"Hi, Toby," she continued, hugging the boy after he had released his seat harness and come to stand on the pavement. "Got a message for your Nan and Grandpop. Your Mum had to go to one of her rentals as someone there has lost their key."

"Hi, I'm Barry Webster and this is Brenda, my wife." Barry was quick to make the introduction, as he had always had an eye for an attractive lady. "Has she been gone long? I should have thought she would have rung me on the mobile."

"No, I told her not to," Aileen said. "We were looking for a chance to meet you and this was it. She shouldn't be long, but I'd love you to come in and meet Larry. I'm sure a cool drink would be welcome. Wine, juice or even a gin and tonic. And I've got some ice cream, Toby. Your favourite, berry fruit."

It was obvious that Toby felt at home with this flamboyant woman, who was carefully made up with understated makeup, wearing a pair of dangly cutwork gold earrings and cerise varnish on her fingernails and toes. He ran ahead to the open door of a rather palatial cream cement rendered house, with an elegant portico and pink tiled entrance. His grandparents followed, quite bemused by this turn of events.

"You must be Laura's parents," cried a very slim, tall, dark haired man with a look of Roy Orbison about his facial features. Dressed in blue board shorts and a blue short sleeved checked shirt, he was smiling broadly as he walked quickly down the pink marble floored hallway to greet them.

"Toby's gone out onto the patio. Come in and I'll get you a cool drink." He led the way ahead of Brenda and Barry, with Aileen trailing behind. "What can I get you?" he asked, going to stand behind a wooden bar in the kitchen area, which was fitted out with brass topped pumps and a sign on the wall saying "Bar Open". He went on to boast about all the different drinks that he could pour for them.

"I'll just have a glass of lemonade," said Brenda, looking around the cherry wood kitchen, which could have been a feature in a women's magazine, and thinking that they must employ a daily, as it was spotless.

"I'll have the same," said Barry. "I'll be driving home."

Larry looked disappointed at their choice, but once he had poured the drinks into tumblers, from a glass jug he took from a small fridge under the counter, he busied himself uncorking a bottle of red wine.

"Aileen, take Laura's parents out onto the patio and I'll bring your drinks out on a tray."

"He likes to make a great show of his knowledge of red wine," Aileen said, once they were out of earshot and they were all sitting at a glass topped table on the patio, overlooking an extensively landscaped garden.

"He's down at McLaren Vale topping up his varied collection whenever he gets the chance. Toby, would you like me to get you a bowl of ice cream?"

The little boy nodded from his place at the table, where he was busy with a box of coloured pencils and a drawing book.

"I always leave them out, if I think there's a possibility of a visit from him. Isn't he a lovely, well mannered young man?"

She got up to go into the kitchen and returned with a bowl of pink and white ice cream and a small teaspoon.

"Here you are, Toby, and here's Larry with our drinks."

So that was how Brenda and Barry found out about the walking group. Apparently, when the couple were not working as dance teachers on the cruise ships or holding keep fit sessions in the local community hall, they kept active by walking. Every Monday morning they would meet like minded people in a car park nearby and, depending on the leader's choice of area for their stroll or ramble, they would drive in their cars to the venue or start their walk from the esplanade.

"We've been all over," said Larry amiably, his foot tapping a little, as there was a catchy tune playing on their CD player, which was kept underneath their hostess trolley.

"Up to Maslin Beach, across the Noarlunga Downs, through the Scrub at Aldinga and next week we'll be ambling around Brownhill Creek. You'll be made very welcome. The Aussies are a friendly bunch."

Laura smiled at the couple, who had telephoned her from the rental.

"Don't give it another thought. We've all left keys in our houses in the past. It wouldn't be the first time for me."

"We just feel so foolish," the woman who was called Mary said. "We try our best to be alert and active and I asked Harry if he'd picked them up off the kitchen work top and he said he had."

"Well, here's another set, Mary. Maybe if you kept these in your handbag all the time? Anyway, how have you settled in? That journey from Manchester is very tiring. I think I mentioned my parents to you when you first arrived. They flew from Manchester."

"We're getting over it," said Harry. "It was something that had to be done if we want to be close to our family. Mary keeps having little naps on the sofa, but I can only sleep in a bed."

"Over here, the Aussies call them "Nana naps," Laura said. "My mum's the same. She can sleep on the sofa, but has trouble sleeping in a bed. Now, is there anything else I can help you with? You've been to Medicare, I take it, and obviously you've picked up the hire car. Have you checked out the air conditioner? You know how that works?"

"Yes, everything's to our satisfaction, Laura," Mary said. " Our daughter's been around this morning and we followed her in the car to the shopping mall. We're trying to get our bearings, as we don't want to rely on her too much. That's why we probably left the key in the house. She kept chivvying us up, because she had to get to work. Her husband works shifts as well, so he's the one who picks the children up from school. Now that we're here, we'll be called upon to babysit. Not that we mind, that's what we're here for."

"You're probably in the same position as my parents then. They're on a tourist visa at the moment, but they've applied for their contributory parent visa. It seems to take a long time to come through."

"Oh no," said Harry proudly. "We're already permanent residents. We got ourselves a migration agent and he dealt with everything. Our daughter and her husband were already on permanent visas, so Steve, that's April's husband, offered to sponsor us. We had to wait two years and in the meantime we sold our house and moved in with Mary's sister. Then, when we got the call, over we came."

"Love's a very strong emotion, isn't it?" Laura said, quoting her own mother's words. "I think it's very brave, the way parents up sticks and travel across the world to be with their families."

"Well, there was nothing left for us in England," Mary said. "Our parents had died, both of us have a sister each and we didn't see much of them. We sat in the house watching daytime telly, or walking around Asda, just to pass the time away. We missed our grandkids, as we'd had a hand in looking after them since they were babies, so we jumped at the chance of coming over to be with them. Look, I've got some photos." She searched in her big black handbag and brought out a small photograph album, with the words "Granny's Boasting Book" on the front.

"This is Talia, she's our eldest. Then there's Ben and Jack. There's only two years between each of them. How our April's been managing, I can't imagine and holding down a job as well."

"Well, they're school age now," said Harry, pointing to another photograph where three cheeky looking imps were smiling at the camera, dressed in school uniforms.

"They're at a school called Woodcroft College. We'll probably find somewhere to live in the area, so they can come to us after school. That's why we had to rent with you, Laura. You can't swing a cat around where they live."

"Oh, is that in Woodcroft too?"

"No, they live in Trotts Park, but their house is too small really. Now we've consolidated, you know, sold the house in England, we'll be thinking of moving nearer to each other. Try to get property nearby."

"If you need any help with real estate, just let me know," said Laura. "I have a friend called Rhonnda who would be pleased to help you." She looked at her watch. "I must fly. My parents took my son, Toby, out after they picked him up from kindy. I arranged for my neighbour to take them in, but they'll probably be fretting by now. No, no, it's not your fault. It was arranged that my neighbours would invite them in for a drink. Which reminds me, why don't we get you and my parents together one day? I'm sure you'd get on very well."

CHAPTER EIGHTEEN

Laura's mobile rang as she was just setting off to do a "service" at the Banksia. The people who were renting the house required a service once a week, as they were in business and out six days working.

The caller was Anne-Marie, the lady who had moved in to the Oleander a couple of weeks before.

"Hi Laura, I'm just letting you know we've found a house to rent in Aldinga. Ray's going to be working in the area, so we thought we'd rent there and maybe buy one of the new houses they're building, eventually."

"Oh, I'm so glad you've found something. It seems to be getting harder to find places. With so many people coming over, everyone's chasing a rental."

"Well, I was just ringing to let you know. Perhaps you and your husband can come down and visit when we're settled and maybe we could fix up a play date for Liam and Toby. And while I'm on, could you direct us to some furniture warehouses? It's rather confusing watching the adverts on the telly, as it seems everyone of them has got a sale."

Laura smiled to herself as she set off in the Rav4 to her rental. The amount of people who had promised they'd keep in touch, with invitations of coffee mornings, barbecues and even play dates. If they'd all been genuine, probably they were at the time, she would have a full social calendar! And perhaps she should be asking for commission from Radio Rentals and Harvey Norman, as her houses were furnished by both of them!

Abbie couldn't get rid of the lethargic feeling she woke up with each morning. Everything was becoming an effort and she walked around the house in her dressing gown most of the day. Sometimes she would pick up her knitting and attempt to work a few rows, thankful that she had at least gone to Sam's Warehouse the week before and bought a few balls of wool.

Molly had been sympathetic, coming home from her placement early one afternoon and offering her mother an immediate facial, saying it would cheer her up.

"Honestly Mum, you drag us across the world so that we can all have better lives and here you are sittin' around mopin'. At least get dressed in the mornin's. Why don't you get a shower, put that kaftan on me and Jason bought you for your birthday then I'll put your hair in rollers before I do yer face?"

"I can't be bothered, queen. I've got to do somethin' about our dinner before everyone gets in."

"I'll see ter the dinner. We'll have a salad again and I'll open up that tin of ham you got at Christmas. Mum, yer not getting' away with it. You're probably feelin' a bit depressed, got a hankering to be back 'ome again. I hear it all the time at work, people feelin' 'omesick, but not being able ter afford the plane ticket. Mum, this isn't like you." She put her arms around Abbie and gave her a hug.

Abbie started crying softly, feeling ashamed that her sixteen year old daughter was witnessing her weakness.

"I can't seem to help meself," she said, dabbing her eyes after Molly got her a piece of kitchen roll. "I think it must be because all the things I wanted back home I've got. I've got a lovely 'ouse with a nice garden, we're livin' in the sunshine and all my kids are doin' well. I'm not struggling for anythin' anymore. I don't even 'ave rows with yer Dad ter get things done, 'cos 'e's gone and done everythin'."

She started to smile then, thinking of all the times she had gone at Wayne for preferring to be in the pub instead of helping her with the kids, or fixing things up at their house in Birkenhead. How she'd been the dominant one in their marriage and he had been the lapdog, whereas this move to Adelaide had been the making of him. He was even known to put his foot down occasionally. Okay, he still went for a drink with his work mates, still went through a twenty pack of cigarettes per day, but he'd done every job in the house she had asked of him and was prepared to do more if she wanted.

"Don't yer ever miss the Mersey ferry, Molly? Do yer remember us travellin' over to Liverpool that time when you were little to watch Cinderella at the Empire? And walkin' down Grange Road on a Saturday mornin', doin' a bit of window shoppin' and eatin' pie and peas at that place in the market?"

"I do, Mum, but as they say, we've moved on and yer 'ave ter put them in your memory box. But I'm wondering if there's something else the matter and you're not just feeling homesick. Would yer mind very much if I asked yer a personal question?" Molly looked a bit hesitant.

Abbie shook her head, looking doleful.

"What if yer went to the docs' fer a checkup? Do yer think yer might be 'aving symptoms of that menopausal thingy?"

It was a pleasant day for it, but Brenda was quite relieved when she and the walking group, minus Fred and Ginger, as they'd gone off to Sydney for couple of weeks, rounded the corner at the bottom of Port Road and found themselves across from the Star of Greece restaurant car park, in Port Willunga.

This was Brenda and Barry's first outing with the walking group. According to the leader, an Aussie guy called Malcolm, it was an easy ramble through the countryside. They had left their cars on the headland above Maslin beach then walked down hill and over dale until they began descending towards the ocean.

There were fifteen in their group that morning, mostly over 55s, wearing walking shorts, T-shirts and comfortable shoes. Fifteen was a momentous amount for Malcolm, as usually there were around eight or nine attendees. He put it down to the more pleasant weather, as they'd been having very high temperatures recently. In fact, he'd had to call off the walk the week before, in case some of the old dears suffered with heat exposure!

"We'll stop off here!" he shouted before making his way to the kiosk to inform the young lady serving that there would be a few of his group wanting drinks. There was a dash for the plastic chairs that were dotted around under a few white tables. Barry managed to get them two.

"I'll just have a lolly ice," Brenda said when he asked her what she wanted to drink. "I've got this bottle of water and I'll have to visit the loo before we set off again."

"It's handy having the Ladies down the bottom of the hill," said a fresh faced woman with pale blonde hair, who looked to be in her early sixties. "Would you mind if I joined you?"

"If you can find a chair, you're welcome," said Brenda, having put her small black haversack on the other chair to reserve it for Barry.

"There's a man bringing some more out. They usually do as they don't want to lose business. Are you having a coffee? Perhaps if I give some money to your husband he'll get me one."

"Oh, I'm just having a lolly ice. This water will do me until we get to our lunch stop."

The woman put her bag on the chair that the man had brought over.

"I'll just go and tell your husband to order me a cappuccino and while I'm there I'll put him right. If you ask for a lolly, they'll think you mean sweets. If you want what I think you're asking for, you need to ask for an icy-pole."

She certainly was straight to the point, thought Brenda, as she watched the woman pushing her way through the queue until she reached Barry. Then she had to smile, as she saw the look of surprise on her husband's face!

Sandra, or Sandy, as she liked to be called, attached herself to the couple from then on, which was difficult, as the pavement was narrow when they walked towards their next port of call.

Their next stop was a café along the esplanade, where they could buy a nice reasonably priced meal or sit outside to eat their sandwiches. Eventually, Barry gave up having to walk in the gutter and began to speak to a man he'd earlier had a short conversation with. By the time they sat down outside the café, after marvelling at the panoramic view across the ocean towards Cape Jervis, Brenda knew everything there was to know about Sandy McLachlan. Starting with her emigration from Edinburgh twenty-three years ago, with husband, Lockie, and two daughters, Lesley and Nan, settling in Sydney, where Lockie worked as a chartered accountant, then him running off with a younger woman ten years ago.

"We were happy in Sydney," Sandy mourned. "We made lots of friends and had a great social life, then he met this floozy from personnel and I was consigned to the bin. Luckily, I got a good divorce settlement, courtesy of Lesley, whose husband is a divorce lawyer, and Nan and I live happily together in Somerton Park."

Even though Sandy had emigrated to Australia all those years ago, she still had a strong Scots accent, which made it difficult for Brenda to understand everything she said. So, when Sandy asked if she could have her telephone number, she thought it was to do with the walking group and gave it without much thought. Barry said later she must have been crazy, because now the woman had their number she'd be on the phone every day!

Laura had got over the sickness stage of her pregnancy and was looking forward to early September when, if she had counted her dates right, she would give birth. Hopefully, her parents would have their permanent visas by then and be there to look after Toby and even keep an eye on her rental business, if Graham was too busy.

The economic downturn didn't seem to be affecting Graham's business. All the houses he had built had been sold and various people had expressed an interest in the block of apartments he was building, including Laura, whose accountant had told her she could go for one of the two bedroom apartments if she felt inclined to do so. She was feeling a little cautious though. What if the forecasts were correct and people couldn't sell their houses in the UK in order to fund their emigration? Not everyone wanted to come out on a wing and a prayer like some did. The apartments were expensive, compared to the price she had paid for the villas. She shelved her decision for the time being, hoping that she would feel a certain confidence in the next week or so. Eddie, who still popped round, mostly on a Friday night to share a bottle of wine with Graham and to chew the fat, said she'd nothing to worry about and if she didn't get a wriggle on the investors would beat her to it. Even Helen was thinking of acquiring one of the apartments.

It was a Saturday morning in late February when Raelene collected Abbie and her two younger children for a day to be spent at the Greenhill Adventure Park, near Victor Harbor. Having been unable to get to the cow racing at Mount Compass in January as she'd promised, because she'd been working, this was to be a special treat. The boot of her vehicle was crammed with picnic baskets, rugs to sit on, footballs, a frisbee, sun hats, and a change of clothing and towels for when the children had finished playing on the water slide.

Her boys, Harrison and Byron, had been to the place before and were telling Kyle and Jodie, in excited tones, what there was to do at the adventure park.

Abbie was feeling upbeat that morning. After visiting a female doctor, who herself had recently migrated to Adelaide and was working at a practice on Main South Road, she was now confident that it wasn't the onset of the menopause that was causing her depression, but a change of position in her family's life. Once Dr Grainger had listened to Abbie's despondent tale, she reasoned that now Abbie's family had settled into life down under, she had begun to get the feeling that there was nothing left to strive for. There were no battles to be fought with Wayne for the control of his money, though he still had his fags and his daily beer, the two eldest were settled in jobs that they were happy in and the house was nearly paid for; all this with the bonus of the sun nine months of the year. Add that to the natural anxiety that came with great changes in a person's life and it was no wonder she was feeling the way that she did.

Dr Grainger had been brisk when she offered the options available to her patient. She could wallow in self-absorption and take medically prescribed tablets to keep her mind in limbo, or take control of her emotions, lose some weight and get herself a life!

Melissa Grainger had been taking control of her *own* emotions recently. Her ex-fiancé had been given the bum's rush and was told in no uncertain terms by email, that she was in a new relationship and couldn't give a fig about his feelings. Which wasn't true really. It was just she felt so angry that here she was carrying through with all the things that she had dreamed about, but without him. Hurt had turned to anger, once her numb feelings had started to thaw.

She and Gary were still an item, but recently there had been suggestions on his part that they should get married and start a family. There had been subtle hints, overt hints and outright broaches of the subject, then on Valentine's Day he had turned up outside the medical centre with a bouquet of red roses and a padded musical card, which played a cheesy love song.

It had been much to her embarrassment, as it had only been a few days before that she had returned to the comfortable fug of general practice. There had been too many calls on her emotions with the emergencies she had been faced with in the hospital, especially when one young unfortunate had been caught up in gangland crossfire. The offer of permanency by the doctors, Beaumont and Brooklyn, was just what Melissa was looking for.

It was the best day of their lives, according to Kyle and Jodie, who, as soon as Abbie had paid their admission, were racing after Harrison and Byron, who had made a dash for the go-carts. There was a height chart of course and both Kyle and Byron were left disappointed as they were less than the 1.35metres required, but they rallied moments later, when they saw the four wheeled motorbikes nearby. There were aqua bikes, paddle and row boats on a calm looking lake, a climbing wall, moon bikes and exciting wave and water slides, which tired the children out.

Raelene was sympathetic when, as the two women sat together by the crazy golf after all four children had gone off for a tour of the park on the tractor drawn train ride, Abbie told her the gist of what Dr Grainger had said to her.

"She's probably hit the nail on the head, Abbie. I've not known you long, but from what you've told me you always were the matriarch. And you're not the type to sit around doing nothing about this depression of yours. Look, why don't you volunteer for things like I mentioned to you before, or better still, why don't you get involved with the school that Jodie and Kyle attend? I'm sure they're crying out for help with things like listening to the children read, or being in the playground at recess and lunch times. And you could still do your knitting for the maternity ward. You don't know how lucky you are!"

"You're right, Raelene, I am a lucky josser, compared to those I left behind in Birkenhead. I'm sure it's just a blip though and I'll soon get over it. I'll look into 'elpin' out at the primary school and I'll even set a date for me garage sale!"

CHAPTER NINETEEN

It was with a sigh of relief on everyone's part which, after waving goodbye to grandparents Marge and Ken, who had stayed in their home since before Christmas, they made their way through to the departure lounge at the airport and the family walked back to the car park. Saying goodbye to someone is always difficult, especially if there is a possibility that you will never see them again and each person felt a different emotion as they got into Rob's X-Trail.

Poppy, the youngest of Rob and Fliss's children, hadn't remembered her Nana Bowden from England, though she had felt a certain warmth towards this white haired lady, who was always giving her kisses and held her hand when they walked together. Granddad was a different matter. He was gruff and she had heard him say that children should be seen and not heard, as it was in his day. She had kept her distance and been labelled as "shy" by him.

Danny, the middle child, had been sad to see both his grandparents go, as Nana and Granddad Bowden had been in his life since he could remember and he missed their presence in his new life in Adelaide. It didn't matter that Granddad insisted on good manners and wanted to watch what he wanted to on the television, Granddad Bowden was family.

Jay, short for Jaydon, the eldest boy, who at ten years old was a good footballer, would miss the coaching his granddad had given him during their "footy practice" on the reserve across the road.

"So, I think we're all ready for a Big Brekky," said Rob trying to lighten the mood, as everyone was looking glum. "They'll ring us when they get home and you'll be able to see them on Skype."

"Granddad said he was glad to go home," said Daniel sadly. "He said he was looking forward to rain and cloudy skies and being able to have a good pint at his local."

"Nana said she didn't want to go home, she wanted to stay with us forever," Poppy said, with tears in her eyes.

Jay said nothing. He wasn't going to start blubbing in front of his younger sister and brother.

"Well, I for one will be glad to get our lives back to normal," said Fliss, who had made up all sorts of excuses to be out of the house or in the study, when they had been hosts to Rob's parents. Her job as a fundraiser and events manager for a charity was only part time and she had really been in the fitness centre "networking", where she had renewed her friendship with Laura, or looking busy working on the computer, when really she had logged onto "Poms in Adelaide" or Facebook.

"You'll be able to have your own room again, Danny. And you, Poppy, can shout to your heart's content, now that your granddad isn't around."

"He wasn't that bad," Rob said, in his father's defence. "He's used to having a bit of peace and quiet now that we've all flown the nest and he's very much set in his ways, with him having been a military man."

Fliss said nothing. She didn't want to start a row with her gorgeous hubby and was looking forward to having his undivided attention again.

They had been together since meeting at Lancashire University. Fliss, who had lived in the Lake District with her parents, travelled in each day in the car that had been bought for her eighteenth birthday. Not just any old banger: she had been allowed to select, within reason, whatever make of small car she wished. Her mother was an artist and her father a sculptor. Both were sensitive individuals, who made a good living from their skills.

Rob, or Robert as his parents called him, also travelled to the university daily, from Preston. Although *his* vehicle, not of his choosing, was an old Morris Marina that his father had kept in pristine condition to be passed on to his eldest son. If it hadn't been for an introduction via Fliss's older brother, who had been on the same degree course as Rob, the couple might never have met. As it was they were ideally suited. Soul mates, they called themselves.

Four years earlier, after Poppy had been born, Rob had begun to have itchy feet. He was not really happy about the daily grind of travelling each day to and from Chorley, where they lived, to a pharmaceutical research unit outside Skelmersdale, and so mooted the idea of emigrating to Australia. Fuelled with a rush of maternal hormones, emigration to Australia seemed fitting to his wife somehow. A new life, in a new country, with a new baby appealed greatly and if she could have signed her name on a dotted line, she would have done just then.

There was much research to be done on the internet, employer sponsorships being the obvious route with having three children. Two years on, after saying goodbye to heartbroken parents and siblings, they found themselves in Adelaide, Rob having secured a research position at a Science Park on a four year contract and Fliss happy to be the homemaker for the time being.

Six months down the line and living in a nice house in Hove, with Poppy potty trained and the chance of working with a girl she had met at the gym, Fliss put her daughter into kindy and Danny into pre-school, Jay having already started at the local primary, and began to work part time. Being a home-maker had become a little boring, especially in the winter months, when you couldn't go walking in the pouring rain, had two children under five to entertain, and could only stand a certain of amount of visits to Fun 'n' Games at Christies Beach and the Beach House at Glenelg.

They had been living in Aldinga for one week when Anne-Marie decided that she felt so isolated that she really needed to have the use of the family car.

There was no problem with transport as far as the children's schools were concerned. The two eldest had slotted in well in the local Southern Vales Christian College and both were thinking of trying out for the junior team at the Aldinga Sharks. There was the

John Nicholl Reserve not far away from the rental house and when the boys weren't using the bike track to do all sorts of wheelies, they could be seen having a kick about on the large field. Her only girl, Emma, was in the last year of the primary school on Quinliven and Liam was in the second year.

Ray had been promised a vehicle by the telecommunication company. It hadn't materialised straight away and so the secondhand Pajero, which he had purchased after the Hyundai Getz had gone back to the hire firm, was his for the moment, to take him around his various ports of call.

Anne-Marie knew that life could become as boring as it used to be back in Denton, after her mother had died. Or anywhere for that matter, once your kids had gone to school. It had been slightly different when they had lived in Perth, as they were only a short ride away from the city and she could jump on the bus with her little one and spend some time in a shopping mall.

Here in the Aldinga Central, after mooching around the Blondies shoe shop, the Chemmart and the surf clothes shop, there was only Coles, the newsagent and the variety shop to while away her time. You could only drink so many coffees in Louis's and she wasn't a great reader to make a lot of use of the library. Public transport seemed non-existent, just a bus to the next town of Seaford or the Colonnades now and again.

Ray had urged her to volunteer or join a club, take daily walks along the esplanade, or go to the fitness classes at the local community hall. According to the *Coastal View*, a magazine that she picked up on a stand outside the supermarket, there was plenty to do in the area, mostly at the community centre at Symonds reserve. She decided she'd have to think about it all, as according to the map Ray had given her, Symonds reserve was quite a plod away.

On the day that Ray had been given his Toyota Hiace, with the name of the telephone company he worked for emblazoned on its side, Anne-Marie, dressed in a smart red and cream tracksuit, with matching trainers that she had purchased from Blondies, was at the wheel of the Pajero, heading up Commercial Road.

A sense of freedom assailed her, though not without a warning in her head from Ray, not to go mad and "max" the credit card. There were still the bills from moving into the rental to settle and the interest free account they had set up with Harvey Norman, who had provided them with their new, hopefully child friendly furniture. She was still hoping that she wouldn't be chased by Laura for the damage done to the coffee table when Liam, in a strop over something, had kicked out and fractured one of its legs! Nor have to pay out for a bucket of paint, as they had scored the hallway wall whilst dragging out their suitcases. Nothing had been said up to now, but she lived in anticipation of Laura's call to her mobile.

The days were becoming a little cooler, now that February had turned into March. The beginning of the "autumn months", as the weather presenter on the television was fond of saying, along with a wish for deluges of rain to fill the area's creeks and reservoirs. She supposed that they could do with a shower or two, as the grass in the back garden of the rental had withered and died, leaving only a blank sandy soil to gaze out onto.

Anne-Marie's destination was the Seaford shopping centre. It had everything a girl on a limited budget could wish for, but she had never had the time to discover its attractions as there had always been her family in tow. Today, Seaford, tomorrow, the Colonnades, she thought as she whizzed past rows of yellow fields and paddocks full of horses, glancing over now and again at the blue of the ocean in the distance. Passing the building site of the new Moana Heights complex and the urban sprawl of Seaford Rise, she reached her goal and turned into the Big W carpark.

She was sitting in the hairdressers' waiting for someone to make a start on her hair, when a woman with short dark hair streaked with red highlights came dashing through the door with a Subway roll in her hand.

"Sorry," she said, after she had gone into a side room and come back empty handed. "I just had to go and get some lunch, I'm starving."

"After this lady," came the reply from the boss, who was working on a head of hair across the way.

"Do I detect an English accent?" asked Anne-Marie, who felt her spirits rise, as she hadn't spoken to an English person since she arrived in Adelaide, unless you counted Laura.

"Yeah, I'm from Yorkshire. Have you been here long?"

"In Adelaide or waiting for you to come back with your lunch?" Anne-Marie wondered if the woman would think she was having a go?

The woman laughed. "In Adelaide of course, you silly muppet. I haven't seen you in here before and I've been working here a couple of months."

"Oh, newly arrived. Staying in rental accommodation in Aldinga. My husband works down there, so it made sense to move there."

"So does my husband. I mean works down there, not moved down there. It's great having all this developing going on. Good for us and good for the economy. Got any kids?"

"Four at the last count. They're all in nice schools in the area."

"I've got two. And we live on the estate they call Seaford Rise."

"So, you'll have a view of the sea then. We were hoping to get a place nearer to the esplanade at Aldinga. You know, a few streets away from the front, but the properties are too expensive. Still, it's only a five minute walk to the sea if you get your skates on. I'm going to do the Lotto."

It was a couple of hours later that Anne-Marie headed back home, with her new hairstyle, compliments of her hairdresser called Cheryl, and three green shopping bags stuffed with all the things she thought she was in need of, from Big W and Cheap as Chips. And what a small world it was; Cheryl had stayed in Laura's very same rental!

Matters came to a head one weekend when Gary asked Melissa if she would like to go to meet his mother and have Sunday tea. Tea, she had found out, wasn't a cup of tea or even afternoon tea with scones and sandwiches. It was what she would have said was dinner, as it could be served from five o'clock on. There didn't seem to be a good reason why she shouldn't accept the invitation. She supposed his mother was bound to be curious about the kind of girl her son was keeping company with.

Gary had virtually moved into the property at Clovelly Park. At least he had a good jacket and a pair of his best shoes in the wardrobe, in case they went to a restaurant. His DVDs hadn't come around yet, nor a set of underwear, but Melissa surmised that it wouldn't be too long before those items resided in her home.

As their relationship had progressed, the standards that would be expected from a man whose intention was to show his girl his best side began to wane. He had started to break wind in her company, he picked his nose and ate the contents and, horror upon horror, he didn't put the toilet seat down after he had used it and failed to wash his hands!

Could she put up with such low standards, she wondered, thinking back sadly to Peter's high principles when it came to matters in the hygiene department. But there again, couldn't she train Gary to conform to her requirements? At thirty-one, time was beginning to run out for her if she wanted to begin a family. No matter who she chose to become her life partner, there would be bits of him that she would have to change.

Gary picked her up that Sunday afternoon in his Ute. Dressed smartly in a green check shirt and denims, he'd had his gingery hair trimmed at the barber and he wore a faint smelling cologne. He seemed a bit nervous as they rode together, as if he was about to visit the dentist. She found out why as soon as they drove onto the drive of what could only be described as government housing, judging by the fact that all the other small dwellings on that road were mirror images.

"Oh, is that your mother?" Melissa heard herself say inanely when she saw a short, rather plump woman with bright red hair, wearing the inevitable black leggings and baggy jumper that seemed to be the uniform of the less well off, standing in front of the entrance door.

"Hmm. Look, Melissa, don't take offence, but I haven't told her you're a doctor. I said you work in Myers on the makeup counter."

"You said what? Do I look as if I spend my days flogging cosmetics to a gullible public? I'm not even wearing makeup for heaven's sake."

"It's your day off. I couldn't tell her you were a doctor. The afternoon would be spent listening to her ailments. She's forever crook and I've told her it's because of all her weight."

There was no time for a heated debate, which Melissa would have insisted on if Gary had told her earlier. Or she would have had him stop the Ute and let her out, which was beginning to be the favoured option.

"Hi, how are ya?" Edie, Gary's mother, asked, putting her hand out to shake Melissa's in a friendly fashion. She hadn't lost her Irish accent. "Pleased to meet cha. Kettle's on, so it is. Gary can make us a coffee."

She wandered off down a small hallway, which, upon following, Melissa found led to an open plan lounge room and kitchen. It was full of clutter, with ornaments, pots and magazines on every available ledge. Patio doors looked out upon a paved area, where a tabby cat was curled up in a corner, taking advantage of a pool of warming sun.

"Have a seat," she said, moving a pile of magazines from the small two seater sofa onto a nearby coffee table.

"Gary, I've set a tray with our cups on. Melissa's is the red one with Nescafé written on it. So, Gary was saying you work at Myers. Is it in the city, Marion Centre or round here?"

Melissa went red, more through annoyance than embarrassment. Now was her chance to put Gary in his place. She wasn't that fond of him that she'd make a liar of herself.

"I actually work in Morphett Vale" she said, looking in amusement at the horror on Gary's face, as he stood stirring the coffee.

"Ah, I must have got my wires crossed then, I was sure he said you worked on a makeup counter. So, are you working at Cheap as Chips?"

Did she look as if she worked at Cheap as Chips? Melissa thought, seeing as she was wearing a rather expensive dress purchased in Rundle Mall at no small cost, and a pair of Jimmy Choo shoes she had brought with her from England. Perhaps she did. Perhaps shop assistants at Cheap as Chips could afford expensive clothes and accessories.

"Coffee, Mum." Gary almost fell over one of Edie's furry rugs in an effort to distract her.

"I said that your girlfriend was to have the Nescafé mug, Gary," Edie said, sipping on the coffee before she suddenly remembered. "Here, I haven't got a cold or anything."

She passed the red mug to Melissa, who grimaced in distaste.

"I hope you like rabbit. I've done a nice casserole with mushies and onions and sweet potatoes as a side. They're supposed to be good for your blood."

Melissa mentally agreed with the woman, sweet potatoes were better for the blood sugar, as they didn't raise it as high as white potatoes did, but rabbit, how was she going to get out of eating rabbit? She'd never eaten rabbit in her life and was not about to do so.

"Do you know, I'm terribly sorry, but Gary said we were coming here for tea." Gosh, her brain was nimble! "In England, where I hail from, tea is served at four o'clock and usually consists of cucumber sandwiches, scones with jam and cream, or a plate of fancy cakes. As I am following the USDA Food Guide pyramid, unfortunately I'm not able to eat the kind of food you're offering."

"Gary! You never said your girlfriend was suffering from a rare condition, poor thing. Is it like diabetes? Sometimes I think I'm suffering from diabetes. I go all light headed and I have to eat a couple of chocolate biscuits. Next time I go to the docs, I'm going to mention it. Look, I'm going for a smoko and when I get back I'll take a peek in the cupboard and see if I've got a tin of fruit or something. Perhaps you could eat a bowl of peaches and a drop of Carnation."

Once she had seen Edie light up a cigarette on the patio Melissa turned to Gary.

"Time to go! Use any excuse you like." She stood up and gathered together the matching beige handbag that went with her shoes and her bolero. "And if she turns out to be one of *my* patients, your head will be on the block!"

CHAPTER TWENTY

The telephone rang just as Brenda and Barry had walked in from their shopping trip to Foodland. Laden with their green bags, as there had been plenty on special offer at the supermarket that day, so they'd topped up, Barry made a dash for the phone on its last ring before the answer phone kicked in.

"Sorry to bother you," the voice said. "Am I speaking to Barry Webster?"

"Who wants to know?"

They were always getting calls from salesmen, who asked could they speak to a certain person and then when you gave *your* name they passed it on to a colleague.

"Oh, my wife and I are staying in one of your daughter's rental houses, until the house we have made an offer on is ours. She said that we should make contact with you, seeing as we are in similar circumstances. Migrated here to be with our loved ones, I mean."

"Oh, you must be Harry, of Mary and Harry. Laura did mention you might give us a call."

"Well, I thought perhaps we could get together while we're waiting for our house to go through. I believe it takes around four weeks and our furniture is due on Adelaide docks in a couple of weeks. Laura said you live in Seacliff, which we know quite well as we've often walked from there to Brighton and back. What say we meet next Wednesday, if you're free? We could do the same as we normally do. Have a walk, have a drink at one of the pavement cafés in Brighton and finish off with a light lunch at the Seacliff Hotel?"

"Why yes, I think we could manage that. Let me check with my social secretary, in case we have another engagement. Wednesday the 12th, Brenda. Are we free?"

"We're free!", Brenda said, in a high pitched jokey voice.

"Then we'll see you around half eleven opposite the hotel. Look forward to it." Harry rang off, leaving Brenda and Barry to unload their groceries.

"Harry and Barry," Brenda said. "You'll sound like a double act!"

Laura was pleased that, at last, her parents might make friends with another couple, who perhaps shared the same interests. At least it was a start that they had grandchildren they could talk about.

"Perhaps they like going to the theatre," she said after calling in to pick Toby up, as she had been cleaning one of the rental houses and her parents had brought him back from kindy.

"They often do shows at Her Majesty's Theatre on Gouger Street. You know, near where we went that time for lunch? And there's the Festival Theatre, where they do more highbrow stuff. Or maybe you could join a bowls club together. There are lots of bowls clubs all over the place. Thanks for picking Toby up. I'm so tired today, Mum, I'll be glad when you get your permanent visa and can come and help me. I usually spend about three to four hours turning around one of my rentals, but these people who have just left mustn't have done a thing while they were there. The kids had left finger marks all over the walls and paintwork, she'd not cleaned the oven or washed the casserole dishes properly, the microwave was filthy and the saucepans, well, I had to throw one of them away. The only thing she had bothered to do was wash some of the bedding, but she hadn't even ironed it, just left it in a heap!"

"Well, if I were you I'd make them pay a cleaning charge, take it out of their bond or something."

"I don't charge a bond, but I think I'm going to have to. I had to replace a whole set of Teflon pans once because they'd used a Brillo pad!"

"Come on, Toby. Take Mummy home and get her to put her feet up. And as soon as we get our visas, I'll help you all I can."

As she watched Laura and Toby drive off down the road Brenda said, "She's doing too much."

"She shouldn't be dashing about at this stage in her pregnancy, she should be getting her feet up. I think I'll offer to help her clean her own house once a week. The government couldn't say I was working then, could they?"

"Probably not," said Barry. "But time's ticking on, Brenda. I think I'll get an email off to see how far we've got up the list."

Harry and Mary's daughter, April, was still having problems finding a house for sale that they all agreed upon. Her husband, Steve, said he wanted a shed, or at least enough land at the side or back of the house that he could put one on. It had to be a two storey house if possible, because that was what they had been used to in England, and as Harry had promised a substantial amount to help pay off their mortgage, as his daughter may as well have some money now, instead of when he and Mary had passed on, they would be able to afford it.

They had all agreed that Woodcroft would be the area of choice, as that was where the children attended school. Harry and Mary had chosen a three bedroom house on a quiet estate called "Hillview", thus named because most of the houses had views towards the Onkaparinga Hills. Although they were waiting for all the legalities to be finalised, the person who was selling the house to them was quite happy for the couple to call to do some measuring, or to see if their three piece suite that was coming over in the Pickford's container would fit in the lounge room, or if the separate dining room would take their large oak table and six ladder back chairs. She was going "interstate" to live with her daughter, as it was warmer on the Gold Coast and definitely more conducive to her arthritic pain.

Steve, their son-in-law, was a cheerful chap who worked on breakdown recovery for the RAA, preferring to work on a night shift so that he could pick the children up from school. His passion was doing up old cars and selling them on for a profit. April was a district nurse, working part time so that she could see the children off to school before checking up on a list of recovering hospital patients, mostly the elderly, who were well enough to be sent home.

There was an Open House that Saturday afternoon and, from the realtor's description in the property section of the *Messenger* everyone decided that this house might be the one. It was on a good block of land; had views across to the ocean; it was at the head of a small cul-de-sac; was near to a golf course and there was enough room at the side and the back of the house for a shed and a swimming pool! It was a little bit more than they wanted to pay, but Norman, the man who Steve had spoken to on the telephone, gave him the impression that he could put in an offer.

It was a little chilly as they entered the rather large hallway, which had real wooden floors that were dull through lack of a good polishing. The house smelt a bit musty and after Harry had remarked on this they were told that the owner had died and there had been some controversy amongst the family left behind. Lawyers had been involved and the house had only been recently put up for sale. The agent left them to wander, so the children ran off to explore each room, Steve went out to look at the garden, which was awash with colourful flowers and April, Mary and Harry were left behind to inspect the separate kitchen, downstairs toilet and laundry room.

"There's plenty of space for everyone," Harry observed, "although I think you'd have to spend a bit on decoration."

"It's all a bit dated," said Mary.

"I think it will need a lot of work doing on it," said April. " A new kitchen, for a start, and did you see the cracked tiles in both the toilet and the laundry room? Anyway, let's go and look at the bedrooms upstairs and see what needs doing up there."

"You have a shower in your room, Mum, but there's only one bathroom," Talia said, as she passed the adults on the wide mahogany lintel staircase. "And if we come to live here, I'm having the front bedroom, 'cos the view to the sea is awesome."

"I can get a huge shed at the back of the house," Steve cried, looking animated as he strode briskly through the door. "There's even enough room to have a separate driveway to it, so I can drive the cars straight in."

He followed the others upstairs, where the boys were quite excited about a large room that wasn't suitable for a bedroom as it didn't have built in wardrobes and in their opinion it would be brill as their games room.

"But what if Grandma and Granddad want to come to stay?" asked Steve. "We wouldn't have anywhere to put them. Anyway, I might want the room as a study, or parent retreat as the Aussies would call it."

Ben was scornful. "Why would Grandma and Granddad come to stay when they'll only be a five minute car ride away?"

"I might have a little too much whisky one night," Harry joked, "and have to totter down the hill."

He was met with an unbelieving stare. Grown-ups said such silly things to a boy who was only eight!

"So, four bedrooms, one en-suite, a family bathroom and a parent retreat," said Norman, who had followed them to where they all stood on the upstairs landing. "And look at that view."

The family stood transfixed at the panoramic view down to the Gulf of St. Vincent. Okay, they had to look beyond the urban sprawl and electricity pylons and stand a little on tiptoe to see over the huge eucalyptus trees that surrounded the property, but it was an awe inspiring view. One that would lighten your spirits if you had got out of the wrong side of bed.

"You should see the orchard," said Steve enthusiastically. "I counted five lemon trees, two orange and three I couldn't put a name to. Then there're all sorts of shrubs and bushes and lots of flowers."

"They were olive trees, the one's you couldn't put a name to," said Norman, who was a keen gardener. "And there are two almond trees over by the neighbour's fence. Have you ever seen almond blossom in July?" The family admitted they hadn't, but said they'd look forward to it. "Any thoughts?" he asked, hoping that they would say that they were interested, because he was having difficulty meeting the target his boss had set him that month.

"Well, from my point of view, I can see me having a great time if I put a shed on that land," said Steve. "I do up old cars for a hobby."

"Oh," said Norman. "Do you sell them on?"

"I think the house needs a lot of work doing on it," April broke in, because if she didn't, Steve would be bending the ear of the poor soul for ages.

"What are the neighbours like?" asked Mary, who had already met one of her new neighbours at Hillview and she had seemed very friendly.

"That I can't say," said Norman. "I don't usually have information like that from the vendors."

"You could always come back and knock on one or two doors and introduce yourself, April," said Harry. "Then if you don't like the look of them, that'll make up your mind."

"Oh, don't say that, Granddad," said Ben. "I like it here and my bedroom would look over the grass at the back, where I could have my goal posts."

"And I could ride my bike up and down the hill," said six year old Jack, not to be outdone.

"We'll think about it," said April, who was the one with her feet on the ground in her and Steve's marriage. Steve could only see what was at the end of his nose and didn't think about consequences.

"Well, here's my card. Give me a ring if you think the house may be suitable. And if you want a second look, you only have to say the word."

"Mum, Dad, there's room for a pool and, do you know, I've just seen a koala bear up a tree!" Talia came rushing up the stairs, her face bright with excitement. "It was awesome!"

Barry came off the computer looking flushed with anticipation.

"According to the person who replied to my email, we've every chance of being included in this year's quota, Brenda. He said not to get our hopes up too much, but a lot of people on the list are dropping out, because of the economic climate. Some are having trouble selling their houses, which they're relying on to pay their contribution payment. Of course, on top of that is the fourteen thousand dollar Centre Link lodgement, though you do get it back in ten years' time."

"That's if we're still here," Brenda couldn't help but say. "All this fiddle faddling is putting up my stress level. They'll put me on blood pressure tablets when we eventually get our medical."

"Well, I vote we should treat ourselves to a nice meal at that place in Old Noarlunga that we've always said we'd visit. We could take a walk along the Onkaparinga River, that should help us unwind."

"You've forgotten we promised to meet Harry and Brenda outside the Seacliff this Wednesday. Don't forget we're pensioners now and can't afford to go chucking our money away on meals out. Anyway, we'll pick their brains. Find out how come they got their visas so quickly."

Considering it was well into autumn, the day was quite warm as the two women stripped down to sleeveless T-shirts and pedal pushers and, with their cardigans tied around their waists, walked along the esplanade towards Brighton. Brenda and Mary had hit it off straight away, both liking the other's honest gaze, the fact they had identical taste in clothing and that they were a similar age. Their two men were chatting together behind them as they strolled, discussing a subject that was close to Barry's heart. How had Harry managed to get his visa so easily?

"Well, to be honest, Barry, I don't think we did get our visas so easily. Perhaps compared to you, because you filled in all the necessary paperwork yourself that you'd downloaded off the Internet. But we employed the services of a migrant consultant, who helped us through the process, advising us which visa to apply for. You know, which one was the best for us? It was an anxious time, waiting to hear back from them, but the feeling of coming through Customs at Adelaide airport, with a permanent visa inside our passports, was the best feeling on earth."

"All right for some," said Barry, though in a light hearted way. "Where we went wrong, according to someone I spoke to, was I thought I could get our visa application changed from offshore to onshore once we'd come to Australia, but it doesn't work like that. We should have got a three month tourist visa, then applied for a bridging one. Now, according to the department at Currie Street, we have to go home once our tourist visa expires."

"What a waste of money. You said you'd bought a house around here as well."

"Well, it's in our daughter's name. We weren't allowed to buy a second hand property and we were worried about going through the F.I.R.B to buy a new one, in case of complications. Anyway, I was talking to a chap by email the other day and he reckons because of the economic climate people are coming off the waiting list. It might be a bit premature, but we could be looking for a flight out soon, so we can validate our permanent visas!"

A similar conversation was being carried out between Brenda and Mary, though it was more along the lines of how devastated the pair would be if they had to leave Laura when she was about to give birth.

"I know I wasn't around for Toby's birth, but I wanted to do the grandma thing properly this time. You know, turn up with a bunch of flowers and a couple of little outfits, hold his or her hand and tell it I'm its grandma."

Mary nodded. She'd been waiting outside the birthing room for each one of her grandchildren's appearances.

"Well, let's hope you shoot up the list and you're making plans to fly off to your offshore processing centre. It would be a shame to have to say goodbye, when we've only just met."

Brenda agreed and said they'd just have to stay positive.

"We can't make up our minds whether to go to a consulate in New Zealand or in Singapore, if we do have to go out to validate our visas. We liked Singapore when we passed through the airport. The place looks clean and we didn't feel intimidated in any way. Besides, the weather appears to be the same all the year, hot and humid with lots of rain, whereas New Zealand will be cold at this time. I don't want to even think about having to go back to England. I mean, where would we stay for a start?"

"Have you no relatives?"

"Not close ones. I suppose we could stay at one of our friends' houses, but I'm sure after a while they'd be sick of us. And who knows how long we'd be waiting for the call?"

"Ah well, we've all got crosses to bear, let's forget our problems and concentrate on a pleasant day out. Shall we go across to the Esplanade Hotel and spend some time on the pokies?"

It wasn't a subject that Brenda and Barry could forget so easily: they would wake up with it on their minds most mornings. Obviously any decision that was made in the next few weeks about their future was of the utmost importance to them and there were still police checks and medicals, once they had been allocated a case officer.

Barry had a moan when Laura came around to drop Toby off for a stopover, as she was going to a get together in a local hotel with some friends she had made through the fitness centre.

"I mean, don't get me wrong, they're a nice couple and your mother and I have said we'll keep in touch as Harry is thinking of taking up golf, since there's a golf club near to his place in Woodcroft, and I keep meaning to join a golf club myself. But I suppose having to listen to someone who has already got their permanent visas and to be honest, is a big smug about it, makes me feel rather annoyed. I mean, what got me, was the way he was going on about having the possibility of "double jeopardy" on his taxes, as he has a works pension in England. I should be so lucky!"

"Well, maybe he will have to pay tax on his pension in England and in Australia as well," said Laura seriously. "I know Graham had a lot of problems when he first came here, with having had investments over there. Anyway, how did your day go? Putting aside your frustrations."

"For the first time in my life I went on a slot machine in that hotel on the Jetty Road corner," said Brenda. "Mary loves to go on them, although she only puts a few dollars in."

"Harry put in more than a few dollars," said Barry. "But it was an experience. We both limited ourselves to a dollar each and of course, the machines won in the end."

"Then after having coffee there, 'cos it's free if you're playing the slot machines, we went to that café that we call Marilyn's and had chicken schnitzel and a salad. And your Dad had pancakes and ice cream. We decided we didn't want a sit down lunch at the Seacliff, with it being so hot today."

"I know the feeling," Laura said. "I'm hoping to just get a plate from the salad bar, rather than having a heavy meal. I thought it got cooler in March, but obviously not this year."

"Grandma. I'd love to have pancakes and ice cream for my supper," said Toby, who had very good manners and hadn't interrupted the grown-ups while they were talking. "Do you think I could ride my scooter along to Brighton and have the same as Granddad did?"

CHAPTER TWENTY ONE

At last! At last Abbie's garage sale was open for business. She had put an advert in the *Messenger*, got Jodie to write "Garage Sale" in large letters on the side of two big shoe boxes, and with arrows pointing in the direction of their house, weighed down by house bricks, as it was a little windy that day, and everything was set out and ready for inspection. Of course, Jason and Molly, who would be possible recipients of any of the cash made that day, had pressing engagements, and Wayne had remembered he had promised the site foreman he'd put in a couple of extra hours, which left Jodie and Kyle, who had been promised a couple of dollars, helping to man the fort.

Their first customer, a man in his late twenties who was very interested in Jenny's old radiogram, wanted to know if it could be delivered, as he didn't want to scratch the upholstery in his brand new car. His address was in Aberfoyle Park, so Abbie agreed to deliver it that evening. Providing he paid upfront, of course. A couple, who rifled through all the LPs that Abbie had put in a box with all the old vinyls she was hoping to get rid of, said she should take them to a Collectors fair, or better still, flog them on eBay, as she'd get a better price. Knowing that she'd never get around to either and the box would still be in her garage a year or so from now, she sold them the lot for peanuts and hoped that Wayne would never find out!

A hour later, after selling most of her old chipped plates, cups and souvenirs from different parts of Britain that members of her extended family had brought back with them and books belonging to the kids that they never read anymore, Abbie heard a young woman talking to Jodie.

"If yer could 'old on ter them, me 'usband could come and pick 'em up tonight."

Was that a Merseyside accent she just heard? She looked up from where she was tidying a box of things that somebody had rifled through and had a moment of deja vu. Surely it couldn't be Jenny. Jenny was back in Liverpool, as far as she knew.

"Can I 'elp yer?" she said, bustling over. It wasn't Jenny, she realised, a little older, but she was a good likeness, especially as she was wearing spectacles.

"I was just sayin' ter the little girl, could yer 'old onto any of the stuff? Me 'usband could come over later and 'elp me ter load it onto the Ute."

"Well, I could 'elp yer," said Abbie, looking over to the beat up old vehicle that was parked at the top of their driveway. "What were you thinkin' of gettin'?"

"The two single beds. I got four mattresses at a sale last week and the kids 'ave bin lyin' on 'em and I notice yer've got some beddin'. That ud come in 'andy."

"Sounds as if yer container 'asn't arrived. Are yer from Liverpool or nearby?"

"Yeah, yer right. We're from Toxteth. And where were you from?"

"On the Wirral. Oh, not from one of the posh areas, before yer say it." That was because if you said the Wirral, everyone assumed you were posh. "No, we were from Birkenhead, near enough ter Bidston." Abbie could feel her Scouser accent kicking in, when she had started picking up an Aussie inflection recently. "Tell yer what, I was just about ter make a brew. Jodie'll keep an eye if yer fancy a cuppa."

"Don't mind if I do. Terry's lookin' after the kids, but he won't notice how long I'm away, 'cos they'll be watchin' telly. We managed ter get a telly from Radio Rentals. That was the first thing we ticked off the list."

She followed Abbie into the house and sat on one of the stools at what Abbie now called her "breakfast bar".

"Tea or coffee? Sorry, I didn't ask yer name."

"Sally Palmer. Most people call me Sal. I'll 'ave a coffee, one sugar please."

"I'm Abbie. Abbie Foley. So 'ow long 'ave yer been over?"

"This is our sixth week. We spent two weeks at Christies Beach Caravan Park and then we found a rental at Christie Downs. It's not much of a place, but the rent's cheap. We're only payin' two hundred dollars a week. Other places we looked at were much more expensive."

"Tell me about it, that's why we bought a house virtually straight away."

"Oh, we can't afford a house. We've always rented. We had to sell off our furniture back in Liverpool, so we could 'ave some money behind us. I'm just 'oping that Terry isn't picky about the job 'e gets."

"So, what does 'e do? Where my 'usband works is takin' on labourers, or I could give yer the number of my ex landlady, 'er fella's always lookin' fer workers."

"'E was a docker. Then 'e went on the dole. Then they sent 'im for retrainin' and 'e got a job as a welder. Then suddenly 'e said, 'Let's take the kids and go ter Australia,' just like that. Next minute he says he's goin' ter one of these 'Australia on Display' recruitment drives at the Atlantic Hotel and 'ere we are. Seems South Australia was lookin' fer skilled workers and 'e jumped at the chance."

"And 'ow many kids 'ave yer got?"

"Well, I've seven, but two stayed behind with their Nana, 'cos they're workin', and one's married, so we brought four across and I've 'ad to tell *them* that we're only here on a year's 'oliday. He just managed ter get in with this age thingy. He was forty five last week."

Looking closely at Sally, Abbie could see the fine lines and crow's feet, though like her, she must have started early with her child births.

"So what are yer goin' ter do fer the rest of yer furniture?"

asked Abbie, handing her guest a mug of coffee then sipping on one herself.

"Well, I've got a double on order from a shop I passed at Junk Food corner – we're just lying on a couple of blow up beds at the moment – and I'll keep lookin' around fer another two singles. Yours are fer the two eldest. Craig's fourteen and Sarah's twelve. I've got them in a high school near to us and the other two, our Ash and Tayla, start at the primary on Monday."

"Well, it looks as if yer gettin' sorted, Sal. It teks a while. We've bin 'ere since last September and I still find meself comparin' things with 'ome."

"Yeah, that's just it. They drive on the same side as us and speak the same language, but somehow yer 'ave ter pinch yerself and remember yer foreigners in someone else's land. I don't know 'ow long we'll stick it 'ere. I miss me other kids and our Julie's goin' ter 'ave a baby at the end of the year. She didn't tell us until we got 'ere, 'cos she knew I'd never get on the plane."

"Oh, I'm sure things will settle down and, who knows, if yer 'usband gets a good job, you could send 'er airfare over."

"Like I said before, I 'ope our Terry isn't picky over a job."

Poor love, thought Abbie as she waved Sally off, having recruited Raelene's husband from up the road to put the single beds, which were made of metal, onto the back of the Ute, along with all sorts of things that Abbie thought might come in handy for the impoverished Palmers, including her phone number. A "pushover for a hard luck story", Wayne would call her when he got in later, but Abbie felt good that she had helped another Pom out.

Gary was beginning to get on her nerves. Not beginning, had been for a while, thought Melissa as she said goodbye to her last patient of the day and wondered what she should cook for dinner that night. He had virtually moved in now, meaning that there were more clothes in the guest room wardrobe than he had at his mother's house and she was finding a lot of his underwear mixed with hers in the washing basket.

How had that happened? She supposed she'd felt sorry for him after he'd had a terrible row with his mother on her behalf, when his mother had called Melissa "Miss Fancy Knickers" and asked who did she think she was, abusing her hand of friendship? Of course, Gary had taken Melissa's side, seeing as he was still in the throes of lust for her and sensed his freedom of nightly leg overs would go down the drain if he took his mother's side.

But how to tell him that she no longer required his presence in her household and her bed? Would the "it's not you, it's me" excuse work on a man who wasn't tuned into the niceties of being given the flick by a well bred young lady? She'd have to give it some serious thought as the smell of his breath, since he was beginning to smoke again, was started to make her heave.

Matters came to a head that evening, although it had to be said, Melissa engineered it.

After feeding him with steak and chips and listening to how he'd been up to his neck in sewage after a toilet pipe had cracked at one of Graham's properties, whilst he and Melissa were eating at the table, she suddenly decided that "good breeding will out" and that that kind of subject should be limited to when they were drinking their after dinner glass of wine at least. He got up to go out onto the patio as soon as he put his knife and fork down, feeling in his checked shirt pocket for his pack of cigarettes.

"Do you have to go and have a cigarette just as soon as you've finished at the table?" she asked in her stern doctor voice. "It would be nice if you could at least move your plate and cutlery into the kitchen."

There, she had said it. How did he react to criticism?

He did as he was asked, though nearly causing a breakage to the plate, which was part of quite an expensive set she had bought from Myers, when he almost threw it into the washing up bowl.

"Can I go and have a smoke now?"

"No, you may not, Gary. When I first met you, you were not a smoker and I don't really know why you've started smoking now. I can give you leaflets on how to stop smoking and I can even give you the telephone number of the Quitline, but I am not happy having a boyfriend who smokes."

"Well, there's nothing more to be said then, I'll be off." And off a huffy Gary went, lighting his cigarette up as he went.

Melissa was left to wonder if Gary had always been a smoker and, as she was a doctor, hadn't dared to light one up in front of her.

Monday morning and Barry and Brenda were off on a jaunt with the walking group.

It was rather cool that morning so both had on a woolly sweater each, fleece body-warmers, jog pants and walking boots. If they were going to do it properly, they may as well be dressed for it. Barry had even found a long wooden stick belonging to the last owner in the garage, which he took along with him.

There were only nine people in the group that week, and once again Fred and Ginger had gone off on assignment, this time to Hong Kong. Malcolm stood in the car park just off the Port Noarlunga esplanade, counting heads as they parked their cars then walked to him. Sandy was there, as per usual. She attached herself to Brenda at each meeting now, regaling her with her imagined hurts and disappointments that had occurred during the week. Barry joked that Sandy had her own shrink in Brenda and it didn't cost her anything, except for the petrol she used in getting to each meeting.

The plan that day was to walk up to the main road roundaboat, along the banks of the Onkaparinga River and across the Noarlunga Downs, with lunch in the small township of Old Noarlunga. The sky looked dark, as they set off on their ramble with great gusto, but Malcolm assured them it was just the clouds blown in from the nearby ocean and the sky would soon be blue again. It didn't usually rain in March and if it did, it would only be a shower. It was all right for him, grumbled Sandy, he would probably have a waterproof in his haversack and she'd forgotten to put one in.

It was pleasant walking along the usually marshy banks of the river, which were now dry as dust with all the recent warm weather.

Black and white pelicans bobbed on the incoming tide of the river, now and again plunging their heads under water if they saw something tasty and interesting. Sandy kept up her usual monologue, this time against a certain supermarket, which would only give discount to Australian pensioners and not to those who only held senior cards.

"I mean, if it wasn't for us pensioners using the place on a Wednesday, they wouldn't have any customers until the weekend," she moaned. Brenda nodded, only half listening as she was sure she had seen something hopping about in the bushes a little way beyond. It seemed that Malcolm had as well.

"Quiet people," he boomed, almost certainly alerting the animal or animals to their presence. The group stopped en-masse, except for Sandy, who was deep in her own speculations.

"Marsupials, Sandra. Nine o'clock!"

Unfortunately she didn't hear him and was amazed when a group of kangaroos came out of the bushes and began to hop off. It took her breath away, quite literally and she had to sit down on a grassy hummock with her head between her legs! It was hard not to laugh, some people had to look away and guffaw into their hankies!

At last they spied the sandstone cliffs across the river, which were home to a multitudes of Corellas, a small white cockatoo that had taken a liking to the area. Quiet now, but at dusk, when they had returned from their foraging for the day they could be heard squawking and cackling and getting on the locals residents' nerves!

"We'll make our way to the hostelry," said Malcolm, after stopping for a breather whilst watching two of his group pretending they were part of the *Raiders of the Lost Ark* as they balanced on the rope walk bridge across the river.

"A bit of interesting history for you. A Cornish man built that little house over there in the late 19th century. Makes you wonder what it would have been like to be an early settler."

"Right up your street," said a woman, out of earshot, who thought that the walk was overly long that day and couldn't wait to sit and eat a good lunch.

"I bet his second name is Hannibal," said another, which was lost on those who didn't know that Hannibal crossed the Alps.

It was after two when the group set off on their return journey. A few glasses of vino had been downed and the attention span of some of them wasn't as good as before they'd been to the Old Noarlunga Hotel. Was it any wonder that one of their number, a man a little on the plump side wearing milk bottle lense glasses, lost his footing on the narrow path and plunged down the side of the riverbank? Luckily, the tide had ebbed and the river was at its lowest, and thanks to the quick reaction of Barry and another man, he was hauled back up again. Shaken, the pace of the group slowed down to match the cautious steps of the unfortunate, so it was well past five as they headed to the car park, just as the rain came down.

Laura hugged her mother tightly. Brenda had telephoned her the minute that Barry had read the email that said the couple had been allocated a case officer. She had dashed around to Seacliff there and then, though she had planned to put her feet up until it was time to collect Toby from pre-school.

"I'm stoked," she said, delighted. "Built in babysitters! What did they say? How long do you have to wait for the visa to come through?"

"Whoa!" said Barry. " Let's not count our chickens. Your Mum and I have to pass the medical first and send off to the UK for our police checks. I'm sure *I'm* all right, but I can't speak for your mother."

He ducked, as a cushion came hurtling across the room. Suddenly their world was coming right.

"We have to wait for an appointment back at Currie Street, but this time we'll be invited. It'll be quite straightforward, a few checks, blood tests and all that kind of thing. We'll have to start looking for a flight."

"You'll like Singapore. Graham and I spent a few days there. There was a lot of building going on, but Mum, they have eight Marks and Spencers. You'll be able to visit every one!"

Melissa thought he had come to plead for her to take him back when she saw Gary sitting in his Ute outside her house, as she returned from work two days later. But she couldn't see a bunch of flowers in his hand or a box of chocolates under his arm, and as he walked towards her he had a stony look on his face.

"I've come to get my things," he said, not meeting her eyes, his whole tradie dressed body stinking of cigarette smoke.

"Of course," she said brightly." I've taken the liberty of putting them all in a bin bag, knowing that you don't own a suitcase, and I've put your DVDs in a carrier bag."

She put her key in the door lock, feeling the tension between them and knowing that, because of his stubbornness, arbitration was not going to work.

CHAPTER TWENTY TWO

It was a Saturday morning and Anne-Marie, Ray and their two youngest were walking around the Willunga market looking for a few bargains. It was a lovely warm day, which was surprising for one of the last days in March, when the cooler weather of autumn could be expected. The two eldest boys were down at the beach with their boogie boards, meeting with a crowd of mates they had got to know at their new school. They had settled well into the area and could be seen hanging around the local Subway most evenings.

Emma, their ten year old daughter, hadn't settled in as well. She missed her friends from her old school and was always on the computer, as soon as the time difference made it possible, to keep in touch with her English friends via the internet. Threats of getting on the plane and going back to live with Ray's mother were mentioned daily. Liam, their youngest, didn't care where he lived, as his nature was very sunny.

Their green bags bulging with local produce, including a whole chicken that was going to be cooked and served cold with salad for their Sunday dinner, a stall caught their eye that sold homemade goods such as cakes and jams, but also a few veggies from a smallholder's garden. Emma, who had the sweet tooth of the family, was attracted by the lurid blue and purple shades of icing that adorned the cupcakes being sold.

"Can I help you?" inquired a pleasant faced young woman wearing a blue and white apron over her white T-shirt and blue denims.

"Four of those cupcakes, please," said Anne-Marie, only ordering cakes for the children, as she and Ray had to watch their figures.

"Is that a Lancashire accent I hear?" asked Ray, who was a lot more forward than his wife, who thought the accent was familiar but didn't like to say so.

"Yes, I'm from Darwen. That's a small town in the north of England."

"Know it well," said Ray, smiling broadly. "We're from Blackburn."

"Well, I never, it's small world. Whereabouts in Blackburn? Me and me husband have still got rellies over there."

"Oswaldtwistle. St.James Road."

"Nooo! Do you know Danny Cheeseborough? He's my brother-in-law."

"Used to go to school with him."

"Well, would yer credit it. Are yer on holiday or have yer settled here? We've been over eleven years. In fact, Holly, that's our daughter, was born in Adelaide. Anyway, I'll have ter keep serving. Here's our business card. Give me a ring!"

She took the proffered money from Anne-Marie, mouthing "ring me" and holding her thumb and finger up, mimicking the handset on a telephone. The family moved off, feeling pleased that they had met a person from their neck of the woods, especially Emma, when she heard that the woman who her parents might get friendly with had a daughter too.

It appeared that Karen, whom Anne-Marie telephoned the following afternoon, ran a smallholding with her husband, John, having bought the land and a shack of a house cheaply with the proceeds from the sale of their house in Darwen. They hadn't wanted to live in a soulless dwelling as they had back in England and as John had worked for Blackburn council as a parkland gardener, he had a little knowledge that he could put to good use. It had been hard work in the beginning, with Karen wondering why they had taken on such a daunting task, especially after their tiny amount of vines were hit by a powdery mildew and their fruit trees were blighted by a swarm of aphids. Luckily there was still a bit in the bank to help them survive and a kindly neighbour, who had been making a living from his produce for years, helped them with sound advice on which sprays to use.

Two children later, now attending the Willunga Primary School, they had a regular stall on the local market, which seemed to be doing quite well, though to make ends meet, Karen also made rather yummy cupcakes and John kept a few local gardens in trim.

It was just after Easter when Abbie and Wayne took possession of their Jayco Expanda caravan. Bought second hand after seeing a similar one displayed at the Caravan and Camping Exhibition at Adelaide Showground, which Abbie had insisted the family went to, it was in such good condition it could almost have been new. The previous owner had only used it to do a short sojourn up to Victoria to visit his relatives in the summer, then found that the world of caravanning wasn't for him. It was just the job for the Foley family though, as besides the double bed which could be made in the expanded part of the caravan at one end, it also had bunk beds. A toilet, vanity unit and shower completed the facilities, along with a built in cooker and space for a microwave.

Of course Wayne had to be persuaded. He couldn't see why they couldn't all bunk up together at their house when Greg and his family came to visit in May. They were only there for a couple of weeks and the purchase of the caravan would be putting more strain on his ever elasticated wages. Abbie stood firm however. There was enough money in the bank to put down a substantial deposit and the salesman at the caravan company had offered interest free terms. It was touch and go whether the Subaru would be able to pull the weight behind it, but for the moment it didn't matter, as the caravan was delivered on a truck and sat in all its splendour on their drive.

Abbie was beginning to feel a bit more positive as Greg's visit neared. He had always been her favourite brother and the thought that he and his family might come out and live nearby spurred her into energetic plans. She planted polyanthus, pansies and violas in the large blue painted pots that she had purchased from Stan's warehouse one Saturday, pruned back the geraniums and lavender bushes that lined her neighbour's fence and planted pea and bean seedlings, rigging up two wooden wigwams in her veggie patch. That was along with the capsicums, which were the only veggies she had managed to grow successfully up to then. All the rooms in the house were cleaned from top to bottom, along with the windows, though everyone said it was a waste of time as they would all need to be done again. They weren't arriving until the end of May and they'd be living in the caravan! Scorn was poured on her plans of trips to Rapid Bay, Goolwa and Victor Harbor when they came, by Raelene. Didn't she know that May was nearly winter and no one ventured to the seaside then? It would have to be city trips and shopping malls to keep her visitors entertained. So Abbie wrote an extensive itinerary, with visits to the cinema, ice rink, bowling alley and the Beach House at Glenelg.

Melissa had coined a new name for the man who, if she had a chance, could be her next boyfriend: "Stud Muffin". He was the locum who was standing in for Dr Beaumont, who had gone on a cruise to Ho Chi Min city for twenty-one days with his wife. A "stud" in Melissa's eyes, was just the type of man Trent Robinson was: tall, dark and handsome, with muscles rippling under the very smart pink Ben Sherman shirt he wore. "Muffin", because he had a dusky suntan the colour of a chocolate cake and she'd love to eat him. She had three weeks in which to attract him into her bed and that night, as she made herself a dish of homemade macaroni cheese with a side plate of sour dough bread and Nuttelex spread, she turned it over in her mind, how she could get him into her web.

It appeared that Dr Trent liked to locum all over the place. At twenty-nine, he preferred to travel the country, rather than tie himself down to a medical practice. Melissa wasn't really looking for a long term relationship, just an uncomplicated quickie now and again.

Of course, one couldn't go up to a person and tell him that, she had to be more subtle. A friendly invitation to dinner from a colleague might go down well. So the following day, before the queue began for the walking wounded, Melissa presented herself in Dr Beaumont's office on the pretext of asking the locum how he was settling in.

"It must be hard," she said, " having to fit in with the day to day running of different practices. But I suppose the treatment will be the same. Have you settled into your accommodation too?"

"No worries," said Trent, smiling engagingly. "I used to live in Adelaide so I know it well, and there's not a lot of difference in the way each place is run. I suppose that's if we're not including Medibank."

"I was wondering, would you like to come to my place for a meal at some point? Perhaps one weekend? This Friday or Saturday, if you're free?"

"Friday would be great. I'm meeting some old uni' friends in the city on Saturday night, so Friday would be fantastic. I like your perfume by the way."

"Oh, thank you. It's *Beautiful* by Estee Lauder. It's my favourite."

After much persuasion from Graham, Eddie and her parents, Laura gave in and got a bank loan for one of the new apartments. One street back from the esplanade between Brighton and Glenelg and the city easily reached by train or tram. She looked forward to a steady flow of occupants from the UK.

Her pregnancy was progressing well, though her doctor had told her to take it easy as there was a five year gap since her last one. Though with still four months to go and feeling extremely well in the circumstances, she couldn't see what the fuss was about and carried on with her daily life as normal.

Brenda, on the other hand, worried herself silly that her daughter was doing far too much for a woman in her condition. On the rare occasion that she was in Graham's company, when he had popped back home for something while Brenda had been helping Laura by vacuuming, she mentioned tentatively that she thought Laura shouldn't be doing as much as she did. He had shrugged and said it was up to Laura and he certainly couldn't dictate to his wife what she should or shouldn't do. He hadn't changed, she thought, when he went on his way without even acknowledging her presence when she had said goodbye. He was totally indifferent to her being there.

But putting aside her son-in-law's sulks, there was the pleasure of helping Laura to choose the furniture that she needed for her new rental. A list had been made between them, but as Laura had to wait for the all clear from Graham, as this was business and things still had to be put on a proper footing, it was agreed that they would look around first before putting in an order at a furniture outlet. Moderation and functionality were the key words in Laura's business plan this time. When furnishing her houses in the past she had bought package deals and in some cases was still paying for them. Meanwhile careless tenants and their children had caused wear and tear damage not significant enough to write the item off but sufficient to make her reassess her game plan.

There were many people, according to the posts on "Poms in Adelaide", that couldn't hack the life down under and were returning to the life that they knew best. In fact, Laura, who sometimes gave her overspill guests to another person who ran a similar business, had heard of one case that made her eyebrows lift in amazement. It seemed that the couple and their children had only been in the rental for as little as forty-eight hours before returning to the airport to get a flight back!

The website was full of people selling furniture, especially if a container had arrived from the UK and they hadn't enough money to ship it all back again. One of her rentals had a large shed in the garden, so her Ping Pong Poms' furniture could be stored in there.

Melissa gave the tikka masala sauce another stir and checked that the pilau rice wasn't drying out. She gave her dining room table a quick once over. Sparkly wine glasses, large and small, shiny cutlery, her white gold rimmed plates, snowy napkins and a condiment set all laid out on a pristine white tablecloth. A bowl of violets, picked from the flower beds that were kept in order by a monthly visiting gardener, gave a dash of colour to her otherwise chaste table and purple lavender scented candles were ready to be lit when her guest arrived.

Her evening of keen eyed preparation had been for the planned seduction of Dr Trent. Dressed in a brown, low cut animal print maxi length gown, with her fair hair hanging loosely courtesy of her hair straighteners, her makeup more full on than during her working hours and wearing sparkly sandals, she was more than a little annoyed that his parting words of, "See you at eight" hadn't been kept to. She took a glance through the master bedroom window, after checking that her blue satin nightdress looked attractively draped over her wicker rocking chair and doing a little tweaking of her pillow shams, to see if headlights could be seen shining up the cul-de-sac. There was nothing to be seen, except for a neighbour's tawny tom cat setting off for a night on the tiles and a teenage boy riding up and down his well lit drive on a large skateboard.

She dropped the net curtain she had lifted hastily, not wanting to be seen as a snoop by the woman who lived across the road. Not that she cared too much about whatever her neighbours thought of the woman who occasionally greeted them if she was in a sociable mood, but more often than not, didn't. Time for that when she'd bought her own place.

Ding dong went the doorbell, just as Melissa was about to take the bottle of red out of the fridge and pour herself a glass. She took her time walking to the door, as he was already fifteen minutes late. Let *him* see what it was like, she thought, but seeing his shadow against the front door glass made her quicken her pace.

"Apologies," her very own stud muffin said as he stood on the doorstep carrying a bottle of white wine and a small box of Cadbury's Roses. "My contribution and sorry I'm late, but my GPS sent me all over the place."

She could forgive him anything were her thoughts, as she ran her eyes over the well built body that wore a tan polo shirt and a pair of beige jeans, no doubt chosen to enhance his swarthy complexion. But it wouldn't do to show her feelings. Time enough for that when they'd had a drink or two.

"That's why I haven't got one," she laughed, forgiving him immediately and looking over his shoulder at the silver BMW 3 Series parked on her drive. "I've heard so many horror stories. Anyway, don't stand on ceremony, do come in."

He followed Melissa down the hall and whistled in surprise when he saw the well presented dinner table that looked as if someone had come over to do a piece for *Better Homes & Gardens* magazine.

"Jeez, Melissa, I didn't know you were having a dinner party. I wondered, when you opened the door and you were all dressed up."

"Sometimes it's nice to make an effort and make an occasion of things," Melissa said, feeling slightly irritated and hoping that Trent wasn't going to be a clone of Gary. "I don't usually go to so much trouble, but it's nice to do it for a colleague and hopefully a friend."

"Well, I'm flattered," Trent said, laying the bottle of wine and the chocolates on the kitchen work surface. "And whatever you have prepared for our tea smells delicious."

"Tea." Melissa felt even more irritated. Gary used to say that and hadn't she got the wrong end of the stick when she was invited for a meal at Gary's mother's.

"I hope you enjoy it," she said. "Courtesy of the cooking classes that were on the curriculum at my old school. Would you like to eat now or would you like me to get you a glass of wine? I have a red I've just opened or we could open the Chardonnay that you've kindly brought."

"I'll have a glass of red, but let's drink it while we're eating. I much prefer to eat sooner than later."

The evening flew by and was an enjoyable one. Both spoke about the universities they attended, Melissa's back in England and Trent, the University of Adelaide, then Flinders. He told of his fascinating work during his two years as a locum around the different states in Australia, filling in for an exhausted medical man in the outback, or for a doctor who needed a well earned break in a country town. Compared to Melissa's selfish flight from her homeland to a cosy medical practice, his story was one of excitement and not a little horror, and at twenty-nine he had witnessed gruesome death from nature's cruellest elements. It took away all Melissa's desires and sexual aspirations, to be replaced with a healthy admiration for this clever, caring man.

"So, here I am, my adventures at an end, and I'm ready to don the robe of respectable general medicine in the not too distant future," he said, suddenly standing up from the sofa, where they had been sitting quite closely, and placing his empty glass on a nearby coffee table.

"Look, thank you so much for a pleasant evening and a beautifully cooked tea. Perhaps we'll keep in touch once I move on to my next place? See you on Monday."

With that, her stud muffin was gone, leaving Melissa with the distinct impression, though he showed no sign of it, that Dr Trent must be gay.

CHAPTER TWENTY THREE

Brenda had insisted that even if the Immigration Department came and took her away in handcuffs, she was going to help her daughter with her ever expanding laundry.

"I just can't watch you lugging that heavy stuff in and out of the washing machine," she had said one morning when Laura was faced with two of her rentals having a quick turn around.

"If I'm not allowed to take it all home and wash it, I'll drop by the launderette in Brighton and the woman there can see to it."

"Mum, I can manage, stop treating me like an invalid. If you want to help me, take our stuff home and wash it for me, then I'll only have the rental stuff to do."

"Well, just be careful," Brenda said darkly. "There's a lot of babies who come out of the womb with the cord tied around their necks."

"Talking of which," Laura said quickly, as she didn't want her mother reminding her of the frailties of giving birth, "I went on the Pom's website yesterday, looking for bits and pieces, furniture and stuff for the nursery, and it's amazing just how many people are going back to the UK, disillusioned with the way of life, work or missing family. I could furnish a whole house if it would all be suitable, not just an apartment. The problem is I'm looking for more Ikea than Harvey Norman, 'cos I'm thinking cheap and cheerful and easy to replace this time."

"Well, I was very impressed with the things I saw when we went," said Brenda, thinking that they could have a mother and daughter day out and have a nice lunch at the café.

"Dad and I have to go for our medical next Tuesday, but I'm free any other day."

"Great, then it's a date. And do you know, there was a post I read about a nurse who had gone back to England for a wedding and was so upset about coming back and leaving all her family, *she's* thinking of selling up."

"It'll be because she's missing her mother, you don't know how lucky you are, my dear."

Anne-Marie, Ray and the two youngest were sitting on Karen's back verandah, looking across the fields and vineyards to Mount Compass and the surrounding hills. There had been a few days of rain previously and the grass was beginning to turn to a verdant green in some places, though the vines were dark with autumnal leaves.

"It's beautiful here," Anne-Marie sighed, looking up to where a bi-plane was circling, about to land at the nearby Aldinga airport. "You are lucky, Karen, to have such a lovely view."

"Well, sometimes I'd swap for a house with mod cons like you have," said Karen. "At one time we had a dunny instead of an inside toilet and I could do with an update of the bathroom and kitchen."

"I can't say that living in our rental is the bee's knees either," said Anne-Marie. "The house is freezing if you don't have the warm air heating on, what with all the tiles everywhere. It was great at first 'cos of the hot weather, but not now. At least you've got log fires to keep you warm. And do you know what our view is? The colour bond fence and next door's bathroom on one side and another fence and someone's bedrooms on the other!"

"Women. Never happy," said Ray to Karen's husband, John, who was setting up the barbecue, as the skies had brightened up again. Ray yelped when his wife gave him a kick.

"Well, it's true, you're never happy. You wanted a modern house with all the latest this and thats, 'cos the house we had back in Blackburn wanted a facelift. Now you've got what you wanted, you're having a moan again."

"Mum, can I go with Holly and have a look at her rabbits?" asked Emma in an attempt to break up a possible argument, as her parents had been arguing a lot recently.

"And can I go as well?" asked Liam, who was fed up with sitting with the grown-ups and being on his best behaviour.

"Course you can, you two," Karen said on Anne-Marie's behalf, feeling sorry for the bickering couple as she'd been through all the same scenario when they'd first come to live in Adelaide.

"It's only a rental you're in, isn't it? You've plenty of time to look around and agree on something. Anyway, you were saying on the phone that you'd met someone else from the north of England. How long has she been over here?"

"Just a bit longer than me and Ray. She's a hairdresser and, would you believe, she was in the same rental as we were? So I've decided to make an appointment with her once a month."

"And have you joined any clubs or classes around the place? Aldinga seems to have a lot of things going on. They've even got a rally next Sunday for 'Cars On The Beach'!"

"No, I wouldn't want to get involved in anything like that, especially if there were cars driving on the beach, I'd be worried about safety, but I did think about going to the centre on a Thursday afternoon for line dancing. I haven't done anything about it yet."

"We could do that together, if you're up for it. I've been looking at joining a line dancing class myself."

Laura could tell from the happy look on her parents' faces that they had something to tell her. She had only spoken to them on the phone that week as Toby had been off pre-school with a cold and it had been decided that in case it was a virus that they would steer clear of him. Now that Toby was better and had gone back to join his classmates, Laura had some time on her hands, as her latest tenants had all moved in.

"So what are you plotting?" she asked as Brenda made her a cup of tea and Barry sat at the dining room table with all his paperwork in front of him.

"Well, it seems that we are fit as fleas. They've received both our medical results and police checks so all we have to do is send them some money and they'll notify any consulate that we signify for preparation of our visas."

"By that, I gather you mean that you've been granted your contributory parent visa and can fly off to Singapore? Oh, that's great, Dad. Didn't seem as long as we thought."

"According to our case officer, there's been a few people coming off the list. Obviously they're having trouble selling their houses in the UK. We're not out of the woods yet. We have to lodge a bond with Centre Link, if you remember."

"Ah yes, sponsorship. Well, I'll look into that one for you. I believe you lodge the bond for ten years in case you should fall on hard times."

"As if," said Brenda, bringing over three cups of tea on a tray. "We'll just have to remember that once our ten years is up, we'll have to claim the fourteen grand back again."

"It's all happening at once," said Laura, happily. "You'll be off in a couple of weeks, before that we'll be furnishing the "Acacia" and, as you know, I'm in the middle of organising a Poms' party, before I get too fat."

"I think it's great what you're doing. Me and your father really admire your initiative, don't we Barry?"

"Well, I was having coffee with Fliss, you know, the girl you met at the Christmas barbecue? Her parents-in-law were over 'til February."

"Yeah, we remember." Barry nodded.

"Anyway, I was telling her about one of the families who had come to live in the Oleander. I haven't told you this yet. She was one of my tenants when I first started the rental business. Nice girl, but didn't make friends very easily. It seemed her kids had settled in okay; her husband was being sponsored by a car repair franchise, just Linda felt she didn't fit in anywhere.

It was quite a bad winter when they got here, rained a lot. I'd only put a couple of heaters in the houses, thinking people would use them if the wall unit in the lounge room wasn't enough. I put blankets in the bedrooms too, but she was telling me that she got so down, sitting on her own everyday. Money was tight so she didn't want to have to pay out for electricity and the only folk she spoke to were her family. So, to cut a long story short, she told her husband that she wanted to go back to the UK. Well, they went back, had to live with his sister 'cos they had nowhere else to live, and then suddenly she wondered what she'd done. It was the same old, same old back in England, but they were in a worse position because they had no house, no furniture and her husband, no job. Luckily, her husband was well thought of at the place he worked at over here and a quick email sorted his old job out. Her mother lent them the money for the air fare and now they're back, but Linda has to make a greater effort to get a social life.

Fliss came up with the idea of having a social night really. She's an events organiser and she fundraises for one of the cancer charities. Anyway, she asked me to ring up everyone who's ever stayed in one of my rentals and put a post on the Poms websites and invite them to the Seaford for a buffet and a get together. She knows of a band who'll play for peanuts and the entrance fee will pay for the food and a contribution to Fliss's charity."

"And long term they should make at least one friend from there that they can keep in touch with.,

"Yeah, Fliss is organising a couple of ice-breakers, but I'll be wandering around introducing various people who I think will get on well. Like, there's a girl called Abbie who I think would get on great with another girl called April. You remember, Harry and Mary's daughter? They're a spit away from each other in Woodcroft, have similar aged kids and the school holidays are coming up. Have you seen Harry and Mary lately, by the way?"

Her parents looked at her a little sheepishly, it had been their turn to get in touch with them again.

"I think they're busy moving house," said Barry apologetically. "We haven't liked to disturb them, have we Bren?"

"And that's another reason why Poms go back to England, parents. You've got to be less reserved and much more sociable!"

Aussie words or expressions you may come across.

Ankle biter – Small child.
Bowser – Petrol pump.
Bub – Baby.
Back door trots – The runs.
Cop A Dump – Cloudburst.
Crook – Ill.
Chooks – Hens.
Doco – Documentary.
Doona – Duvet.
Firies – Firemen.
Larrakin – Rascal.
Lollies – Sweets.
Manchester – Bedding.
Nudge a bottle or two – Had a few drinks.
Pollie – Politician.
Root – Have sex.
Rug up – Wear warm clothes.
Soapies – Soap operas.
Salvos – Charity shop or Salvation army.
Sticky beaking – Being nosy.
Slow mo – Slow motion.
Soursobs – Yellow wild flower.
Sparky – Electrician.
Take a Punt – Take a guess.
Towies – Men who operate tow wagons.
Tradies – Skilled workmen.